THE NEW SISTER

Lucilla Andrews was bo... daughter of an Englis... mother. Her late father was then a manager of the Eastern Telegraph Company. At three she began her education in an English private girls' boarding school in Sussex and when she was eleven she wrote her first novel – an epic of love, lust and banditry in China. Unfortunately the manuscript was discovered and ended in the school incinerator.

During World War II, Lucilla Andrews entered the Nightingale Training School at St Thomas's Hospital in London and five years later left with an S.R.N. and S.C.M. Part One. She married a doctor, had one child, and when her husband's illness necessitated that she become the family breadwinner she returned to nursing.

Her first book, THE PRINT PETTICOAT, was written while she was working as an assistant Night Sister in a small Sussex hospital. Since that time it has never been out of print.

Over the years Lucilla Andrews has established herself as one of Britain's leading popular novelists. She created what was virtually a new genre – the hospital romance – written against an authentic and detailed medical background drawn from her own experience.

Readers who would like to know more about Lucilla Andrews are recommended to read her autobiography, NO TIME FOR ROMANCE, an account of her life and training as a nurse in wartime London.

Lucilla Andrews lives in Edinburgh.

Also by Lucilla Andrews

HOSPITAL CIRCLES
A HOSPITAL SUMMER
THE LIGHTS OF LONDON
MY FRIEND THE PROFESSOR
THE PRINT PETTICOAT

and published by Corgi Books

The New Sister Theatre

Lucilla Andrews

CORGI BOOKS

THE NEW SISTER THEATRE

A CORGI BOOK   0 552 99279 8

Originally published in Great Britain by
George G. Harrap & Co. Ltd.

PRINTING HISTORY
George G. Harrap edition published 1964
Corgi edition published 1965
Corgi edition reissued 1968
Corgi edition reprinted 1973
Corgi edition reissued 1978
Corgi edition reissued 1987

This book is set in 15/16pt Plantin.

Corgi Books are published by Transworld Publishers
Ltd., 61-63 Uxbridge Road, Ealing, London W5 5SA, in
Australia by Transworld Publishers (Australia) Pty. Ltd.,
15-23 Helles Avenue, Moorebank, NSW 2170, and in New
Zealand by Transworld Publishers (N.Z.) Ltd., Cnr. Moselle
and Waipareira Avenues, Henderson, Auckland.

Made and printed in Great Britain by the
Guernsey Press Co. Ltd., Guernsey, Channel Islands.

CONTENTS

CHAPTER ONE

One Quiet Theatre Evening

Sister Theatre came back into the theatre proper just after seven that evening. I was sitting on a high stool drying and polishing the great stack of instruments spread on the top shelf of the glass trolley in front of me.

"My poor Nurse Lindsay! Still at it?"

"And one more lot still to come out of the sterilizer, Sister." I eased my turban a little farther back on my head. "Those men must have used every single instrument in the General Surgical Unit Theatre to-day."

"I certainly got that impression handing them out." She looked round the quiet theatre, at the empty table, then up at the silent gallery. "It's been one of those days. In a way I'm glad. I've had no time for 'am-I-really-doing-the-right-thing?' thoughts. But how I am going to miss you all!"

She had been in charge of that theatre for the past ten years. To-day was her last day. Next

7

week she was flying out to West Africa to take over the theatre block in a new teaching hospital. I had been one of her theatre staff nurses for two years; senior staff nurse for the last eleven months.

I said, "And how the Unit is going to miss you, Sister! This theatre just won't be the same after to-day."

"That's probably a very good thing, my dear." she replied briskly. "We've all been jogging along in a nice, pleasant rut. It's time for a jolt. And having a new Sister Theatre from St Martha's, across the river, will have everyone on their toes. You nurses will want to show Miss Davis that no theatre nurses are as efficient as those trained here in St Barnabas' Hospital. Miss Davis will be just as determined to uphold her training school. It should all work out very well" – she smiled at my expression – "once a few corners are rubbed off. As senior staff nurse, getting busy with tactful sandpaper will be your job."

We had become great friends in the last eleven months. So I was honest. "Thanks very much, Sister, I can hardly wait."

"It shouldn't be too bad, Lindsay. Miss Davis is a pleasant woman and an experienced Sister Theatre. Our Staff Nurse Brown may be a shade tricky at first, as she hasn't attempted to hide her resentment at the job being given to a non-Barny's nurse. She'll just have to get

8

over that. The fact remains that, with the exception of yourself, none of my other staff nurses have had sufficient experience, or – in my view – are temperamentally suited to taking charge of the busiest theatre in this hospital." She took a pair of sponge-holding forceps off my trolley, tested their grip reflectively. "I must admit that chip on Brown's shoulder is very much larger than I had anticipated. I always wanted you to succeed me, but I am beginning to feel it's just as well our Mr de Winter made you a far more attractive offer first. You could manage the work and administration perfectly, but Brown's being only one year your junior would have presented you with no small problem in her present frame of mind." She put down the forceps. "It's a very good thing that you are shortly to become Mrs Senior Surgical Officer. Incidentally, what news of that flat?"

"We can have it from February. It's pretty expensive. Joe's brooding on it."

"He'll come up with the answer you want. And I'm sure you'll be very happy together. I mean that, Lindsay. Your clever young man has worked so hard during his time as S.S.O. He needs someone like you to look after him and stop him working himself to death. Also," she added slowly, "some one who will always understand how much his work means to him, and how much he'll mean to Barny's. I have not said this before, because it is not the kind of thing a theatre sister should say about one specific surgeon, and I don't believe in using the word 'brilliant' idly. I will use it now. I consider your young man the most brilliant young surgeon I have ever had in this theatre. I think he will be one of the great names of modern surgery, and that one day I shall say with tremendous pride, 'I worked with Mr de Winter of Barny's.' And after all that I must get off to supper or I shall be very late, and then you will be very late, and Sister Dining-room will be very cross!"

"That would never do, Sister. And, Sister – thanks."

She did not answer. She just smiled and took herself off.

Alone again, I let myself think of my future with Joe. It was all so perfect that at times it scared me. My engagement ring – as always on duty – was pinned inside the big pocket of my uniform dress. I fingered it now through my theatre gown. It was real enough.

A theatre junior pushed in an empty metal trolley. "Sister asked me to tell you Nurse Brown is doing the autoclaving, and she has sent all the other nurses to supper. I am to go later."

"Right. How's your tidying going?"

"I've finished the surgeons' room, glove-room, linen-room, tin-room" – she ticked them off on her fingers — "and Sister's duty-room. I thought I'd do the gallery next."

"How about the anaesthetic-room? That's more important."

She looked worried. "Dr Delaney's in there writing notes. I didn't like to disturb him."

She was in her second year of training and third week in the theatre. Mark Delaney, the Resident Anaesthetist to our Unit, had registrar status and wore a long white coat. Our house physicians and house surgeons wore short whites. At her stage I had been nervous of the short coats, scared stiff by the long.

"I'm afraid that room has to be done. Dr Delaney won't mind being asked to move into the surgeon's room. But as I do want to ask him something about that last man we did this evening, could you ask him to spare me a moment? That'll get him out, and you can nip in and tidy fast."

She beamed. "I will, Nurse. Thanks." She spun herself and trolley around, and into Sandra Brown, who had come in behind her.

"When are you going to learn to look where you are going, Nurse?" snapped Sandra. "You're not pushing a luggage trolley round Waterloo Station! This is an operating theatre!"

The junior apologized nervously and scuttled off. Sandra turned her scowl on me. "I can see you think I was too tough on that girl, Maggie. But the juniors are supposed to be getting a training. Have you forgotten how we got pushed around?''

''No. Nor what we called the people who pushed us around. Come down off that soapbox, honey. She's only in her third week. You needn't take her too seriously.''

''It's all very well for you,'' she retorted. ''You never take things seriously – perhaps because you've never had to. You've always been dead lucky – had everything handed you on a plate. Like – like those two girls directly above you getting married in the same month, and Matron making you an official theatre staff nurse in your fourth year! And then you just shot up to senior because Angie Forbes decided to take that job in Australia in the middle of her two years on the top! I've had it the hard way.''

''You'll be senior when I leave. Only two months.''

She shrugged. ''This creature from Martha's will probably have her own ideas on that.''

I had been six years in the hospital, known Sandra for five of them. We had worked together several times during our training, and although we never had, and never would, become friends, we had got along fairly well on the whole, and very well when there was a crisis on. She was magnificent at rising to surgical occasions, but even in a constantly busy theatre life was not one long crisis. We had days, sometimes weeks, of routine operations, when theatre ran like a well-oiled machine, and there were regular quiet intervals which allowed us to get on with the vast amount of cleaning, testing, restocking, and resterilizing that had to be done whether we were quiet or not. In general it was infinitely preferable to be able to do all that in peace – unless Sandra happened to be on duty.

It was during those periods that her conviction that she was being put upon, unloved, and unappreciated made her the one difficult member of the present theatre staff. If she had not had such a talent for theatre work Sister Theatre would probably have had her moved months ago.

I murmured some soothing bromide about the new sister from Martha's being certain to appreciate a good theatre girl when she saw one, and changed the subject. "Is the autoclave's safety-valve still whistling? It nearly burst my ear-drums last night when I was doing the gloves."

An autoclave is a machine that sterilizes articles by subjecting them under pressure to intense heat. In common with the five other surgical units in our theatre block, we had our own autoclave, and did all our own sterilizing.

"It had a bit of wool or something jammed in the works. Sister was going to send down for a repairs-and-works man this morning while you were off. Mark Delaney came in and fixed it. He said it had upset you." She folded her arms, leaned against the sink. "Of course, he couldn't have that."

"Nonsense, Sandra! You know Mark's passion for machines. He adores taking things to pieces and putting them together again." Then, as her scowl had returned, and the one person who could bring her to explosion-point in record time was our R.A., I switched the conversation again to what I thought was the safe subject of the next day's operations.

I thought wrong.

"No point in our discussing who'll do what, Maggie. The new creature will be here by then. Incidentally, why hasn't she arrived? I thought she was supposed to be coming on this evening for an hour. We run out of red carpet?"

"Could be. Or she could have missed a train. She was due in at five. Sister didn't know why she hadn't turned up. If the Office do they haven't told us."

"It's a wonder Matron hasn't gone to the station to meet her! It really is too bad. Shoving some ghastly woman from Martha's in over our heads! What's so wrong with Barny's girls?"

We had been through all this so many times that I left her to chat it out with herself as she drifted aimlessly round the theatre.

Theatre clothes suited Sandra Brown. She was tall, very slim, had good eyes and excellent legs – two useful assets for any theatre girl, since for hours of any working day they are the only

14

two visible portions of the anatomy. She was more striking than pretty – her features were too strong – but occasionally, when she smiled, she could look very attractive.

"If you'll forgive my intruding, ladies," drawled Mark Delaney from the door, "there's a fine scent of cooking rubber out there in the corridor." He held open one of the thick, soundproof swing-doors as Sandra shot past him, then let it swing and strolled over to me. "An over-sensitive olfactory nerve can be highly convenient to a man on occasions."

"That was a false alarm? Mark!"

"Now, did I give any alarm? Did I not merely announce there was a scent of cooking rubber out there? And will you tell me, Maggie, my love, when does an autoclave packed with glove-tins not give out with its inner secrets?" He draped his large body not ungracefully on a high stool. "I've already had to listen to the sultry Sandra doing her nut about this new Sister Theatre twice this evening. If I've to hear it again I'll go crazy. But as that cute little doll with the big blue eyes said you wanted me, here I am. I am all yours But you, alas, are not mine! Tell me, darling, what has Joe de Winter got that I lack?"

"I'll tell you one thing. More sense than to tease Sandra. She doesn't enjoy it." He grinned unrepentantly, and, knowing him so well, I gave up. "That cute little doll with the big blue eyes wanted to tidy the anaesthetic-room. You're a Big Doctor to her and she didn't dare throw you out. As I have to get the log straight, and am not clear what you used for our last man, I thought we might kill the two birds with one stone.''

''So the little thing thinks I'm a Big Doctor, eh?'' He laughed. ''She'll learn, the darling girl that she is. Just a flipping anaesthetist. The lowest form of life in the theatre.'' He paused reflectively. ''She's got good legs too.''

''Mark dear, you are nothing but a wolf in a white coat. Date that junior later if you like — but I'll warn you she has a boy-friend amongst this present set of dressers. Right now, let's get back to business.''

''A wolf, am I? How right you are, Maggie! Now, about that chap . . .'' He produced an envelope. ''I'll write the details down for you.''

I was very fond of Mark Delaney. He was a good anaesthetist and a nice man. We had been friends since he was the student with the broken ankle in the third bed on the left in Albert Ward and I was a harassed first-year in my first ward. He had been unofficially engaged to a physiotherapist student when he broke his ankle on the rugger field. When he left Albert he was unofficially engaged to the Albert fourth-year nurse. Both girls had been tall, curvy blondes. Since then he had been involved with a whole series of similar blondes,

16

and twice reached the stage of giving them rings. Those engagements had later broken off. Mark had remained on the best of terms with his two ex-fiancées and all his ex-girl-friends.

Back in Albert he had asked my advice about that fourth-year. He had gone on asking my advice about his love-life until I got engaged to Joe. Joe knew all about our old friendship, and once admitted to having been very worried by it. I had explained that never in a hundred years would anyone need to worry about Mark and me.

"We just like each other. No more. He only dates me when one of his blondes lets him down. His murmuring sweet nothings doesn't mean a thing. He can no more help doing that to any female than he can help breathing."

That was true. Mark was great fun, providing he was not taken seriously. Sandra, I had lately suspected, did that in more ways than one. That was why she was so violently anti-him on the surface. I did not yet know whether she herself realized why he made her so edgy. She was one of those people who spent so much time analysing other people's motives that she had none left for looking under her own personal stones. I was quite sure Mark was well aware of the effect he had on her and why, without ever discussing that specific subject with him. I had not mentioned it to Joe, either. I had long reassured him about Mark, but there was a limit to how much the nicest man wanted to hear about his fiancée's other male friends.

Mark heaved himself off the stool. "Time I got me down to Casualty. I am on medical call this night. Who knows? The customers may be queueing up to see me."

"If they were that walkie-talkie in your pocket would be blasting off like the autoclave last night."

"So it would." He took out his little receiver. "An electronic slave-driver, no less." He put it away, flexed his huge shoulders. "Old Achilles Delaney is on his way to hold the hospital on his manly shoulders."

"Wouldn't you mean Atlas?" The light being switched on in the gallery made me look up. The junior was above, bustling round the benches, straightening the hard cushions. "Wasn't Achilles the man with the heel?"

"So he was. Blame my subconscious, darling. Guilt will out."

Sandra appeared in the gallery and looked down on us. The gallery was cut off from the theatre by a glass wall, connected during cases by an intercom. It should now be switched off – one of the junior's jobs at the end of the day's list. The junior had gone up there earlier, when the watching students filed out, but as I had not yet had time to check her tidying there was a chance she had forgotten, and it might still be switched on. The obvious course

18

of calling up to find out, and then telling her to turn it off if it were on, was out, as Sandra was there. With her passion for getting things wrong, and if possible taking umbrage, to do that now would be to convince her I had some secret criticism to make of her to Mark.

I caught his eye to warn him we probably had an audience who could listen as well as observe.

His smile said plainly, "Let us not disappoint 'em." His voice said brokenly, "You don't think me a heel? Honest to God, have I not been right the times I've told you you're the only girl I've ever really loved, with you understanding me the way you do." As ever when his tongue was in his cheek he produced a superb brogue. "I have to leave you now – I give you this." He handed me the old envelope with the anaesthetic details I needed for the theatre log-book. "From my heart. It'll tell you all you have to know."

I was nearly choking with suppressed laughter. I had to suppress it. The junior had vanished, but Sandra was still up there. If I laughed, and the intercom was off, she would be sure I was laughing at her. "Thanks, Mark. That's big of you."

He blew me a kiss and ambled out. The light in the gallery went out a few seconds later.

The junior came into the theatre about five minutes afterwards. "The Assistant Matron would like to speak to you on the telephone, Nurse Lindsay.'

The Assistant Matron sounded perturbed, but did not tell me why. "Sister Theatre is with Matron and will be late back. I have asked Sister Dining-room to keep your supper hot. Will you carry on in charge of the theatre for the rest of the evening?"

"Yes, Sister. Thank you."

Sandra joined me as I rang off. I handed on the message.

She sniffed. "Reception committee for the new creature, no doubt," she remarked, as the telephone rang again.

"Casualty switchboard here, Nurse. You got the S.S.O. there?"

"Sorry, Charlie, no. He hasn't been back since the list ended. Why?" I asked. "Case for us?"

Charlie said as to that he couldn't say as he wasn't sticking his neck out, he wasn't, not after twenty-one years in Casualty. "But I got a gent from St Martha's Hospital on the line for the S.S.O., Nurse Lindsay – sounds real anxious – but I can't contact that Mr de Winter nowhere. Rung all round I have, and buzzed his signal time and time again, without getting no answer. Reckon he must have a fault in it, like."

"He must. He's probably talking somewhere between wards. You've tried the dining-room and his rooms?"

"Tried the lot, Nurse. He has to be somewhere in the hospital, seeing he's not left word he'll be out and I've never known that Mr de Winter to go out without leaving word, nor switch off his receiver long as he's been here. But where he's got to beats me."

It did me. I had never heard of Joe vanishing either. "How about the terrace? He sometimes goes out for air."

"That's an idea, Nurse. Ta. Much obliged."

Sandra had been listening. "So Charlie's joined the hue and cry for the S.S.O.?"

"Is there a hue and cry on? How did you know?"

"Some one from Martha's wanted him a little while ago." She looked down her nose. "Some female. That's why I was up in the gallery. I thought he might be in the theatre."

My mind was on Joe. It was so unlike him to be out of touch. "Why go up to the gallery?" I asked absently.

"And have Mark Delaney think up another excuse to get rid of me so that he could have you to himself? No, thank you. I preferred to use my eyes."

It had been a long day; my feet were aching; I was very sorry Sister was leaving; rather bothered about Joe. "Sandra, for heaven's sake relax. You know quite well Mark Delaney nourishes no passion for me. He just likes playing the fool."

She turned scarlet. "I know a whole lot more than you may think, Maggie! I can see you imagine you are being very clever the way you handle the men in your life – being engaged to one and keeping the other on a string. I just happen to know you are not quite so clever after all. You see, I was at school with her. If you're interested, her name's Frances Durant!"

The ill-suppressed violence of her outburst disconcerted me far more than what she had actually said. This Frances Durant was probably Mark's latest heart-throb.

I said, "I don't think I'm being at all clever standing here nattering with a mass of instruments still to finish. You ready to go to supper?"

She had enough sense to take the hint and disappear.

Instrument-drying was a soothing occupation. After a little time at it I decided Sandra was just het-up over the new Sister and Mark, had been ready to explode all evening, and it was pure chance that I happened to be around when she exploded. The name Frances Durant floated through my mind. Nice name. I wondered if she was a curvy blonde.

"Nurse Lindsay, I'm most awfully sorry. . . ." The junior was doing her jack-in-the-box act again, and this time holding out a kidney dish filled with instruments. "These were in the anaesthetic-room. I forgot to give them to you."

"Oh, no! I've just turned off the instrument-sterilizer. Never mind. Let's have 'em."

"Thanks, Nurse. Er – is it all right now I've tidied all round if I go and write up those notes Sister gave us this evening? If I leave them until I get off," she added honestly, "I'll forget."

"Then get them down. Do them in the duty-room, and you can listen for the telephone at the same time."

She removed herself. I rinsed the instruments she had brought, put them in a large kidney dish and the dish into the smallest instrument-sterilizer, and turned up the heat. When the water began to bubble, I closed the lid, adjusted the heat, then set a large wooden-framed egg-timer on the closed lid. The first grains of sand began to trickle through the narrow waist.

"This theatre," said Joe's voice just behind me, "seems the one quiet spot in the entire hospital."

I turned, and a wave of sheer joy at seeing him swept over me. He never had to do or say anything as far as I was concerned. He just had to be there. From the way he often looked at me I knew he felt the same.

He was not looking at me now. He was watching the egg-timer.

"Joe. Casualty wants you."

"I know. It was only to take an outside call. Wasn't important. I was on the terrace. My receiver had a short. Mark Delaney's just fixed it for me in Cas."

I smiled. "Handy man to have around, our Mark. If he ever had to chuck medicine he could always get a job with our repairs-and-works boys."

He looked up. "Why the devil should he have to chuck medicine?"

"No reason. I was just waffling."

He glanced round. "Sister back from the Office?"

"So you know she's there? No. Want her?"

"No. You. I have to talk to you, Maggie" – he hesitated – "about us."

"Us?" I echoed, surprised. He was generally so careful to avoid our private affairs on duty. He said that was the only way he could work with me. "Joe. Something wrong?"

He did not answer. His attention was back on the egg-timer. I watched him with sudden anxiety. He looked more tired than I ever remembered. I would have thought I knew every line of his intelligent, sensitive face by heart. There were now new lines at the corners of his eyes, and shadows beneath – shadows nearly as dark as his hair, and that was as close to black as any Anglo-Saxon's can get.

He did not give the impression of being a huge man like Mark, even though he was nearly as tall. In a white coat he looked long and thin. In a theatre T-shirt he was not so much thin as without an ounce of extra weight. Physically he was strong as they come. Good surgeons need stamina. He was a good and apparently tireless surgeon. He had not had one day off through sickness all his years at Barny's, and the only ailment I had ever known him admit was an occasional touch of rheumatism.

"Joe, is something wrong?" I repeated. "You look so tired."

"I'm all right. What's in the sterilizer? Sharps?"

"No, an assortment of forks."

"Then another run through won't hurt." He flicked the glass over and faced me. He was not wearing a mask, but he might well have been. "Yes. Something is wrong, Maggie. Do you know why Sister Theatre is with Matron?"

"No. The Ass. Mat. didn't say."

He told me Miss Davis, the new Sister Theatre, would not now be arriving, as the taxi in which she had driven to a railway station that morning had been in a collision with a lorry. "The poor woman has a fractured base and right clavicle. She was concussed, and didn't come round until late this afternoon."

"Joe, how wretched for her! I am sorry. Was that why Martha's wanted you? Did they hear first?"

"You know Martha's rang me?" he asked curtly. "No. I told them. Miss Davis is up north. The S.M.O. at the hospital that admitted her rang our Matron at her — Miss Davis's — request after she came round." He put his hands in his coat-pockets. "Matron told me. She's going to ask you to take the job, Maggie. You'll have to do it."

"Must I? I don't want it."

"I don't think you'll have any alternative. Our Sister Theatre's plans are all fixed. She can't stay. This theatre has to have a Sister. Matron can't produce some one with the right qualifications and experience" – he snapped his fingers – "just like that. You'll do nicely. And as you know, she would have offered you the job originally if we hadn't fixed up our future."

"That's true." I thought it over. "Perhaps I could cope for the next two months. That'll give time to see if Miss Davis is going to be well enough to come on to us later, or for Matron to find some one else. That poor woman! What a thing to happen on your way to a new job!"

"A tough break. It's too early for any prognosis, but from what Matron told me I doubt she'll be fit to work anywhere inside of six months." He paused. "Maggie, Matron wants you to take this job for at least six months."

"Six? Joe! She can't ask me that! I'll help out – but we've got everything all fixed up."

He said very slowly. "We had. However, I'm afraid" – and he seemed to have to drag the words out of him – "I feel the time has come to do a little unfixing. That's why I wanted to see you now. Before Matron sends for you."

The theatre was very quiet. In the quiet the gentle bubbling of the sterilizer was ominous as distant thunder.

We looked at each other in silence for perhaps ten seconds. Or hours. Or years. I could not have said which. Possibly pride should have made me realize immediately what he was trying to say and give him the right civilized answer. I loved him too much to waste time on pride. Also I knew him too well. We had not just seen each other in our free time, as most engaged couples do; we had worked together daily for over two years – in the very early mornings before breakfast, in the late evenings when emergencies came in at the end of long, heavy days, in the cold darkness of the small hours when we had been called up, in the colder greyness of countless dawns.

Anyone could keep up an act for a limited period. No one could act successfully through all the hours he and I had spent together. He had loved me. Nothing would persuade me to believe otherwise. I was too shattered to understand what had made him say what he had just said. My judgement registered the blunt fact that he must have fallen out of love with me. Yet every instinct I possessed was insisting that for the first time he was now putting on an act with me.

I broke the silence. 'Joe dear, what is all this about? I just don't understand.''

His face tightened as if I had hit him. "Isn't that obvious—" He had to break off as the little receiver clipped to his breast-pocket suddenly buzzed like an infuriated bee. He reached for it instinctively, pressed the switch.

"Senior Surgical Officer wanted in Casualty at once, please," chanted Charlie's voice thinly. "Acute abdomen. Male. Age forty-eight. Senior Casualty Officer suspects perforation. I will repeat: Senior Surgical Officer—" and Joe switched off.

Training made me say calmly, "You'll have to go."

"Yes." His face was nearly as white as his coat. "We'll have to finish this conversation later. I'll have to look at that man. May have to operate."

"The emergency setting is ready. I'll turn up the steam. We can always turn it off later."

"Right. I'll let you know as soon as I've seen him." He walked towards the double doors. I suddenly thought; that's how he'll walk when he's old.

"Maggie." He turned back momentarily. "I'm sorry this had to happen."

I said, "I don't yet know what's happened or happening, Joe. But I'm sorry too."

The nurses-in-training returning from supper came in as he went out.

"Trouble brewing, Nurse Lindsay?" asked

28

the senior, Nurse Bachelor, cheerfully. "That why Mr de Winter's just gone down our corridor as if jet-propelled?"

"Possibly." I explained briefly. "Will you ring the students' room and warn our four dressers to stand by? Both our porters are down in Cas. They'll bring themselves back, if necessary."

Ten minutes later Mark rang from Casualty with the confirmation. "Up in twenty minutes to you. Then on to Henry Carter Ward. A riproaring perforation."

"Right." I reached for the memo pad. "Name and so on, please?"

"Peter Arthur Worth. Age forty-eight. 30 Water Street, SW3. Religion C of E."

"Hang on . . ." I wrote fast. "Next of kin known?"

"Very well, to our Maternity Unit. Mrs Sylvia Worth – his missus – produced twin boys this morning. They've three more kids, all boys, and the lot under seven. This chap was looking after the trio, and that's why he delayed calling in their family doctor. They're Australians. Haven't been over here long. No handy relatives, but the neighbours have rallied."

"Good. How is he?"

"Dodgy," said Mark. "With luck – he'll get away with it."

Sandra came in quickly as I put down the receiver. "Case?"

"Yes." I gave the details, asked if she had

heard about Miss Davis.''

"It was all round the dining-room." She pressed her lips together. "Matron'll have to promote you."

I said wearily, "Then you'll be promoted too. Now, about this case. Bachelor can 'dirty.' I'll take it. Will you keep an eye on the inside and out? As the man has already perforated, we may run into snags. Will you see the juniors get off on time? Home Sister will go up the wall if they are as late off as they were last night."

"All right." There was an emergency on, so she shed her prickles like an old coat. "What about your supper?"

"They'll keep it hot. I'm not hungry."

She hurried off to change back into theatre clothes. I returned to the theatre proper to carry on with the necessary preparations.

The operation, though an emergency, was a routine emergency. A few minutes after the recalled dressers (senior students working temporarily in the theatre) had taken their places Joe came in with his registrar and houseman. As he walked over to his sink he gave me the brief nod he always gave the instrument nurse when entering the theatre for any operation. At the sink he glanced over his shoulder.

"This man Worth is heavily built. I may need our special skin-retractors, Nurse Lindsay."

"They are ready, Mr de Winter."

"Thanks." He concentrated on lathering

soap high over his elbows.

He looked and sounded so normal, everything else was so normal, that for a fleeting moment I let myself wonder if that interrupted conversation really had taken place. Then the double doors opened. The two porters, Sandra, a ward nurse, and Mark wheeled in the unconscious man on the stretcher trolley, and also the attached anaesthetic machine.

Joe got into his gown, waited while Bachelor tied the back tapes, then eased on his gloves. "All well, Mark?" He checked to see if his assistants were ready. "Right. Let's get started."

A very short while later a porter, disguised behind mask and gown, came in with a note. Bachelor took it from him, glanced at it, then came to my elbow and held it out for me to read. It was a message for Joe. My job included handing on all messages for any surgeons during an operation.

"Casualty are on the telephone for you, Mr de Winter. They have a Dr Durant from St Martha's Hospital down there asking about a medical case which may have been left in your car. Dr Durant apologizes for disturbing you while operating, but requires that case urgently."

He did not look up. "If it is in my car it'll be on the back seat. My keys are in the inside pocket of my jacket hanging in the surgeons' room. Could you ask some one to look and send them down, please? Oh, yes – and my apologies to Dr Durant for her having to come back.''

I had already caught Sandra's eye to ask her to deal with this. I had given the message, heard most of the answer without taking any of it in. It seemed unexceptional. The senior residents of most London hospitals were frequently in touch with each other about rare cases, the need for a special serum or drug, or the shortage of beds. Then that ''her'' and the sudden blatant triumph in Sandra's eyes made me feel exactly as if I had had an electric shock.

I had to ignore it. Later it could and would register. Not now. I caught Bachelor's eye and nodded at the twin bowls of sterile saline in the stand by my instrument trolley. The saline was growing lukewarm. It was time for their first change.

CHAPTER TWO

A New Sister Theatre

The theatre was warm, and grew warmer. The dressers shifted from one foot to the other surreptitiously, flexed their shoulders, and as they were only watching and not assisting (as occasionally happened) edged a little farther away from the powerful lights.

The surgeons' gowns seemed clamped to their shoulders, and their masks tight against their bent faces. They were directly under the shadeless light. The house-surgeon, Tom Ross, being the most junior, felt the heat the most. His forehead was purple. Joe and his registrar, George Ellis, were too accustomed to working in that temperature to notice it.

Bachelor again changed the saline bowls, one at a time. She balanced the fresh, hotter bowl on the open palm of one hand, removed the old bowl on the palm of the other, sliding one out, one in, without touching the bowl-stand or the sides or lips of the bowls. She was an efficient and neat-handed 'dirty,' and never forgot to keep one eye on the instrument nurse while going about her job as liaison between the sterile-gowned and gloved operating team and the – to them – untouchable world of sterilizers, tap-handles, cylinder knobs, electric switches, hypodermic trays, drugs, telephones, and anything else that might be required.

Joe worked swiftly, surely, his neat gloved hands moving as if they had an independent existence of their own. He never talked much while operating, but whether he talked or not his hands worked on.

The registrar followed his moves, clipping off each cut blood-vessel, ligaturing each in turn, then unclipping the artery forceps. Tom Ross held various instruments in the necessary position, sponged the wound occasionally, or adjusted the angle of the sucker, but was more often required to stand holding, watching, and learning. There was a maxim in Barny's that applied to the medical and nursing staff alike: first you watched, then you assisted while being yourself watched, then you taught others.

When each instrument was done with for the moment I removed it from the operating table, rinsed it in hot saline, replaced it in its recognized position on my trolley. The order of my trolley, another Barny's rule, was upside down in relation to myself, and facing the surgeons. And since the official order of the various types of instrument never changed, the surgeons always knew exactly where to find what they needed if, for some unlooked-for reason, the instrument nurse was not free to hand this over.

In all our theatres it was a much cherished tradition that none of our surgeons ever had to name the precise instrument. When we were trained as instrument nurses we were trained to follow the operation as closely as the surgeons, and so anticipate their wants. This was never easy at first or when working with a strange surgeon, but experience made it perfectly possible, and resulted in the theatre serenity being undisturbed by grunted demands for instruments. And not only the theatre serenity; all Barny's junior surgeons soon learned that the one sure way to make one of their own instrument nurses bristle with indignation for an entire list was to demand "Clamps . . . retractor . . . needle-holder" – and so on.

I had worked so often with Joe that I knew instinctively when his hand was going to stretch out my way, what he wanted, what he was going to do next, whether he was satisfied or anxious, without a word passing between us. When a patient worried him he had a mannerism of tilting his head slightly to the right as if listening for a sound no one else could hear. Our retiring Sister Theatre once asked, "Are you listening for a heart without a stethoscope, Mr de Winter?''

On that occasion he had just shaken his head and worked on. The patient had suddenly collapsed ten minutes later. Later still Joe had told me he had been as suddenly convinced something was going to go very wrong. ''Some people smell danger. I sort of hear it.''

Now his hand stretched my way again. I set in it the first of the two final arterial clamps he was going to need.

''Thanks, Nurse.'' His fingers closed over the clamp. ''All well your end, Mark?''

''Taking it like a text-book.''

''Good.'' He worked on in silence for a few minutes. Then he put down the scalpel. ''No wonder this poor chap had such a rough time.'' He glanced up, beckoned the dressers closer. ''Take a look at these adhesions, and those old scars. This is what an appendix looks like when it turns acute after years of being chronic.''

A dresser asked. ''Why did he let it go on so long, sir?''

''He had had attacks of pain before and got away with them. The body has very tough defences. And most people have strong feelings about operations and surgeons. ''They don't want anything to do with either. I don't blame 'em.''

The dressers were amused. ''Surely there's nothing very much to having an appendix out?'' suggested another.

Joe asked, "You ever had an abdominal operation?"

"No."

"Presumably at some time in your life you've cut some portion of your anatomy? Superficially? With a penknife? Climbing over a gate?"

"Lord, yes, sir!"

"Did it hurt?"

"A bit."

"Then how much more do you suppose all the cutting through delicate tissue and muscle I have just had to do hurts? A wound," Joe added thoughtfully, "doesn't cease to hurt because it's surgically inflicted. We can and do see our patients here through the worst of the pain. We can't keep them drugged. The aching and general discomfort that follows most operations – and certainly all abdominal ones – is worth putting up with in the long run, but by no means insignificant. It's not something any surgeon can dismiss as a triviality, unless he's content to forget he ever qualified in medicine, and settles for just being an efficient technician with a knife."

Teaching the boys was as much a part of his job as operating. He went on explaining and demonstrating as he stitched. He was dealing with the final layer of muscle and explaining why he had used the specific drain he had, when his hands and voice paused together. He tilted his head to the right and ignored the question on the elasticity of scar-tissue from one of the dressers.

Mark looked up, recognized that mannerism as I had done. "Trouble?"

Joe said, "Not this end. All gone like that text-book you mentioned. How about your end?"

"Heart's fine. A nice steady *lubb-dupp*." Mark's fingers throughout the operation had been on our patient's right temporal artery. He checked the many recording instruments on the anaesthetic machine again, as he had been doing constantly, then momentarily raised a corner of the anaesthetic mask. "Colour's fine. Why?"

Joe shrugged, went back to his stitching. He still seemed to be straining to catch an unheard sound.

Our dressers, though senior, were new to the G.S.U. Theatre that week. They looked at the clock and then at each other expressively. The registrar noticed, frowned them to immobility. They waited until his attention returned to the patient and then exchanged some more resigned glances amongst themselves.

"Hold it! Just one moment there!" Mark's voice a minute or so later was soft yet urgent. "Something's cooking with this pulse."

The surgeons froze to statues. The dressers' four heads jerked towards Mark as if they were puppets and he had tugged their strings.

Bachelor came quickly to my elbow. I nodded at the emergency hypodermic setting on a tray on a near-by shelf. We might not need it. If we did it would be in a hurry.

Mark was altering the various knobs on his machine fast. There was a little green rubber bag attached to the anaesthetic mask. It had been rhythmically inflating and deflating ever since the man was wheeled in from the anaesthetic-room. It had lost its regularity. It was moving more slowly. Then it fluttered. Then it stopped.

Until Mark's "Hold it!" the work had been progressing at its usual orderly pace. Then all but Mark were still. When that bag stopped the theatre atmosphere was electric and the tempo speeded up like an over-fast film.

Mark had the anaesthetic mask off, the small anaesthetic tube out of the patient's mouth, and a long intratrachael tube in, in a matter of seconds. Joe swiftly seized a bundle of large abdominal gauze packs from my trolley, dipped them in the hottest bowl of saline, wrung them out, laid them over the still uncompleted wound. Bachelor had brought me the hypodermic tray with the dish lids removed. I fitted together a large syringe and long needle. Joe took this from me as Mark pulled off his stethoscope.

"Sorry," grunted Mark. "He's gone. Probably a coronary."

"Probably." Joe glanced at the clock. "We've got about two and a half of those three minutes left." He looked at the label on the rubber-capped phial Bachelor had swabbed and was holding up for him. "Right." He plunged in the needle, drew up the fluid. "Let's hope this has some effect."

It was an accepted medical law in our hospital that three minutes from the moment a patient's heart stopped was the maximum time we had in which to get the circulation going again safely, if it could be got going. An injection into the heart muscle might be enough. I had known it be; I had known the reverse.

Joe put down the syringe. "No. I'll have to massage." He took the scalpel from the dish I was offering him, and opened the chest wall between the lower left ribs with a long, careful incision from right to left to avoid cutting the main arteries – even though for the moment there was no bleeding, as the circulation had stopped. He dropped the scalpel back in the dish, then eased in his whole right hand between the ribs. "This man's ribs are like a vice," he muttered. "That's better – I'm there. Watch out for those bleeding-points, George. All hell's let loose if one gets it going again. Now – let's see."

He had cut carefully. Even so, a fast-increasing scarlet stain soaked his gown sleeve, chest, and the sterile towels covering the patient. George Ellis worked as fast with his many artery forceps, with the houseman sponging and responging for him.

Mark said, "I can just get his pulse at the neck."

"Good." Joe's forehead was tight with effort. 'I'm afraid that's me. His heart hasn't taken over yet. It's early. We'll just have to keep on." He looked at the registrar's work. "Good. You're getting it under control. You keep on with that. Tom – you keep that site at blood-heat."

Sandra wheeled forward the dressing-trolley and a second double saline bowl stand she had set for that purpose. I said, "You'll find everything just behind you, Mr Ross," and took the large, steaming kidney dish Bachelor was holding between two pairs of long-handled bowl forceps. "The rib-retractors are ready, Mr de Winter."

"Fine. Thanks. Shove 'em in, George. How's his pulse now, Mark?"

"It could be worse. Heart doing anything?"

"Not yet."

The rib-retractors were self-retaining. Once they were in position the registrar offered to take over. Joe said he could carry on *pro tem*. "Now his ribs are off my wrist my own circulation's getting back to my hand. This may be a long job. We can start up shifts later."

He went on massaging for another half-hour,

then George Ellis took over, then Joe again, then George Ellis, then again Joe.

Cardiac massage for any length of time is always a physically exhausting feat. Of the two men now, George Ellis clearly felt the strain more. Bachelor was kept busy mopping his damp forehead with the special hand-towel reserved for that purpose.

The shifts were cut down to fifteen minutes each. It was around three hours from the moment of failure when Mark asked, "Are you going to get anywhere?"

"God knows," retorted Joe wearily.

George Ellis noticed the time. "You've done overtime. My turn now."

"I'm all right for a spot longer. Got my second – or is it third? – wind." There was silence for a few minutes. Then, "By God! The bloody thing's stirring! Come on, you bastard," muttered Joe, "come on, you lazy lump of good muscle – do your stuff! You know the form. You've been pumping for forty-eight years – pump, damn you, pump! That's it!" He sighed deeply. "That's it, chum. You can do it all by yourself. Just keep it up. Just keep it up." He mopped his forehead with the sleeve of his free arm. "Don't worry about the towel, Nurse, I'll have to change anyway before we go on."

His sigh had been echoed round the theatre. The tension of the last three hours vanished. Mark pushed his cap back a little with one

thumb; the dressers mopped their own fore-
heads with their gown sleeves; Bachelor's eyes
were like stars; Sandra and I smiled at each
other over our masks. No one said another
word.

When it was all over Mark went up to Henry
Carter with the patient, the porters, and the
attendant ward nurse. I pushed my trolley
towards one of the sinks. Joe walked slowly
towards his, peeling off his gloves.

A dresser broke the silence. "Obviously if
you hadn't applied cardiac massage that case
would have died, sir?"

He was very young, so he used textbook
words. He would learn later that they were a
hallmark of the young and inexperienced. He
would also learn there was a time for not
asking questions.

Joe untied the top strings of his second gown,
removed it, and dropped it on the surgeon's
table before answering. "That wasn't a case,
Hall. That was a man. Yes. He would have
died. Five kids would have lost a father. And
a young woman up in our Mat. Unit would
have had to face bringing them up on her own
and an immediate future in a strange country."

The dresser was persistent. "But does one
– I mean – should one think of people as
people when one has them on the table?
Doesn't it disturb one's concentration if one

allows oneself to become emotionally involved?''

George Ellis was trying to catch the boy's eye to tell him to be quiet. Teaching during a case was one thing. Few surgeons could bear chatting at the end of an exhausting operation until they had had time to get to their own room, have a cup of tea, perhaps a cigarette, and slowly relax.

Joe was no exception to this. The strain was clearly telling on him now. He looked even more tired than he had done earlier. He pulled off his cap, added it to his mask and gown on the table, pushed a hand through his hair. ''In my experience there is no way of forgetting the human angle. It does not disturb my concentration.'' He glanced as if involuntarily at me. ''It just hurts like hell. Well. That's that.'' His tone was final. ''Thank you very much, everybody. I hope we don't have to trouble you again to-night. Good night.'' He walked out of the theatre without looking back. The thick doors swung soundlessly shut behind him.

George Ellis took off his long rubber apron. ''Hey – boy!'' He turned on the dresser. ''You don't know how lucky you are to have an S.S.O. who's a patient man. But if you persist in asking ruddy tiresome questions at the end of ops any ideas you may have about specializing in surgery can go out of the window. Any other surgeon in this hospital would have taken you apart just now! And don't think,'' he added sternly, "that because Mr de Winter dealt with you gently there is no limit to his patience. Watch out in future! And when in doubt, belt up!" He stormed out after Joe.

It was half-past eleven before I took the theatre keys along to Night Sister. She told me Matron was waiting to see me in her flat.

Matron offered me cocoa in a fluted cup, shortbread, and the job of Sister Theatre for a certain six months. I accepted.

"I am most grateful to you, Nurse Lindsay. This will give me time to find a suitable substitute should Miss Davis not be fit to return. Such an unfortunate and most distressing accident! We must hope for the best. I knew you would understand my position, and realize," she went on sincerely, "how much I regret having to ask you to postpone your marriage like this. But I cannot pretend you could combine the post with marriage. That might be possible in a smaller, less busy hospital. Not at St Barnabas's."

That was true. I did not dare comment on it. I told her why I was so late, and then we went on to discuss the theatre work in detail. Before I left she gave me a new Sister's belt. "You must be measured for your new uniform in the morning. Sleep well, my dear. You look tired."

I was tired. Too tired to risk thinking. I fell asleep directly I got into bed. The theatre haunted my dreams. All night long, men with masked faces, rows and rows of instruments, and a creeping, growing scarlet stain no one was able to control floated through my sleeping mind.

Sister Theatre came to say good-bye to me when I was dressing early next morning. There had been no time last night. ''You musn't let this unexpected promotion frighten you,'' she said, after we had talked over Miss Davis's accident. ''You are perfectly capable for the job. As for Brown, you'll just have to be firm with yourself as well as her.'' She watched me buckle on the new belt that automatically raised me to the rank and title of Sister. ''You won't have realized this yet, but from this moment you are in a new world. You are on the other side of the tallest fence in any hospital. It'll be a little lonely at times. No more sitting gossiping with the other staff nurses in the dining-room or canteen. No long natters behind the linen-room door when Sister isn't looking.'' She smiled. ''And don't forget to look behind those doors now. It'll be expected of you.''

''Sister, I don't feel anything like a Sister.''

''It takes some time before one does. When you get into dark blue you will keep getting a shock when you see your reflection unexpectedly. Shattered me.''

''Sister! I didn't think anything could do that.''

''Indeed, many things still can. I've just

learned to hide my feelings, even when not wearing a mask. We all have to learn that as we turn senior."

I thought of Joe last night. "Yes."

She stood up. "I must let you get over to breakfast, my dear. One last and very minor tip. That new junior's a nice child, but she's got a memory like a sieve – particularly about microphones. She's always leaving them on. She did tidy the gallery last night?" I nodded. "I thought so. The intercom was still switched on when I was up there having a final look round."

That removed any doubts about Sandra overhearing Mark's nonsense about my being the only girl he had ever loved. I could not worry about that. The only person I was worried about was Joe.

I said, "Sister, I hate saying good-bye."

"Me too. I'm going to take your young man's advice. I'm sure he's right that when one has to leave a person or place one loves the only thing to do is get away fast before one has had time to be missed."

I touched the ring in my bib pocket. I did not know if it had any right to be there. It was there because I could not bear to be without it – until I knew beyond all doubt that I had to. "When did Joe say that?"

"Last evening. On my way to supper."

There was a sealed envelope in Joe's handwriting waiting for me on the desk in the

47

theatre duty-room. As S.S.O. he had duplicate keys to all our theatres. He must have put it there during the night or early this morning. Habit as much as apprehension for its contents made me hesitate to open it. I knew Sister Theatre would not really object to my using her duty-room to read it – and then I remembered. No one could object to my reading my own letter in my own duty-room. It was a queer sensation.

It was not a proper letter. It was just a few lines signed with an initial. It ran:

> 'I would like to finish that interrupted conversation some time to-day, if possible. I cannot get out until the week-end, but if I can manage it, will ask Bill Swan to stand in for an hour or so to-night. Possibly around nine. I hope you will be able to manage this.'   J.

There was no 'love,' not even a 'yours.' Just 'J.' And then a one-line afterthought: ''Good luck, Maggie.''

I was still looking at those last three words when Sandra tapped on the open door. ''May I take the dispensary order book'' – she hesitated deliberately – ''Sister?''

''Do.'' I was too preoccupied with my private life to waste time or energy worrying about her tone or the way she was looking at my belt. ''By the way, Matron wants to see you at eight-thirty

48

this morning. As you guessed, I'm temporarily in charge."

"Only temporarily? So your leaving date hasn't been altered?"

"Just postponed six months."

"That all?"

I nodded as if life was a song. "Now I had better get down to the day's lists."

She did not move. "I knew there was something I had to tell you about last night. That medical case *was* in Joe de Winter's car. The porter told me when he brought back the keys. The world's quite a small place, isn't it?"

"Very. Particularly the medical world." I sat down at the desk. "I've just remembered it's stores-replacement morning. I've got to fill in the miserable form in triplicate before I do anything else."

"I suppose I'd better get the dispensary done."

"Yes," I said, and this time she moved off.

I had just finished my forms when Bachelor appeared in the doorway. "Nurse Lindsay – I'm so sorry!" She smiled attractively. "I mean, Sister. Sorry to disturb you, but do you know how many size-eight glove-tins we had ready last night?"

"Three. I saw them on the shelf in the autoclave-room. Why?"

She said she had thought we had three tins

when we went off last night, but there were none this morning. "There was a note on the shelf from the Orthopaedic Theatre. They ran out during the night, came up and borrowed two tins of eights. See? It doesn't explain the third."

I looked at the note. "Unless that figure's a three and not a two. If it is a three I'm going to make one big fuss. I don't mind our helping them over a crisis, but it isn't fair to clean us out. We'll need some eights for the list this morning."

I reached for the telephone on the desk. The line to the Orthopaedic Theatre was out of order. I asked Bachelor to slip downstairs to them. "Sister is having a day off. Staff Nurse Watt is in charge." Ellen Watt was one of my original set of nurses, and my greatest friend amongst the girls. "Would you tell Nurse Watt the truth, ask if we can have a return of one sterile tin of eights at once, please. And you might also ask her from me how many large-fisted surgeons they had up in the night. Three tins each holding a dozen pairs take a lot of using."

"That's what I thought, Sister!"

Mr Partridge, our consultant gynaecologist, operated in our theatre on two mornings a week. He was a square, gentle man, with a bumbling voice and the charming manners of every gynaecologist – or, come to that, obstetrician – with whom I ever worked. Not unreasonably, since we had ample warning of all his cases and requirements, he always insisted everything should be ready for him. His registrar and houseman took eights in gloves. If he arrived for his list this morning and found we had run out of his assistants' correct size he would be very annoyed, and rightly.

Bachelor returned with two tins. "Nurse Watt says she's very sorry these had not been returned as soon as she arrived on this morning. The Staff Nurse on call last night says she only took the two."

"That's fine. And where's our third?"

Sandra came in. "May I go along to Matron?"

"Of course. But first . . ." I asked her about the tins.

She could not explain why one was missing. "I know I sterilized three dozen eights and left the tins on the shelf to cool. They were there when we went off." She studied her hands. "I didn't lock up. I don't have any keys, not being a sister."

Bachelor went off to check again after Sandra had gone, without discovering the missing tin. I returned to my administrative work.

"And what price glory now?" Mark filled the doorway. "How does it feel to be sitting there thinking, my Unit – my office – my desk?"

I smiled slightly. "My headache, Doctor!

51

Something we can do for you?"

"Not one thing. I just looked in to wish you the best of British luck in your fine new job, and to hand on some news you'll be wanting to hear."

I braced myself. "What news?"

"What else but the latest on the man Worth and his wife? Not to mention the twins. Making steady progress, the lot of them. Can you imagine, four of one family, and all in Barny's at the same time! A record, no less." He turned to go, turned back. "That was a good job your revered ever-loving did last night."

"Yes. It was. Does Mr Worth know?"

"He does that. Joe was up in Henry Carter early, to explain why he's got not one but two fine rows of clips holding him together. Devil of a shock for a man to wake up and wonder if our surgeons thought they'd find his appendix under his heart. No end bad for morale."

"I believe you. How did he take it?"

"Quietly. An intelligent man, that. I'll tell you this" – he grinned with pleasure – "you know those twins? Know what the poor little devils are going to be called if their old man has his way? Joe and George. And God help the general surgeons when the midwifery boys get to hear of it! They'll be out for more blood than the little lot that made a shambles of your theatre last night!"

It was Thursday, the one day on which we had

no official General Surgical list. Most Thursdays we had a steady stream of General Surgical emergencies to compensate. None came to us that day. That afternoon was quiet for the first time in weeks, and we were able to get ahead with extra chores like marking, glove-mending, and turning out cupboards.

The missing tin of gloves turned up amongst those waiting to be autoclaved. The seal was broken, but all twelve pairs were intact. None of the nurses could explain this.

Sandra blamed the new junior. "The girl's hopelessly absent-minded, Maggie – so sorry – Sister. I know it's none of my business, as Admin problems aren't the concern of a mere staff nurse, but, frankly, I should get rid of her fast."

I did not want to turn the chip on her shoulder into a boulder, so I answered mildly, "Alcott's not all that hopeless. She may forget things – who didn't as a junior? But she is very willing, and always admits her mistakes. She may have got muddled over the tins, but she says she didn't touch them. I can't see I've got any grounds for doubting her."

"Which means you doubt me! Why not go straight ahead and ask Matron to transfer me? That's what you really want isn't it?" she insisted, as people do, through lack of imagination, intelligence, or both, when assuming that any person whom they dislike must share their own standards of behaviour, thoughts, and motives.

I would have preferred not to sound like a sister on my first day in the job, but had nursed long enough to see the future dangers if I now sounded like anything else.

"If I ever do want that I shall go straight to Matron. Admin problems, as you've just reminded me, are my concern. Now. About teas. Will you go down to yours now and take Bachelor with you, please."

She opened her mouth as if to explode again, then swallowed. "Yes, Sister."

Alone, I thanked heaven for our mutual training. Barny's nurses had ingrained in them the fact that authority must be respected no matter how much it might also be disliked or resented. My belt had won that round for me. But I was very much more shaken than last night by the strength of Sandra's dislike of me. I had thought we got along fairly well. Fairly well! She loathed my guts.

When I returned from my tea Sandra was checking stores. "The S.S.O. came in, Sister. He wanted you. He'll be back, or ring."

"Thanks." Formality was my defence in more ways than one. "A case?"

"He didn't say."

The telephone on my desk rang as I was counting sets of scalpel-blades. I seized it. "General Surgical Theatre."

"Maggie – Ellen here. I haven't had a moment to ring you before – oh – can you hold on?"

"Sure." I left the receiver tucked between my neck and right shoulder and went on counting blades. Then I heard a faint voice and held the receiver closer. "Ellen?"

No one anwered. There was a series of clicks in the background, then a woman's voice talking: "I have to tell you I think you're wrong. You should tell her the truth. She has a right to it."

It was obviously a crossed line. I was about to put down the receiver when Joe's voice froze me physically. "I'm doing this my way. And I know what I'm doing."

"If that's how you feel I'll say no more. Will I see you the usual time to-morrow?"

"If you are sure it's all right for you, Frances."

"My dear man, what a silly question!"

I put down the receiver then. I was still gripping it on the rest when the bell rang again. I had to answer it. That was my job. "General Surgical Theatre. Sister speaking."

"Sister, de Winter here. I'm up in Obstetrics. Does that time I suggested suit you?"

His formal manner could just mean he was not alone. He had not been formal two minutes ago. It was a defence for him too.

I said, "I'm not sure yet. Something may come in."

"In which case I'll probably be busy too. If you can get off, could you manage it? Please?"

I felt hollow with misery. I had to believe my ears. But I loved him. I could not turn off that love like a tap. "If I'm free – yes."

"Thank you." He rang off.

Ellen Watt rang again a few seconds later. "Sorry about that, Maggie. Now, about those gloves . . ."

I listened to her apology without really hearing anything until she asked how I was enjoying life amongst the upper classes. "Taking a bit of getting used to?"

"Yes," I said. "Yes, it is."

CHAPTER THREE

An Engagement Ends

The Senior Medical and Surgical Officers at Barny's, being top residents, had their own private sitting-rooms. The remaining sixty-odd assorted registrars and housemen had to share three large communal sitting-rooms. There was no official division of those rooms, but an old unwritten law reserved one for the senior registrars, one for the middle grades, and the last for the most newly qualified house-physicians and -surgeons. These rooms were all on the top floor of the Doctors' House, a neat wedge of a building standing at right angles to the Medical School and way off from all the main blocks.

The latter was a mixed blessing. It did give the residents a chance to feel they were getting right away from the wards, but as they were constantly being called back on the job it made a lot of extra walking. I had never noticed how much extra until that night.

Joe called for me at my Home, and we walked back to the Doctors' House in silence. We seemed to be walking for hours.

The hospital had provided the main furniture in his room. It was good, solid, and dull. His piano, radiogram, dozens of records, hundreds of books, and a few pictures transformed the place into an extension of his personality. Music was his great passion and safety-valve. He was a very good amateur pianist, and in moments of stress took to the nearest piano where another man may have taken to a double whisky. As S.S.O. in a large, constantly busy hospital, alcohol was out, for obvious reasons, while he was in residence. Our top residents were on call twenty-four hours a day, seven days a week, apart from their alternate week-ends off and holidays, throughout the two years of their appointments.

I had loved that room. Our residents were allowed to entertain female guests in their sitting-rooms until 11 p.m., and I had spent hours up there with Joe talking over our future, theatre shop, hospital gossip, or just listening while he played the piano or to his records. Yet that night when we finally arrived I had to brace myself to go in.

· We talked about the weather, Miss Davis, my predecessor's new job, who was going to win the next election.

Suddenly I could tolerate no more small talk.

I sat in one of his armchairs, folded my hands in my lap, and asked what he had meant about us getting unfixed.

He had on his white coat, because though off temporarily he was as always on call. He put his hands in the pockets. "You want it just like that, Maggie?"

"Please."

A muscle twitched high in his cheek. Otherwise his face was expressionless. "Right. I'm sorry about this, Maggie. Would you mind if we ended our engagement? I can't marry you. I'm sorry," he said again, "but that's the score."

It was only what I had expected. But how it hurt!

"Then, of course, our engagement's off."

"You don't mind?"

"I mind like hell. But I'm not crazy enough to want to marry a man who doesn't want to marry me."

He sat on the arm of a chair, offered me a cigarette, and when I refused lit one himself, watching me over the flame of the match. "I – I have to thank you. I don't know the right words."

I said flatly, "I shouldn't bother looking for them. Just tell me something. Why haven't you asked me this before?" He stiffened, perceptibly. "Or is this a spur-of-the-moment decision?"

"No. It came to a head last night because of that business in the theatre."

"But you've wanted us to break off for some time?"

He met my eyes and nodded.

I had thought nothing more could hurt me. I discovered I had been wrong about that, as so many other things. "How long, Joe?"

He folded one arm on the other. The knuckles on his exposed hand were white. "There are times when the calendar and the clock don't make sense. This is one of them."

"I see." I unpinned the ring from my bib pocket. "Then there's no more to be said. Here. This is yours."

He said quickly, "I'd like you to keep that. Please."

"No, thank you." I flicked down the corners of my apron (I was on call too), and stood up. I walked over, stood in front of him. "I don't want it."

He took it from me then, held it in his open palm, looked at it as if it was the first ring he had ever seen and he found it clinically interesting.

"I'm sorry about all this, Maggie. You probably won't believe this – and there's no reason why you should on present showing – but I hate hurting you."

He did not have to tell me that. It was in his face. He was a good doctor as well as a talented surgeon. All good doctors detest hurting people. That being one of the points that sets them apart from the other sort.

"I believe you. I'm sorry about this too." I went back to my chair. "I only wish I had known the set-up before I spoke to Matron last night. Sandra Brown is a trifle temperamental, but she's very efficient. She could have managed my job. Now I'll have to stick it for six months, as I've promised that. I like keeping my promises. Once the six months are over I've finished with Barny's."

"No." He got to his feet. "You can't do that, Maggie. You must stay on. I know I've no right to ask you anything now, but I wish you would."

"You want me to stay on?"

That astonished me more than anything else that had happened in the past twenty-four hours. He could fall out of love with me, fall in love with another girl, and still be the intelligent, sensitive man I had always believed him! Broken engagements did occur; people could not stay in love to order; but no really intelligent or sensitive man could pretend it was going to be tolerable for us to go on working together indefinitely.

He said, "I want you to stay on as Sister General Theatre for the whole two years if Miss Davis isn't fit, which I'm afraid is possible. Good theatre sisters are precious. You could be very good, Maggie." Briefly he looked and sounded his old self. "I'm fond of our theatre, Maggie. When I leave Barny's I'll like to think it's in your hands."

"Leave Barny's? Joe!" I gasped. "What the devil are you talking about?"

"Something else I've got to tell you to-night. I've decided to resign." He went over to the piano, put my ring on the top, sat down, raised the lid. "I had a talk with old Robbie this evening. He's going to get the Board to accept my resignation at their next meeting."

"You're resigning?" I echoed. "And Robbie's letting you go?" He nodded, and began softly to play one of Chopin's slower waltzes. I moved to his side. "Joe? Why? Because of me? Because of my new job?" The expression that flickered through his eyes before he could control it answered me better than words. "It is!" And I was so concerned by this new turn of events that I forgot everything else. "Joe, this is absurd. If anyone has to leave it must be me. Sandra will have to take over. She can do it – and she'll love it. I'll see Matron tomorrow, tell her the truth. She's an understanding woman. It'll make sense to her."

"I think not." His hands stopped on the keys. His face hardened. He did not now look or sound like himself. "It's kind of you to be so heroic, my dear, but quite unnecessary."

"I am not being heroic!" My voice cracked. "You must know that!"

"I only know you are behaving most admirably, my dear." His drawl reminded me of Mark in his most affected mood.

"Joe, stop acting! It doesn't suit you."

A small light flared in his eyes. It was not anger. It puzzled me. "I'm not the one who is acting, Maggie."

That hit me hard. I stopped being puzzled. I had been nearly falling over backward in my efforts to behave like a civilized adult. My civilized veneer was wearing thin. "I am *not* acting!" I snapped. "I mean what I say! You are not now going to have to live with me. I have to live with me. Consequently, I don't propose living with the thought that it was to save my pride – or some such rubbish – that the great Joe de Winter, Master of Surgery, Fellow of the Royal College of Surgeons, the pride of Barny's surgical side, and the white-headed boy of the even greater Sir Robert Stanger, walked out on his own hospital!" I paused for a long breath, then added more calmly, "Also, I'm not just thinking of me. I'm thinking of Barny's. A hospital is only as good as its bright young men can make it. You are one of our brightest. You matter to this hospital. It taught you all you know. It has a right to expect you to use that knowledge here."

I saw that had gone home. But he only said, "Which is precisely why I want you to stay on."

"Our positions are not comparable. No," I insisted as he was about to interrupt, "and you know that as well as I do. I'm well trained, quite efficient, and should be able to cope with my new job. But I am not an inspired theatre sister. I'll never be in the same class as our last Sister Theatre, just as George Ellis will never be in your class, no matter how many higher degrees he collects. My leaving would mean a minor inconvenience for Matron. It would not leave an unfillable gap. That's what there will be if you walk out.''

"Then I'm afraid we'll have to agree to differ on that. It's all fixed.''

"It is? Really?''

He nodded in silence.

I had to sit down. "Is Sir Robert furious?''

"He didn't give me that impression this evening.'' He sat on the sofa. "He seemed to think I was doing the right thing.''

I felt as if not only my private world, but everything I thought I knew about the back-stairs politics of the G.S. Unit, was crashing round my head. Sir Robert Stanger, our Senior Consultant General Surgeon, had never troubled to hide his opinion that one day Joe would be the man to succeed him. Joe had been one of his students, his houseman, registrar, and finally S.S.O. on Sir Robert's glowing recommendation. That I had from the last Sister Theatre. I would have expected him to be my greatest ally. And I was wrong again.

I said at last, "I don't understand any of this. Where will you go?''

"The States. The money's better. A change

of hospital will be useful experience."

"But where are you going to get it? The Mayo? John Hopkins? If it's all fixed, presumably you must know? And won't you have to take another set of exams?"

"Possibly. I've looked into everything. I'm just not ready to talk about it."

I felt as if he had slapped my face. "I see, I'm sorry. Can I ask who's taking over from you? Or is that another Top Secret?"

"You can know. Keep it to yourself until the official announcement. Bill Swan."

That, at least, made sense. Bill Swan was Sir Robert's present registrar. "When does all this happen?"

"If Robbie can persuade the Board to let me out ahead of time – and he says he can – in a week or two. I hope no longer."

That finished me. I felt utterly defeated, with good reason. I had lost. Possibly, that was how I was able to ask, "Joe, would all this have anything to do with a Dr Frances Durant?"

He did not answer at once. He stared at me, and a slow, dull flush crept up his face. "Yes."

"Are you going to marry her?"

"As I was engaged to you until twenty minutes ago that's scarcely a question I can answer."

That should have silenced me. But I was in no mood to be warned off. I had nothing more to lose where he was concerned, and if he and Sir Robert were apparently united on his

65

committing what could well be professional suicide, I still wanted to know the reason why.

"Does Dr Durant understand what you are giving up? Does she want to work in the States? Is that the driving force?"

He said coldly, "I'm sorry, Maggie. I can't discuss Frances Durant with you. You must see that."

I remembered that telephone conversation. He could discuss me with her. And that, I realized, answered me.

I stood up. "Time I went. I hope you're doing the right thing. I don't think you are. I'm probably wrong. And as you've made up your mind, I'll most likely stay on here if Matron asks me. I don't at the moment give a damn either way."

The sofa was lower and deeper than the armchairs. I noticed absently that he seemed to be having a little difficulty getting on his feet. I put that down to a combination of the habitual late-evening weariness of all our residents and the present tension. He certainly looked as emotionally exhausted as I felt, and the new shadows I had seen under his eyes last night had deepened. In view of his late night, that was not surprising either. And then the way he used his hands to get off the sofa, and a slight rather odd stiffening of his back, stirred some memory at the back of the trained part of my mind. I did not bother to investigate the memory then. I had other things to think about.

The rules of established civilized behaviour made him offer to walk me back to the Home. "No, thank you. I would rather go alone."

He did not press the point. "Thanks for coming over," he said politely.

It was the end. So I was equally polite. "Thanks for asking me. Good night, Joe."

"Good night, Maggie."

He opened the door for me. I did not look at him as I walked out. Every one has his limit; I had reached mine. I walked along the red corridor carpet to the lift without glancing round. I did not hear him close the door.

From that evening onward with every day that passed I thought, That's another day – another night – gone; soon it will be better; it must be better.

It wasn't. I went on loving him, and I could not stop. And the more I thought things over the more puzzled I became about Sir Robert's attitude. Joe was not the first man to chuck aside a golden future because he had lost his head over a woman, but why a shrewd man like Robbie Stanger should encourage him into folly was beyond me. Certainly he could make a lot of money in the States, and no doubt do very well. But he was a Barny's man. To all Barny's men (and nurses) there was only one hospital in the world – St Barnabas' Hospital, London.

If I had still been a staff nurse I would have discussed this with Sister Theatre. I would have been grateful for some disinterested but informed advice. There was no question of my being able to mention it to Sandra. My two other staff nurses, Nurse Garret and the newly promoted Bachelor, were both considerably junior to me. They would have been horrified if their new Sister Theatre suddenly burdened them with the problems of her crashed love-life.

I moved into a new room in the Sisters' Home in the following week — a very splendid room with two armchairs, a rosewood writing bureau, well-stocked crockery cupboard, a french window opening on to my own private balcony, and a tiny kitchen which I shared with my next-door neighbour, Sister Henry Carter Ward.

Ellen Watt was away on holiday that week. She came up to see me the afternoon she got back. She was in mufti. The Sisters' Home was out of bounds to all nurses in uniform unless specifically delivering messages.

"Wow, Maggie!" She whistled appreciatively. "Talk about giving you plenty of room at the top! This is dreamy!" She went out on the balcony. "You look right over to the men's house. Isn't that Joe's sitting-room window? You and he wave to each other?"

"No." I explained why not.

She reacted much as I had done. "Is the man

68

mad? His future's all laid out here! Robbie Stanger must be absolutely furious!''

"Joe says not." And I told her just what he had said in that context.

She was a very fair, very tall girl, with large myopic blue eyes. She blinked at me through her slanting-rimmed spectacles, then went back and sat in one of my armchairs. "Tell me all that again, Maggie. Slowly."

I repeated myself. When I had finished she again blinked at me in silence for some seconds. Then she shook her head. "I don't understand. Men! God save us! At times I've thought I understood 'em, but, by God, I do not! They call us illogical, but when the sex-bug bites 'em bad enough there's nothing they won't do, stoop to, or chuck up! And to think I've always thought Joe de Winter a sensible, well-balanced individual! I dunno. This Frances What'sit must have hit him so hard he's lost the ability to think or see straight. Mind you," she added reluctantly, "I've known that happen. Remember Charlie Jones?"

"That pathologist who took off with a lab. technician a year or so back?"

"That's right. He'd been married eight years – reasonably happily, one heard – had four kids. He forgot the lot."

I shrugged. "These things happen all right."

"And what is the Frances woman? Seen her?"

"No. I gather she's a physician at Martha's

69

and was at school with Sandra Brown."

"You haven't discussed her with Sandra?"

I said, "I'm not the one that's crazy, dear."

"That's a relief. That girl's got a wicked tongue. She can't have guessed anything or the whole of our table would have had the story from her."

I said I doubted if Sandra or anyone else in the theatre could have guessed my engagement was off, as Joe was behaving exactly as he always had done. "On top. I can spot the difference."

She said if it was any confort to me Sandra would never bother to notice Joe, or any other man, while Mark Delaney was around. "You do realize she's utterly obsessed with that man? She can't talk about anyone else these days, or blacken him sufficiently. A classic love-hate fixation, if I ever saw one." She smiled briefly, "I suppose you know you have been dangling him on a bit of string for years?"

"Oh, yes. The *femme fatale* of the General Surgical Unit. That's me."

We were silent for a little while, then I asked, "Ellen, why is Robbie letting Joe go?"

"You've only got Joe's word that the old man was so co-operative. Sorry, Maggie – but isn't that true?"

"I hadn't thought of that. I've got so used to believing him."

"One does, dear," she replied drily, "particularly in our job. One gets so accustomed to hearing the truth and only the truth from patients, because as we all know nurses are the only people patients don't bother to lie to. One gets to believing patients represent the normal human race. Of course, they do nothing of the sort. They just represent the human race when frightened. Fear strips off the layers. They come back on again as soon as the patients climb out of bed. But because we have so little time for having any contact with the outside world, we nurses trust people. A very dangerous habit.''

''Yes. Very.''

The theatre was extra busy during all that next week-end. If it had not been for my private affairs I would have enjoyed that enormously. It was Sandra's free week-end. Rose Garret stood in for her well; all my nurses rose excellently to the occasion. I wished my predecessor could have seen the result of her training, and then realized uncomfortably how much the future theatre efficiency would depend on what I taught the juniors now.

''To think we thought sister had it easy!'' I told Ellen on another evening in my room. ''When I'm not handing out instruments, filling in those wretched forms, soothing irate ward sisters because the times of their patients' ops have had to be altered, or coping with consultants who always want to borrow the

71

theatre at the same time, I'm holding snappy little classes for the girls. I've never worked so hard in my life.''

''Wearing, but ideal therapy for you at this moment.''

When I had walked out of Joe's room that night I had thought I would never be able to stand the strain of working with him again. Training helped as much with him as in my dealings with Sandra. Our both being senior had another great advantage. The hospital grapevine never buzzed in the hearing of senior residents or sisters. Ellen heard all the buzzes, and told me that for once the grapevine was behind with a story.

She said now she had begun to suspect the silence. ''I think the Doctors' House has clamped down on it. The boys must know Joe's going, and who is taking his place and his stand-in's place, yet not one word has got round.''

This was an unexpected relief, and another puzzle. ''Ellen, why?''

''Could be just that the boys like Joe. He's been a good S.S.O., has always seen his juniors get time off even if it meant his doing their jobs as well as his own. I think that's probably it. The boys aren't going to spread any gossip about him. And when doctors don't want to talk they can make clams look like blabber-mouths.''

''You haven't even heard our engagement's off?''

"Only from you. The girls in general are just wondering how long you'll have to go on postponing things. That includes Sandra. And you know this Frances Durant? Well, at lunch yesterday Sandra said something about being at school with some one by that name, and then grumbled on about old school friends who promised to keep in touch and never did. I don't believe they are still friends. She was on one of her soap-boxes about it."

"She's got a good supply of those. Luckily, now she's my deputy we alternate off-duties, and though we are on together a lot, it is seldom in the quiet of the evening, when she does most of her tub-thumping."

Ellen smiled. "So there is some consolation for being at the top, Sister Theatre?"

I might be at the top in the theatre. In the Sisters' Home I was a very new, very junior girl. I often felt far more junior than I had in my first year. And I had no set of fellow-juniors amongst whom to take refuge.

The only person outside the hospital who had to know of my altered future was my father, who was at present working in the New York branch of his business. I was an only child, unlike Joe, who had brothers and sisters strung out all round the world. My mother had died too long ago for me to remember her. My father had made a terrific success of being both parents. He had met and liked Joe very much.

I had his reply by return air-mail. He wrote that he was extremely sorry, but, having heard from Joe also, thought we were doing the only sensible thing. My father and I were very close. He had not written one word against Joe. I was grateful for his insight.

I was officially off duty at five on the day I had that letter. I was not able to leave the theatre until ten to eight that evening. At five next morning Night Sister called me. "Sorry to wake you, Sister. An emergency appendix. I shall now wake Nurse Bachelor."

The three staff nurses and myself shared the night calls. As Bachelor was the most junior, she was paired with me; Sandra with Rose Garret.

Bachelor came into the theatre a few seconds after me, yawning her head off. "Why do people have to burst their appendixes in the small hours, Sister? There should be a law against it."

"This one hasn't burst yet, Nurse." Joe had come in behind her. "It will if we wait. Morning, Sister. Sorry to get you both up." He disappeared into the surgeons' room.

Bachelor looked after him and spoke my thoughts. "He looks whacked. He been up all night, Sister?"

"Possibly. Let's get things ready" – I looked at the corridor clock – "and if you have a spare moment could you make some tea – good and

74

strong – and take it along to the men."

She was a quick worker, and found that moment. Later, as she waited by one of the glass windows set in the double doors for the arrival of our patient, she asked, "Sister, why does Mr de Winter write notes leaning up against a wall when there's a table handy? Is it a habit he's got into from so much standing?"

If it was it was a new habit. "In the surgeons' room?" She nodded. "Perhaps because he didn't want to risk falling asleep. There's less chance on your feet."

"I never thought of that. Here they come!"

The appendicectomy was perfectly straightforward. Mark came into the theatre when it was all over.

"Twenty to six on a frosty morning! I ask you! What a hideous hour for a decent man to be up! Why did I take up medicine?" He stretched himself lazily. "And where's the ubiquitous Dolly Bachelor got to?"

"Shoving used gowns and towels down the linen chute. Why? And why is she ubiquitous?"

"Because she pops up wherever I go." He produced an enamel powder-compact from his pocket. "I have this for her. I was at a party across the river last night. She was there with some wild man from Wales. And then it turned out our hostess was her cousin, and she asked me to return this, as the Welshman had removed the lady earlier." He helped himself to a high stool, rubbed his eyes hard. "I must be getting old. I can't take this late-night-early-morning lark the way I used to."

"Poor old man." I finished scrubbing dishes, collected them on a tray, stacked them in a large bowl-sterilizer, then returned to deal with the instruments. "Good party?"

"I've known worse. Not bad for a Martha's show."

I stiffened inwardly, then told myself not to be an idiot. Martha's had been standing across the river from Barny's for the last four centuries. I had seen it daily for the last six years. It was a little late to let the very name of the place upset me, even if Frances Durant did work there. "I didn't know Bachelor had a cousin at Martha's."

"She has not. The cousin is married to a Martha's man. A decent man from Dublin called Hugo O'Brien. Head of their Pathological Department, no less."

"And how do you come to know him?"

Apparently he had met Dr O'Brien at some recent medical convention, discovered they were both Dublin men. "And that's not the whole of it. His mother's sister's husband's first cousin − or it could be second − is my father's brother's wife's aunt's sister-in-law. You follow me?"

I smiled. "Roughly, Doctor, roughly."

He groaned. "How can you look and sound

so revoltingly fresh at this ungodly hour? You're as bad as your ever-loving –" he corrected himself quickly " – as old Joe the Knife himself. There he was just now, after being up all night, saying there was nothing he needed more than a fine walk by the river in all this cold and then a bath and shave to set him up for the day's work."

"What kept him up?" I asked, to give myself time to decide whether to take him up on that slip or not. Joe must have told him. I had not yet mentioned my private affairs to him, partly through lack of opportunity, partly through lack of courage.

"Three road smashes coming in one after the other. The orthopod boys were snowed under – if that would be the right word for all the blood that was flowing round Cas. They had to have a spare pair of hands. And where else would they get them but from the S.S.O. himself?" He jerked a thumb downward. "Your pal Ellen Watt was down there until five this morning."

"No wonder Joe looks so tired."

"A strong man, but no machine." He watched me put the clean instruments on to boil, then arrange a trolley for their drying. "So all is over and done between the two of you?"

I faced him. "Yep."

He took that impassively. "He'll be missed when he's gone."

"You know that as well? Why haven't you mentioned it before?"

"Tell me, now, Sister Theatre," he drawled, "have we had so much as five minutes for quiet talking together ever since you acquired that fetching little lace bow under your chin?"

That was true, yet not all the truth. Because of my own reticence, I let it go and asked his opinion of Joe's leaving the country.

"The man feels he wants a complete break. And why wouldn't he? He's given some good years of his life to this hospital. Why shouldn't he walk another set of wards – and earn the hell of a lot more money for walking them? Let me tell you something, darlin' Sister. Over on the other side of the Atlantic they actually pay their doctors big money! Would you expect a man to ignore that?"

"If a man wasn't prepared to ignore that he would never have worked ten years in Barny's as Joe has done – or taken up medicine in this country in the first place. It's scarcely a short cut to riches."

He said I could be right, but what in hell did it really matter why Joe was going? "Point is – he's nearly on his way. Which leaves you free to get out and about – live it up. Which reminds me, have I told you how much I love you?"

"Not for a couple of weeks – and not now! It's indecent before breakfast. I've got to get this clearing finished, and I'm in no mood for a jolly laugh."

"That doesn't surprise me." He took my shoulders in his hands. "Hurts bad?"

"Worse than bad." I leaned against him momentarily, forgetting my new job and where we were. "I don't know what to do about it, Mark."

"And the boy with all the answers has no answer for you." He rubbed his face against mine. "I guessed it would be like this for you." He used a voice I had not heard him use before, then muttered something under his breath.

"What was that, Mark?"

"Nothing I can repeat to a lady, my sweet." He let me go. "When's your next free evening off?"

"Not sure. Can we talk about it some other time?"

"We'll do that. And we'll do the town on that evening." He looked round as Bachelor returned. "I'll be on my way or Nurse will be shoving me down the laundry chute. I see the light in her eyes!"

Bachelor smiled after him with the expression of an adult with a playful but tiring small boy. "Mr de Winter's been waiting for him out in the corridor. And he asked me to tell you, Sister, that he'll be starting his afternoon list an hour later than usual. The wards have been warned."

"Thanks." I checked the time, switched off

the instrument-sterilizer, began fishing out the steaming instruments. "Why an hour late?"

"He didn't say, Sister. Oh — was it all right to make more tea? He looked so queer. I don't remember his looking like this after other all-night shifts. Would you say," she added absently, "those injections he's having in Martha's tropical lab. are affecting him?"

I glanced at her sharply. She had clearly no idea she was giving me news.

"Injections can be upsetting. Depends what they are, obviously."

"Oh lor'! I forgot!" She clapped a hand to her masked face. "Hugo — he's my cousin's husband — told Sylvia, my cousin, but no one, no one at all, should discuss those new injections for rheumatism! He'd be livid with me! I'm terribly sorry, Sister! I shouldn't have said a word! I haven't to anyone else! I promise. It just sort of slipped out!"

"Things do in the early morning. It's the same as late at night. Don't worry." I changed the subject even though I would have liked to pursue it. So Joe was having injections for his rheumatism? That was possible, and yet why go to Martha's, when we had our own very large pathological department? Unless Martha's path. lab. was on to something new and he was willing to be a guinea-pig, because he suspected he might have one of the more unpleasant forms of rheumatism.

I had changed the subject to Bachelor's connection with Martha's, then asked about the tropical lab. she had mentioned. "Big as our own?"

"Much bigger. Nearly as big as the Tropical Medicine place. One of Hugo's assistants is top girl there. She's a great friend of Sylvia's. A fantastic woman. She looks like a pin-up, and is loaded with brains. She's got Membership and an M.D. and isn't thirty yet! And – which is really quite maddening in a crazy way – she's awfully nice. Her name's Frances Durant."

I concentrated on my instruments. "I've heard the name. I believe she was at school with Nurse Brown."

"She was? I'd never have thought it! Frances isn't at all bi—" she corrected herself – "a bit like Nurse Brown." And to cover her embarrassment she took the subject back to Joe's injections. "I honestly can't think why Hugo made such a fuss when he heard Sylvia telling me Frances was treating Mr de Winter. After all, he is our Mr de Winter. And, as for being an injections victim, that doesn't make him news! I'm a human pin-cushion, what with being vaccinated, anti-polioed, anti-TB-ed, anti-typhoided, and God knows anti-what-else-ed! Home Sister's only got to see me to send me to the nearest path. lab. for another shot of this or booster of that! I suppose poor old Hugo, being such a Big Doctor, just has to be hot on ethics?"

"Lots of doctors are," was all I said.

We finished the clearing and the resetting in silence. The theatre was always left ready for immediate use in an emergency. We had everything in order just in time to go to early breakfast. Bachelor said she was starving. "My stomach's flapping against my spine, Sister! These early calls are ruining my waistline!"

"They do give one an appetite," I agreed. As we sat at separate tables in the dining-room she would have no opportunity to observe that on this occasion they had not had that effect on me. Her description of Frances Durant had fixed that.

CHAPTER FOUR

An Invitation From Mark

A few days later one of the dressers was racing along the theatre corridor on his return from lunch.

"Hey, Dolly! Have you heard the latest? Old Joe the Knife's leaving and Bill Swan's taking over at the end of –" His voice stopped suddenly, and there was a scuffle of steps as Dolly Bachelor swept him into the sanctuary of the at present empty surgeons' room.

I was at my desk. I went on with my writing, pretending I was deaf. It had been the best-kept story I had ever known at Barny's, but every story has to break some time.

By evening it was all round the hospital. At dinner my fellow-sisters cast me discreetly speculative glances, but, as we were fortunately still on the most formal terms, refrained from mentioning the subject to me. Ellen came up to my room that night and told me the staff nurses had discussed little else at their meal.

"The only staff nurse whose views I haven't had is Sandra. She having a day off?"

"Yes. She hasn't got a late morning, so she'll be back tonight."

She said, "I don't know whether this'll amuse you, but thanks to Sandra the girls are all convinced Joe's mainly getting out of the way to leave the road clear for Mark Delaney. Doing a Galahad, in fact."

"That so? Nice to know."

I took myself on duty extra early that day. We had very long lists scheduled for both morning and afternoon, and I wanted to get most of my paper work finished before breakfast. Sandra, my senior staff nurse, was in charge of the department until I came on officially, after breakfast, at eight-fifteen. I reached the theatre just after half-past seven. At that time she would be in the theatre proper organizing and supervising the early cleaning. The fact that the theatre had been cleaned and reset after the last case last night made no difference to the early-morning work, the theatre being a department in which one cleaned the clean. I knew she would take umbrage if I looked in on the cleaning to say good morning, and assume my presence must show the juniors I considered her incompetent to be in charge, so I let myself in quietly, went along to my duty-room, and got on with the forms.

It was some little time before she came into the duty-room. "Oh! I should have knocked. I didn't know you were on, Sister."

"I'm not, officially." I explained why I was there, handed her the dispensary book. "Wanted this?"

"Yes; thanks." She lingered, frowning. "Is it true about the S.S.O. leaving and Bill Swan taking over?"

"Quite true."

"I just couldn't believe it!" She went very red in the face. "I've been expecting something to happen – not this! I must say – I'm sorry – but I think it's downright wicked his having to chuck up so much just because you're in love with Mark Delaney!"

I had had enough – and no breakfast. "I may or may not be in love with Mark Delaney," I snapped, "but I am well aware who is! So I don't think we'll continue this conversation. I came on to work. And you had better get on with your dispensary order."

If I had not been so angry I would have been interested on the effect Mark's name was having on her vasomotor system. She had gone red, white, then red again. She tore off like a starched tornado.

A little later a trolley was trundled to the tin-room next door. "How many gowns are we going to want this morning, Rose?" asked Dolly Bachelor's voice.

"Nurse Bachelor!" Sandra must have bounced out of the stock-room. "Are you incapable of doing simple arithmetic? I have already told you Mr Partridge has seven operations on his morning list. That means six gowns per op: three for the surgeons, one for Sister, one for the dresser, one spare — as you very well know!"

"Sorry, Nurse Brown," apologized Dolly.

"I should think so! How many more times am I going to have to tell you to think for yourself? And how many more times am I going to have to hear you using Christian names on duty? Now you are supposed to be an acting staff nurse, will you kindly act like a staff nurse?" The dispensary basket creaked as she deposited it violently on the bench to await removal by one of our porters. "Nurse Garret," she added icily, "I am now going to do the needles in the theatre proper, if I should be needed."

There was silence until Sandra's rubbered footsteps vanished behind the soundproof doors.

"Dig her for a crazy, mixed-up staff nurse!" remarked Rose Garret. "Watch it, Dolly. Our Sandra's out for blood this morning, and if you're not careful you'll be first donor."

"I don't see why she has to be so narked," replied Dolly plaintively. "It isn't her man who's leaving."

"Don't be dumb, duckie! Do a little of that

simple arithmetic she was bleating on about. It adds. Of course she's doing her nut about old Joe leaving. That'll mean the end of all hope for her – and heaven knows she never had any – with the massive Mark. We all know he's nuts about Sister.''

''Is that why old Joe's vanishing? Is he being that old-fashioned square – a little gent?''

Rose said she wouldn't be at all surprised. ''Old Joe's a cutie.'' She sounded as if he was two inches high and made of sugar. ''Sister has to have what it takes, having both those men in her pocket. Yet she doesn't look a sex-pot to me.''

Dolly Bachelor assured her Women Never Could Tell. ''Evan thinks Sister's terrific.''

I did not know whether to laugh or cry. I did know it was high time to make my presence known. I picked up the telephone, asked for the Orthopaedic Theatre. Ellen answered. I asked if she had any Forms XLVI to spare. ''No, don't bother to send them up. I'll collect them on my way to breakfast.''

There was an embarrassed silence from the corridor when I replaced the receiver. Then the tin-trolley was trundled away.

Later, when I called in on Ellen, she said. ''What did I tell you, Maggie?'' And then, ''Those girls work with Mark. Do they have to be so wrong? He is rather nice; you have always liked him. Why not – well – just keep an open mind? I hate to say this, dear, but you aren't always right in your judgements on men.''

I could not answer that one. Thinking it over in the quiet of Sisters' breakfast, I was as convinced as ever that Mark was no more in love with me than I was with him. He had more or less dropped his act about loving me more than life itself when I first got engaged to Joe, but before that, whenever it had suited him in between girl-friends, or because there was some particular girl he wanted to impress, he had gone into the old routine. To give him his due, he knew I never took him seriously.

I was not clear now why he had again decided to give the impression I was the love of his life. As far as I had observed, there was no girl in my theatre whom he wanted to make jealous. The fact that he was doing just that to Sandra was incidental. For her – and the theatre's – sake I wished it was not, and that Mark would grow out of his tiresome teenager tactics.

Directly after breakfast each morning I made out the day's work-list. Sandra knocked on the open door as I was studying the off-duty rota for this purpose.

''Sister, would it be possible for me to be off this morning instead of this afternoon?''

''It would suit me far better if you did change. This afternoon's is going to be much the most difficult list. Sir Robert's having one of his days. Every single op is a major, and this abdomino-perineal means his usual double team. Sir Robert and Mr Swan the top end, the S.S.O. and Mr Ellis the bottom.''

She studied the list over my shoulder, formally yet attentively. Despite our earlier scene, and her personal animosity to me, theatre work fascinated her. ''Should be interesting. Pity to miss it. You'd like me to take for the S.S.O.?''

''Very much. I must take for Sir Robert. Garret'll be on, and is shaping nicely, but knowing Sir Robert's speed I would infinitely prefer having you behind the other instrument trolley.'' I glanced at the time. ''We are starting early this afternoon. Could you go off now and come back at twelve-thirty instead of one? That suit you?''

''Please.'' She flushed. ''If you're sure that's all right?''

'Couldn't be better.'' I was astonished and relieved by this wholly unexpected olive-branch. After my outburst, which I now regretted, I had expected her to sulk for days. ''Thank you very much for offering to change.''

''That's all right,'' she mumbled uncomfortably. ''And – er – incidentally, Sister, Nurse Garret has asked me to give her a lift up West. She wants to meet her mother and go shopping, or something. Could she leave now and come back early too?''

''Certainly. Bachelor and I can manage Mr Partridge between us. Go and collect Garret now. And thanks again."

She looked as if she was suddenly regretting her offer, but she only said, "Back at twelve-thirty then, Sister."

I could not conceive what had brought about this change of heart, but was too thankful to waste time looking for reasons. That afternoon list had been on my mind because of Rose Garret's comparative inexperience. Sir Robert was such a swift surgeon, and Garret was slow. Slowness infuriated Sir Robert. On occasions I have known him order a tardy houseman or dresser, "Out! Out, boy! Go on. I've got work to do! If ye can't get on, get out!" In general he was less fierce with nurses, but even so I remember the time in my early days when he had asked me in the middle of a case if I was married. "Ye not, eh Nurse? Just so, just so. And if ye'll forgive me, just as well if you're going to take as long darning y'husband's socks as ye are getting those needles threaded for me! I'm not doing a tasteful bit of tapestry-work, gel! I'm trying to stitch up a ruptured bit of gut!"

That had had me nearly weeping into my mask, but at least it had been a late-evening operation and the gallery had been empty. Sir Robert was due to teach all afternoon. If Garret annoyed him there would be a packed gallery to hear as well as see his reaction.

I finished my work-list, pinned it up, went along to change into theatre clothes. A junior tapped on the door. "Please, Sister, Mr Swan would like to speak to you on the telephone."

I took the call on the corridor telephone. "Sister Theatre here, Mr Swan. Good morning."

"And to you, Sister. Now, about the new order for to-day. The S.S.O. asked me to contact you as he's had to go along to Cas. Point is this: Sir Robert's apologies and so forth, but as he has to be in Paris this evening for that International Surgeons' Conference, he wants to operate this morning. Starting at nine-thirty. Any objections?"

I closed my eyes. "Oh, no, Mr Swan," I said weakly.

He said if I would forgive him saying so I was the answer to a hard-working surgical registrar's prayer. "The ward sisters are all raising hell and Partridge is furious! Heaven will reward you, Sister, even if I don't."

"Thank you, Mr Swan. Sir Robert is teaching as previously arranged?"

"He is. You can put up the 'House Full' notices right now, Sister. The gallery'll be packed with any of our top brass who can make it, apart from the student men, as my boss will have four V.I.P.'s watching from the floor with him. They are all flying over together this afternoon." He reeled off the names of three surgical Knights Bachelor and one plain Mister, all of whom were household names in any English-speaking theatre. "Useful to know who's behind the mask, eh, Sister?''

"Very, Mr Swan, very. Thanks for the tip-off."

He rang off. I put down the receiver and thought, Good God! I had let my two best staff nurses go off. I rang their Home instantly to get them back. If Sandra objected it was just too bad. I had never felt so much like a Sister Theatre. I wanted my trained nurses back. If they could be reached I was going to have them.

They could not be reached. The portress said they had left the Home in mufti a few minutes before, and she had just seen them driving by in Nurse Brown's car.

"Never mind, Mrs Jason. Thank you."

I stayed momentarily by the telephone, thinking fast. I had previously arranged to be the sole instrument nurse needed for the gynae list, with Cotton, our third-year, as my 'dirty.' Dolly Bachelor had been down to take charge of the department generally and anaesthetic-room in particular while I was tied up with the list. The two juniors on that morning, Alcott and Jones, were expecting to double up with Cotton and Bachelor, watching and learning all they did.

That would all have to be scrapped. As there was no alternative, Bachelor would have to be second instrument nurse for that first complicated job. Cotton would have to be 'dirty' for her, as she was good and Bachelor would need all the help an efficient 'dirty' could give her. Jones, being senior to Alcott, would just have to preside over the anaesthetic-room – I could ask Mark to keep an eye on her – and run the outside for me. Little Alcott would have to be 'dirty' for me – and Heaven help both of us if she was in one of her absent-minded moods.

"Here's a sweet prospect." Mark had come in. "Why so pensive, angel?"

"Not pensive. Plain worried." I explained, and asked him to look after Jones.

He said there was nothing he would not do for me – when he wasn't doing for old Robbie. "A full-time job that! And which is Jones? The skinny bird? Why can't I have the doll with the big blue eyes."

I said tersely, "Because Jones is more senior and more use."

"Careful, sweet! You're sounding like a sister!"

"Unfortunately, that's what I happen to be here this morning."

He was amused. "You are worked up! Relax. Surely you knew Robbie was throwing this demonstration?"

"Not until Bill Swan told me."

"Sandra didn't hand it on? When I myself whispered the rumour that the lists were going to be switched into her shell-like ear when you were at breakfast? When I came in to take a gander at your off-duty rota. I wanted to be sure you had a free evening to-morrow. There's a fine party we mustn't miss, and you owe me a date. How about it?"

"No dates now, Mark."

"And why not? You're free, as Sandra herself pointed out when I told her about this party."

"You told her?"

He read my mind and began to laugh. "So she held out on you about old Robbie? Well, well, well!"

"Mark," I said quietly, "don't be so bloody silly. It's not well at all – and I haven't time for more nonsense. Do you want anything?"

"Do we have this date?"

I would have agreed to anything to get rid of him. He said I would never regret it and strolled off chatting to himself about young women who were going to grow old before their time through taking their careers too seriously.

I called Bachelor from the theatre.

She was openly horrified. "Sister, do I have to? I'm even slower than Garret, Sir Robert'll eat me alive!"

"You'll be taking for the S.S.O., not Sir Robert."

"But he's just as quick."

I said, "I know, my dear. You'll just have to manage. I think you can." I sounded far more sanguine than I felt, but the poor girl needed all the encouragement I could give her. "Cotton'll be a great help."

"I'll do my best, Sister, though I don't honestly think my best is anything like good enough. Could you – would you mind – perhaps asking the S.S.O. not to mind too much about my being slow?''

In the past I would have done that already. ''I may not get a chance, but if I can – ''

''Sister! Here he is!'' Her eyes lit up with relief above her mask. ''Shall I see about the resetting, and telling the others?''

''Please.'' I waited as Joe came quickly down the theatre corridor, the skirt of his white coat floating out behind him. ''Morning, Mr de Winter. Mr Swan has just rung about the changes.''

''I know. Can you spare me a moment, Sister?'' He held open the duty-room door. ''If you please.''

He was our S.S.O. I had no alternative but to make time for him. I went into the duty-room. He shut the door. ''Maggie, do you realize what Robbie's going to do this morning?'' I nodded. ''Then what the hell were Sandra Brown and Rose Garret doing driving out of Casualty yard in outdoor clothes just now? Aren't they your two best seniors? You'll need at least one of them for Robbie's list.''

''I know that now. I didn't when I let them go.'' I sat down. ''I rang over directly Bill rang me. It was too late. Bachelor'll have to take the second instrument trolley.''

''Which one is Bachelor?'' He came over to the desk. ''That chubby one outside just now? With the brown eyes? The new acting?''

"Yes. Fourth year. She's very good, but too inexperienced to have her speed up yet. She's convinced Robbie's going to eat her alive."

"Poor little thing." He sat by me. "Will I have her then? She afraid I'll eat her?"

"She's not so much frightened of you as your speed. Will you guide her along without Robbie catching on?"

"Sure. She should be all right. She doesn't dither." He picked up the list of cases on my blotter. "And what about your 'dirties'? They up to this V.I.P. show?"

"One's good, one's hopeless." Slowly we smiled at each other and the clock turned back. "It's not the poor child's fault. She's just too junior as yet. She's very willing, which is what worries me this morning. She's perfectly capable of rushing in helpfully to pick up a dropped sponge or pair of forks and then laying either on the table or my trolley. You tell her something one moment, she says, 'Yes, Sister, of course, Sister!' and forgets all about it the next. Did you by chance hear about our lights failing momentarily during the urological list on Tuesday? Between ourselves, that was our Alcott. You know the main switches are all outside? She was supposed to be writing up a lecture, had finished, and thought she would help out by doing some extra dusting. So she turned off all the switches before wet-dusting them. She said she knew it was dangerous to wet-dust with

96

the switches down. She had forgotten they controlled the theatre lights."

"My God, Maggie! Can't you send her off duty or something?"

"Not without leaving myself 'dirty-less. Besides, I feel safer when I can see her. I'm just hoping the good angel of all theatre sisters will be on the job with me."

"You and me both. Now, back to business. This third chap'll need the portable boys along. Rung X-ray?" He waited while I dealt with that at once.

"This fourth chap with the chest aneurysm," he went on, "is bound to leak. The ward have got three spare pints of his group. Get them to send the lot down with him." I made that telephone call. "As for the girl at the end, I've a notion Robbie'll finish her off by slapping on a plaster."

"On that? Why? I thought he was agin slapping hands in plaster?"

"He is, on the whole. But when he saw her yesterday – her proximal and middle phalanges are the two crushed – he said he thought he would have her in plaster for a few days until the fracture line gets sticky. The old routine."

"We'll have a plaster trolley ready. Thanks."

"Not at all. By the way, Robbie is back from France tomorrow. He'll be doing that hole-in-the-heart girl from Christian on the morning after." He paused. "Possibly my last day."

The clock shot forward again. I said, "I'll get my end organized."

He nodded and stood up quickly. Or, rather, he tried to stand up quickly, and stuck halfway. He leaned both hands flat on the desk top, grimaced involuntarily, then heaved himself upright.

"Joe, are you all right?" I watched him anxiously. "You stuck."

"I know. My back's stiff. Probably a touch of lumbago."

"If it was, then you'd still be stuck."

"Then it's just as well if it isn't," he retorted shortly, "as I still have two more ward-rounds to do before Robbie's party begins."

That should have warned me off, but I could not stop being anxious about him just because he had stopped loving me. And again, as in his room, I thought: I've seen some one do just this before. Again, I could not place whom or where. "Have you talked to the S.M.O., Joe?"

"Because I get the odd twinge of rheumatism? Don't be absurd, Maggie. Half the country suffers from it, the other half's getting it. Our own fault for living in a perpetually damp climate." He opened the door. "I've got to get moving. See you later."

"Yes. And Joe – thank you very much."

"That's all right. My theatre too. I told you I was fond of it."

"Yes, you did. Thanks all the same."

Sir Robert was still working on the girl with the crushed hand when Sandra and Rose Garret returned to duty. When the operation was over and the surgeons had retired to their room the two staff nurses came in to report back to me and help with the clearing. Sandra's eyes above her mask were defiant and wary. Rose Garret was openly upset. "Sister, was there a change? You've had Sir Robert?"

"We have indeed. And a most interesting and pleasant morning." I smiled across at Dolly Bachelor, who still looked two feet above ground with relief and pleasure and her own success. "Nurse Bachelor managed splendidly, and so did Nurses Cotton, Jones and Alcott. It's too bad you girls missed it all." I named the V.I.P.'s "Sir Robert was at his best. Now, I'm afraid we are going to leave you to clean up while we go to lunch."

Rose said, "Then it didn't matter our being off, Sister?"

"We missed you," I said truthfully, "but everything went very well, so the switch-round really did not matter. Come along, Nurses. Get changed and off to lunch. Mr Partridge wants to start at two."

Sandra, for the first time since I had known her, was speechless. I did not comment on that, or on Mark's unofficial message which she had failed to hand on. There was now no point, and her action had quite fortuitously shown me that in Dolly Bachelor I had another staff nurse with a talent for rising to theatre occasions, and that young Alcott under pressure and a sister's eye had the makings of a very good theatre nurse. It had also shown me the one person I needed to keep a constant eye on was my senior staff nurse. I had made the mistake of underestimating how far her dislike of me would take her. After this morning, rightly or wrongly, the mystery of those size-eight glove-tins was no longer a mystery to me. I did not like mysteries any-where. I was determined there would be no more in the theatre – my theatre.

That made me smile faintly to myself. I was beginning to think like a sister. It was only a question of time before I began saying the modern nurses were not what nurses had been in my young day. And then I remembered I was a sister. For the first time, as I walked in to lunch that day, I genuinely felt like one.

The mood was still on me when I returned to the theatre. I decided not to waste it, called Sandra into the duty-room, asked her to close the door, and then told her how pleased I was with the juniors in general and Bachelor in particular. "We have the makings of a really good team, now. And in no place is teamwork more essential than in the theatre. A patient's life may quite literally depend on that. But you know that. So I won't keep you any longer. Will you take for Mr Partridge? Garret can see to the comings and goings in the anaesthetic-room, and Jones can 'dirty'.''

"Yes, Sister." She stared at the floor. "Was that all?"

"Yes, Nurse Brown."

She went out without meeting my eyes.

I would have preferred not to have gone to that party with Mark, but when the next evening came the theatre was quiet, and I was not on call, and had no excuse for staying on duty in my free time.

Mark was uncharacteristically punctual. In the taxi he said it was time I caught up on how the other half lived. "There are more things in life, my cherished Sister Theatre, than are found within the green walls of your elegant department."

He had booked a table for dinner at a very expensive restaurant. I asked if he had won the Pools.

"Indeed I have not! But I said we'd live it up, and that's what we're doing. Now, no more talk about money. Sordid, my sweet, sordid."

The party was being given by some friends of his. Their name was Smithe-Grey. They lived in a pent-house on top of a new block of flats overlooking the river. On the way up in their private lift I asked Mark how he came to know them. "I don't remember your mentioning their name?"

"And how long is it since we have been out together?" he demanded severely. "Too damned long. So is it any wonder there are whole pages in my life that are a closed book to you? But if you must know all my secrets, Hubert Smithe-Grey was carried into our Private Wing one night last year with a busted varicose vein. He may be a tycoon, but he bleeds good red blood like the rest of us!"

"Good red? From a vein?"

"Will you stop being a theatre sister, darlin'? Have it your own way. But he bled – like a stuck pig, if that suits you better. So there was no time for waiting around for the top brass. I gave him gas. Joe stitched him up. He asked us both to look him up. I don't believe Joe took him up on that?" I shook my head. "Not as far as you know either? Well, now, it's fine to scorn money. But I love the stuff. So I came along to say hallo, and have been coming along from time to time ever since."

Mr Smithe-Grey was a small, neat man with a tired, young-old face. Mark murmured, "He'll be into Barny's again. Ulcers, no less. Did you ever see a more classic gastric?"

Mrs Smithe-Grey had pale pink hair and a pink spangled dress. She said we were her precious lambkins, warned me she was just crazy about my adorable boy-friend, and vanished as hostesses do at parties.

Mark said he must find us the necessary.

"Wait just here like the sweet girl you are."

I waited and waited. The room was full of smoke, people, and noise. My eyes began to sting. My face felt ready to crack with my fixed smile. I backed against a wall as the crowd grew thicker and noisier, wishing Mark would return and rescue me. Through the smoke faces drifted by, disembodied, then one stopped directly in front of me. The face of a very good-looking young woman with fair hair dressed in a high chignon and with really beautiful green eyes.

"Hallo. You look as lost as I feel. Don't you know anyone here beyond our hosts either?"

"Not apart from the man who brought me. He's disappeared. I don't know how, as he's so huge. I wish he'd come back, as I can't honestly claim to know even our hosts."

She edged herself against the wall beside me. "The Smithe-Greys are sweet, but whenever I get to any kind of a party like this, I start wondering what on earth persuaded me to come. I usually try not to come alone, but the date I had fixed for tonight fell through at the last moment."

"That's tough luck." I looked her over, covertly. That look amused me. She was exactly Mark's type. Her left hand was bare. Her missing escort – and how any man could back out of a date with a girl with her looks was beyond me – might well find he had made a big mistake letting her come to this party alone.

We talked fashions. We were discussing skirt lengths, when she suddenly broke off the conversation. ''Mark Delaney! Hallo!''

Mark had returned, balancing two glasses, a dish of olives, another of nuts. I thought the lot were going down. Then he recovered his grip in more ways than one. ''Hallo there! And why wasn't I told you two girls know each other?''

My companion said, ''We've covered a great deal of ground, but not names.'' She held out a hand to me. ''Frances Durant.''

I glanced at Mark. He was looking at her with something close to awe. Since the reason for that was plain to anyone who knew his taste in women, I had no way of knowing whether he suspected how I felt. I said I was Margaret Lindsay.

Her expression did not alter. ''Anything to do with Barny's? Like Mark?''

Mark took over. ''Is she not! A Sister Theatre, no less! And Frances here, I would have you know, Maggie, is one Big Doctor from Martha's. She works for my old pal Hugo O'Brien.''

I had been prepared to detest her. I could not do that now we had met. She was the kind of woman women would like nearly as much as men. Dolly Bachelor was right. Frances Durant was a nice person – and that fact was maddening.

CHAPTER FIVE

Swan-Song For Joe

On the way home I asked Mark if he had known Frances was going to be at that party.

"The Smithe-Greys ask her round often. They've taken quite a shine to her."

"And not only the Smithe-Greys," I said drily. "Joe. Or didn't you know that?"

"These things get around."

"Was that why you were so determined to drag me to the party?"

He asked, "Would you think me a heel if I said yes?"

"I'd rather you were a heel than a liar. Maybe you were right."

"Useful to know the strength of the opposition?"

"Opposition?" I shook my head. "No."

"I don't follow you, Maggie. I thought you loved the man."

"I do. That doesn't mean I'm prepared to do battle. I'd fight with him. Not for him against another woman. He's not my property. He wouldn't be that, even if we were married, but I might be prepared to put up a fight then to save a home, or for our kids. Not for a man alone. If he wants her he can have her. I may go on loving him, but I still don't want a man that doesn't want me."

"So there's no truth in that 'Hell hath no fury' routine?"

I thought of Sandra. "I wouldn't rule it right out. Like most generalizations it's based on truth, but doesn't always apply." I turned to him. "But you'd fight for a woman?"

"With no holds barred, sweetie." He patted my hand. "And no nonsense about keeping the fight clean. Haven't we long agreed I'm that heel?"

"You have. I'm not so sure. No –" I pushed him away – "you don't have to prove things. I want to ask you something." And I went on to talk about Joe's rheumatism. "Would it be some form of arthritis?"

He shrugged. "More likely simple fibrositis. Who doesn't get the odd twinge?"

"That's roughly what he said. Would you know if he's having anything for it?" I could not mention those injections without giving Bachelor away. "It's some time since I was in a medical ward. What's the latest in drug therapy?"

"You should have asked Frances that," he

replied casually. "That's her line of research. They keep bringing out new things. I doubt there is yet anything to touch the good old aspirin tablet. But talking of medicine, have you heard who's giving the gas for that hole job *mane*? Old 'Hearts' himself. And the boy" – he tapped his chest – "will be assisting. Going to be a toughie, that job."

We were always given ample warning before an operation to repair a hole in the heart because of the vast amount of organization necessary beforehand. Once the time was fixed and the theatre reserved, there was no question of the operation being pushed to a later hour to make room for a sudden emergency either blowing up in one of the wards or coming in from outside, as so frequently happened with our normal lists. As surgical emergencies continued to occur whether or not the G.S.U. was free to deal with them, while we were occupied with our scheduled case the Orthopaedic Theatre, after adjusting its lists accordingly, dealt with all the general surgery for us. That inevitably meant warning the Orthopaedic Theatre about the situation at the same time as the G.S.U.

Very early next morning our corridor was blocked by the slow train of expensive electronic machines being wheeled into their appointed positions in the theatre proper by the small army of physicians and technicians who would preside over them during the operation. Dr Malling, the senior member of the automatic-heart team, came into the duty-room. ''Would you object to a couple of post-grads whom we're training being on the floor with us, Sister? They would be most grateful.''

''Of course, Dr Malling.'' I found Bachelor, whose job that morning was to look after the team. ''Ten, not eight, sets of gowns, caps, masks, boots, Nurse.''

Alcott stopped me in the corridor. ''Please, Sister, I know I'm off at nine-thirty, but may I stay on and watch?''

''By all means, but from the gallery. I'm afraid there'll be no spare room on the floor.'' We stepped aside to let another machine go by. ''There's still more equipment to come.''

''More?'' Her eyes were round. ''Sister! I know in that class you gave us yesterday you said the automatic heart was big, but surely it isn't all this?''

''A bit more than all this. The human heart is a highly complicated organ, Nurse. Any machine that has to do its work isn't something you can just pick up and clip on.'' I looked at the time. We were well ahead, so I took her round. ''We'll start here. This is the heart-lung. These rubber pipes carry the blood to and fro once it's in action.''

''Why all these dials, Sister?''

''Pressure gauges. This one'' – I pointed

without touching anything – "is the thoracic aorta; this, superior vena cava; inferior vena cava, and so on. The physician working this machine will call out the various pressures in the arteries and veins constantly. It's something the surgeons have to know, as I explained yesterday, but can't see for themselves."

Bachelor was at my elbow. Behind her Nurses Cotton and Jones hovered hopefully. Bachelor asked if they could join in. "We have finished our routine, Sister."

She had seen two other previous hearts repaired, but it was the first time for the other three. I had another glance at the clock. "Right. Let's have another look at the heart-lung."

A minute or so later we moved on. "This machine you all know. Well, Nurse Alcott? What is it?"

"Electro-encephalograph, Sister." She sounded doubtful. "But why? This isn't a brain operation."

"No. But the oxygen supply to the brain has to be under constant check. It musn't fail. This'll tell us what's going on."

Nurse Cotton asked, "If it does fall, Sister, or if the blood pressure drops or something, who makes the decisions? Dr Malling? Sir Robert?"

"No. Not in this operation in this hospital. The anaesthetist is in charge of everything apart from the actual surgery. Next to Sir Robert he is the most important man in the theatre.

That's why Dr Homer is giving it himself today. Either Dr Homer or the Senior Medical Officer preside in these operations here. Of course, every member of the team looks after his or her own machine, but Dr Homer has to keep an eye on the lot. That's why we use this particular anaesthetic machine with all these recording instruments.''

The girls considered the rows and rows of dials. Cotton said, ''Place looks like the cockpit of a jet aircraft!''

Nurse Alcott liked to get her facts clear even if she seldom remembered them, and asked Cotton how she knew what the cockpit of a jet aircraft looked like.

''Saw it on television.''

We moved on again and stopped by a transfusion trolley and stand. ''Why blood, Sister? Will she lose a lot?''

''We hope not. We have to be prepared. And it is sometimes necessary to transfuse while the machines are working. The right volume of circulating blood must be maintained, it mustn't clot, and may need an extra pint – or less, or more.''

Nurse Jones said she had been wondering about clotting. ''How about the coronary artery, Sister? Isn't there a hideous risk of a coronary, if it's clamped?''

''A clot's one of the dangers, as I explained yesterday. These suckers here deal with the coronary. One's high pressure, the other low. Sir Robert's assistants will use them to stop the coronary blood getting in his way.''

"While he's stopping the heart?''

"Not only then. Throughout.''

Alcott said slowly, "Sister, if the heart is stopped, isn't some one technically dead?'' Her eyes were worried. "I mean – supposing it doesn't want to start up again?'' She hesitated. "Does it? Always?''

The few men already there had been listening casually. Suddenly they all looked at the floor, like a well-drilled chorus.

I said, "Not always, Nurse Alcott.''

Her eyes stopped being worried and were fearful. "So this child Sir Robert's doing could be going to die?''

"She will die very shortly, if she doesn't have this operation, or if it isn't successful. Physicians don't advise, and surgeons don't undertake this repair lightly. It's only done when there is considered to be no alternative.'' I was briefly silent. "You seen a blue baby, Nurse?'' She nodded. "How old?''

"Only babies, Sister. In Charity.'' (Charity was our infants' ward.)

"You remember how they gasped for breath? Well, this little girl is nine. Apart from her heart, Dr Homer says she's a very nice, very normal child. But she can't go up stairs without collapsing. She can't run, jump, play games, dance, go to a normal school, play with normal children. If she lived long enough to grow up, which is very doubtful indeed, she couldn't risk marrying, having children, running a home of her own. Would you say the poor child was living? Or just existing? This is a dangerous operation, and it doesn't always succeed. When Sir Robert opens up the heart he may find the lesion is too extensive for repair. But if it can be repaired and he can stitch in that gusset I showed you yesterday, which will later be absorbed by the body, then although she'll have to go carefully for six months or even a year, after that she can be a normal little girl doing the things all normal children do. Her parents know the risk – everything has been explained to them. They have decided it's worth taking. I think they are right. I also think they are showing the most tremendous courage and unselfish love. She is their only child.''

The girls nodded dumbly. Then the irrepressible Alcott asked impulsively, ''Does she understand, Sister? Of course, she's only nine.''

Bachelor turned on her fiercly. ''My little sister's nine! Of course she understands! Kids of nine always understand what's going on!''

Alcott looked as much shaken by the good-natured Dolly Bachelor's explosion as she had been by what I had previously said. I pretended not to notice and dismissed the class.

Sandra came over from the sterilizers. ''The

112

S.S.O. rang while you were teaching the nurses, Sister. I didn't interrupt as he only wanted to let us know Mr Ellis is to be registrar on call for any G.S.U. emergencies this morning and won't be coming to us. He has let the Orthopaedic Theatre know."

"Thanks." It was just a routine call. Despite everything, I found I still wished so much that I had been free to take it, just to hear his voice and perhaps manage to ask if this really was his last day, that it was just as well my job had prevented me. "Now all we have left to do is get scrubbed up, and wait for the job to start."

"It should be a fascinating case." Her eyes were shining over her mask. "I wish we did more hearts."

"They are very interesting." I did not tell her I could not share her elation at the prospect ahead. Cases were simply 'cases' to her. Academic exercises requiring the utmost technical skill, and nothing more. If she had heard Bachelor snap just now, she would have thought her unnecessarily dramatic, and myself unnecessarily indulgent, for not slapping the girl down with some reminder about our being there to think and do, and not feel. If I admitted sharing Bachelor's dread of seeing a child's heart stopped, it would only add to her conviction that I was unfitted for my job. Nothing would persuade her that I could love and yet be hurt by the theatre. Pain did not cease to

113

be pain because it was inflicted with good intent, any more than a wound ceased to be a wound because it was inflicted with a surgeon's knife.

Our patient's name was Pauline Dawson. She had very fair hair and was smaller than the average nine-year-old. Unconscious she looked like a waxen doll, and when Sir Robert laid bare her heart it looked too large to be fitted back in her narrow chest.

I stood behind my usual trolley, close to Sir Robert's right hand. Joe, Bill Swan, another registrar, and two housemen were assisting. One of the housemen was a spare. He waited, gowned and gloved, in case an extra pair of hands was needed. Qualified hands. Our dressers were all banished to the gallery.

In the mirror above the table the waiting heart-team were able to watch everything that was going on in the wound. The heart-beat began to slacken, then flutter like a trapped butterfly. Then it stopped.

"Right," grunted Sir Robert. "Right. Total by-pass, gentlemen."

Almost immediately, as the machines hissed, sucked, heaved into motion, Dr Malling's slightly monotonous voice began chanting the various arterial and veinal pressures. Occasionally Sir Robert broke in to explain briefly what he was doing to the packed gallery above. Every now and then he paused to look at the clock. The machines could keep that child alive for so long, and not one minute longer. The exact time for that particular operation had been previously worked out by Dr Homer, and Dr Malling and his team. Sir Robert had agreed to do what must be done within the time set. He did not query the cardiologists. He was on their ground now.

The tension in the theatre increased as the time limit grew closer, then reached its maximum as the final stitches were put in several minutes the right side of the danger line.

"Right," muttered Sir Robert. "Right. Now, let's see . . ."

The exposed heart gave a little shudder, then the ventricles stirred almost sleepily. The beat was irregular, but it was beating. Then, very slowly, its rhythm adjusted itself and settled into a reasonably strong, but above all steady, motion.

No one spoke. The surgeon's concentration was still too intense for spoken relief. Dr Homer looked up at Mark, who had been towering over him throughout, and nodded. Mark mopped his forehead with the sleeve of his clean but unsterile gown.

When the chest wall was stitched up Joe replaced his scissors on my trolley. Momentarily our eyes met, and we smiled at each other. The past and the future were unimportant. The present was sheer, exquisite joy.

It was not our private joy. The automatic-heart men were flexing their shoulders, beaming at each other, and Dr Malling patted his specific machine affectionately. Dr Homer supervised the moving from the table to the bed with the portable oxygen tent that was brought right into the theatre by the porters and the senior staff nurse from Christian Ward. "You take her up, Mark, I'll be up to see her parents directly." He walked over, slapped Sir Robert on the shoulders. "Thanks, Bob. Nice child, young Pauline. Her parents are going to want to thank you."

Sir Robert nodded heavily, looked round. I guessed what for, and pushed forward a high stool.

"Thank ye, Sister. Thank ye." He sat down, removed his cap and mask, dried his face with his cap. "Thank yourself, Hearts. And you, gentlemen. And your good self and nurses, Sister. Must be getting old. These things take it out of me more than they used to. But it all went very well. Capital," he said wearily, "capital." He noticed his assistants. "Go and get yourselves some tea, you boys. I'll be along in a moment."

Slowly the theatre began to clear. Joe remained, talking to Sir Robert. He had removed his mask, gloves, and gown, but forgotten his cap and long white thin-rubber operating-apron. It flapped round his overboots as he came over to me. He looked nearly as tired as Sir Robert.

He stopped in front of the trolley I was clearing, glanced round. We were for the moment alone in that particular corner of the theatre.

"A good case, Maggie. Your predecessor couldn't have run it better."

"I don't know about that. But it was good. Oh, very, very good."

"Yes. I'm glad about that. A nice swan-song." He pushed at his hair, felt his cap, took it off, dropped it on my trolley-top. "I won't be here this afternoon. I'm off."

I held on to my trolley. "For good?"

"Yes." He touched my gloved hand as it held the trolley very lightly. "Good-bye." He walked out of the theatre before I could say another word.

Sir Robert got off his stool. "Much obliged, Sister." He went out after Joe.

I was Sister Theatre. The case was over. I could walk where I wished in my own department. I followed the men out. Sir Robert would have no objections to my having a private word with a retiring S.S.O.

But Dr Homer was in the corridor by the open door of the surgeons' room. "There you are, Joe! What's this I hear about your leaving us this afternoon? I thought Sir Robert told me you weren't going in to Martha's yet?"

"What did I tell ye?" demanded Sir Robert before Joe could answer. "What's that, Hearts?"

The three men vanished into the surgeons'

room before I heard any more. I was very tempted to knock on that closed door and demand a word with Mr de Winter. It would cause no comment, as I might well want to know the answer to some professional query. Dr Homer's remark made me decide against it. I was badly shaken about Joe's going, and I now had to have time to think. Joe had not mentioned working at Martha's; no one had mentioned it. He was officially off to the States. All Barny's knew that. All Barny's also knew that when you work in any hospital you go 'on' the staff. You go 'in' as a patient.

I went back to the theatre and my clearing to think things out. A few minutes later Bachelor told me the surgeons' room had been emptied in a body. ''Mr Swan asked me to tell you he'll be in early for this afternoon's list as he'd like a word with you, Sister. He said there are no changes on the list.''

Bill, as I had expected, came to tell me he had taken over officially. He was one of Joe's greatest friends. We had always got on well, on and off duty. After we discussed the various changes in the G.S. Unit resident staff resulting from his moving up the ladder, I repeated the remark I had overheard. ''Why did Homer say that, Bill?''

''Don't ask me, Maggie.'' He looked through some notes he was carrying. ''Why should Joe want to work at Martha's? Barny's is a much better hospital.''

''I didn't say work, Bill. I didn't get the impression that was what Homer meant, either. I heard him clearly. He said 'going in.' He must have meant as a patient.'' I watched his expression. ''Mustn't he?''

He studied me thoughtfully. He was a quiet man, not given to much talking, with light brown hair and a long, pale, English face. ''Why would he want to do that?''

''I'm asking you. For his rheumatism?''

''You suggesting he's got acute rheumatism?''

''Of course not! He'd have been warded with that. But'' – I shrugged – ''I just don't know, Bill. That's why I'm asking all this.''

''Sorry, Maggie.'' He shuffled the notes together like a giant set of playing cards. ''I can't answer any of this. Would if I could.'' He looked at his watch. ''If you'll excuse me and I move I can get down to Cas. to see how things are shaping there before I have to start here.''

Sandra was off that afternoon. She took over a quiet theatre from me that evening. As I was on call from nine for the night and had a sisters' meeting at eight, I told her I would not be going out.

Etiquette forced her to escort me to the outer door. ''So Joe de Winter has left us?''

''Yes. He has. Good night. Hope it stays

119

quiet." I had to get away fast, or crack. I raced down the block stairs as if the roof was falling in.

I wished I was free to get right away – to a movie – anything outside. The thought of my room, with its view of the Doctors' House, was intolerable. Once on the ground floor I walked the full length of the bottom corridor to kill time.

That was a mistake. There were too many white coats about, too many tall, dark-haired men. I went out on the terrace. That was even worse. Joe and I had spent hours on that terrace; every corner of the stoned flags, every bit of the balustrade dividing Barny's from the embankment, jeered and jarred.

My feet had taken me in a circle and back to the theatre block. I knew I was being stupid and childish, that it was useless to try to run away from my thoughts, but I still could not face my room. I went up in the lift to the Obstetric Theatre on the top floor, and went up the remaining stairs to the roof.

In summer that roof was the pride and joy of the whole block. It was ornamented with coloured sunshades standing in painted tubs, straw mats, lounging theatre staffs and dressers off duty, enjoying the sun and one of the finest views in London.

On that cold evening it was deserted, but the view was better than ever. The river was a black silk ribbon, and the thousands of lights on the far bank sparkled in the cold air with a gaiety that jarred. I hugged my cloak more tightly round me, leaned against the balustrade, and found I was staring at the tiers of lights that was Martha's. I thought back to that conversation with Bill, and then again to Homer's remark. I had been very het up. Maybe I had misheard. Maybe. And then I thought: does it matter? Joe's gone.

Some time later, as I was thinking of moving, I heard men's voices on the fire-escape bridge that connected the theatre and surgical blocks. My eyes had long grown accustomed to the darkness up there above my own hospital's lights. I recognized Mark and George Ellis, and backed quickly. I thought the men had not seen me, then I heard Mark tell George to go on in and get cracking on suffering humanity. "Seeing I'm off the hook until eleven, I'm going up there to enjoy the view with Maggie Lindsay."

I waited until his broad shoulders loomed up the top flight of the fire-escape. "You see well in the dark, Mark."

"The result of being raised on all those home-grown carrots." He leaned on the balustrade beside me. "My old man may never have had much of a talent for raising the lolly, but he has no equal at raising vegetables." He put an arm round my shoulder. "I don't see why you have to weep on that cold stone when I'm at your disposal, angel. And it's far too beautiful a night for weeping alone."

That finished me. "Mark, I'm sorry," I sniffed, and wept into his jacket.

I had done with weeping, but was still leaning against him when we heard the roof door behind us creak. He looked round as I moved away fast, and muttered, "Wouldn't you know it?"

Sandra had come out on to the roof. She was bristling with such obvious indignation that on any other evening I would have been amused.

"I'm sorry to intrude, Sister," she said icily, "but when Mr Ellis told me just now you were up here I thought I ought to tell you Mr de Winter has been trying to contact you. He's rung the theatre twice since you left. He said he had tried the Sisters' Home. I couldn't suggest where you might be. When he rang last he said he wouldn't have time to try again. He didn't say why not, or leave any message."

I could have wept all over again. When she removed herself I asked Mark if he had known Joe was still in Barny's up to a short time ago, and why he might have wanted to reach me. "I had the impression he left this afternoon."

"The man had to pack." He knocked out his pipe against the stonework. "He'd no time for that while still on the job. I expect he was ringing about his radiogram and records. He said he was going to ask you to take them off

122

his hands. Like his piano. Old Bill's got that."

"Why?" Surprise shook me out of my disappointment. "It's quite easy, if expensive to take all that across the Atlantic. My father took his desk and a few other cherished pieces. Joe's not rich, but he hasn't had time to spend money for years, and, unlike yourself, hasn't any family he has to help. His brothers and sisters are all comfortably off. He could afford the transport bill. And he loves that piano and the other things."

He said, "You'll forgive my saying this, darling, but couldn't it be that he doesn't care to be cluttered up with old loves in his new life?"

That would have hurt me far more if I had not known Joe so well.

"His love of music isn't part of me. It's part of himself. I can't understand his wanting to cut all that out. It makes no more sense than what Homer said."

"And what did my respected boss say?"

"Of course, it was Bill I told, not you." I explained myself. "Bill obviously thought me daft."

"I should think so! And what in hell would a Barny's man be doing in Martha's? Don't we have a fine hospital of our own?"

"We do. But I heard him say –"

"That Joe was going over to Martha's! Maybe you did!" he snapped. "And maybe he is! And

123

why not? You'll have heard it's a hospital? And quite apart from the odd social attraction, you'll have maybe heard the place has surgeons? I'm not saying they're much good, but no doubt at all they do their best! And they have meetings – get-togethers – 'let's-all-have-a-ruddy-good-time-telling-each-other-what-fine-fellows-we-are' affairs! Have you never heard, my sweet, imaginative, thick-headed Sister Theatre,'' he demanded, ''of a surgeon from one hospital in London visiting those in another in his off-time, to thrash out the latest technique of shoving in a knife?''

''Yes,'' I said weakly. ''Yes. I have. Of course. I never thought of that. Is there something on to-night?''

''Sure there is. Joe was talking of it only this morning. There's some man who's thought up a new way of whipping out gallstones or something. I forget the details, being no surgeon. But talking of surgery, how many times did your heart skip the old *lubb-dupp* this morning?''

We talked shop until we were both very cold and had to move. On the way back to my Home, Mark talked about his family. One of the things I liked most about him was his great affection for his parents and five brothers and sisters; another was the way he had helped his parents financially from the time he had qualified, and accepted his responsibilities as

124

the reasonable consequences of his being the eldest son and only member of his family at present earning a living.

His father was a retired schoolmaster who had never risen above being an assistant master in a minor English public school. He had married late, retired to Eire with his still very young family on a small pension. Fortunately all his children were clever and, I gathered from Mark, ambitious. Mark had never made any secret of his intentions to stay on the Barny's medical ladder and get to the top rung. He had taken his present job when his first medical registrar's year ended, solely as a means of staying in the hospital. He was a good anaesthetist, but he wanted above all to get back on the medical side in Dr Homer's cardiac firm. He loved Barny's, refused to contemplate working elsewhere. I had once thought Joe felt that way, too.

I refused to think of Joe, so asked Mark about his second brother, Sean. "Hasn't he nearly finished that catering course at his Technical College?"

"He has. He's doing fine. One of these fine days I've a notion Conrad Hilton'll have a rival."

"I hope so. For your sake, as well as Sean's and your parents. In a way your being such a good son – no, you are – has done you a good turn, professionally. Homer likes you. I noticed that this morning, and it wasn't for the first time. I'm pretty sure that when you finish your term as our R.A. you'll be able to get into his firm.''

''You think he'll approve of my filial devotion to duty?''

''I think he'll approve of the fact that you've never been able to afford a wife. He doesn't like women, unless they are patients or ward sisters. He's even scared of nurses. I guess he sees them as potential dangers to his resident's peace of mind. I don't believe he's ever taken on anyone who wasn't a bachelor. Has he?''

''He has not. And wouldn't I like to tell that sex-starved bastard what he could do with his views of the celibate life,'' he retorted with rare bitterness, ''if he wasn't just about the best cardiologist in the business.''

We had reached the steps of the Sisters' Home. I faced him. ''Does it worry you that much?''

''You really want me to answer that?''

I shook my head. ''Sorry. And, Mark – thanks.''

''You've not one bloody thing to thank me for, my love,'' he said, and walked back across the road with his shoulders hunched and hands in his pockets, ignoring the oncoming traffic. The driver of the double-decker bus coming towards him slowed his vehicle and waved the traffic behind to a crawl. It was typical of Mark, I thought, to cross a busy road with the care-lessness of a thoughtless schoolboy, even though

126

like anyone who had worked in a Casualty department, he knew precisely what the consequences could be. In his work, and to his family, he acted like a responsible adult, yet off duty he could – and often did – behave like an irresponsible ten-year-old. In spite of all he had told me about loving Barny's and his plans for his future, I would never have been surprised if one of his sudden crazy impulses had caused him to chuck the lot for a better job, or some woman – and then, inevitably, regret it. I had been half expecting that all the time he had been doing anaesthetics, since he did not really care for the job. Yet he had made, was making, an excellent R.A. And, particularly lately, he seemed to have at last outgrown his previous need to boost his ego with a series of girl-friends, and was showing a new stability of purpose in his work and general attitude to life that must have impressed his colleagues as well as myself – with the obvious exception of Sandra. But then, I decided, she saw people as she was, not as they were. And then I thought: only Sandra? What about me? With Joe. And Mark.

Home Sister came out of her office on the ground floor. "Ah, Sister General Theatre! Good. I hoped I would catch you on your way in. The radiogram and record cabinet are safely in your room. Mr de Winter asked me to say he was so sorry to miss you when he came over to say good-bye to me. I was very sad to see him go. We are losing so many of our good men to the Americans. But one cannot blame the young men for going where the opportunities are brightest.''

Up in my room there was an envelope addressed to me in Joe's writing on the lid of his radiogram. I had to sit down before opening it.

The letter inside was written on Barny's writing paper. There was no forwarding address. It was not meant to be answered.

Joe wrote:

I am sorry to dump my things on you without your permission. I had hoped to ask you first, but thought there was plenty of time, then found it had run out. I have tried to reach you this evening, without success.

Would you mind my leaving the radiogram and records with you? I hope not, as I had to tell Home Sister you were expecting them. If you have strong feelings, give or chuck them away. I don't want them back. Transporting them won't do them any good – and think of the fortune they'd cost as excess luggage by air!

Again, sorry to be so high-handed, and thank you for everything.

Yours,

JOE

I lowered the letter, stared at the radiogram as if it was the first one I had ever seen. Then I went over to the record cabinet, slid back the doors. The many records were listed and numbered. I took one out, checked with the list. As I would have expected, it was in its appointed place. Joe was a methodical man – most surgeons were. It was not like him to leave either his packing, or these arrangements about his possessions, to the last minute. Why this sudden rush? Was it just an act to avoid the embarrassment of asking me to my face? That was possible, and yet would not explain his last-minute packing. Mark explained that as "no time." Joe, being a perpetually busy man, had always known how to make time. Busy people always did.

I looked at his letter again. Why had he written it? Even if he had been in a hurry to get over to this meeting at Martha's, he had to be staying somewhere to-night. In some hotel? All hotels had telephones. Why not ring me later?

I went back to the cabinet. There were records there he had had since he was a student. They were not part of his life with me, as I had told Mark. They were part of himself, important to him, yet he had left them with me. Why? Because he wanted me to have them? As a placebo, in exchange for my engagement ring? Or because, being a surgeon, he knew there were occasions when it was necessary to cut away good tissue as well as bad, to ensure a complete cure?

129

CHAPTER SIX

A Pundit Shares A Problem

Some one knocked on my door. I opened it to Sister Henry Carter Ward.

"I saw your light on, Sister Theatre. Coming over for our meeting?"

I asked if she would mind waiting while I put on a clean apron. She came in, admired the radiogram. "I never knew you had one in here."

"It's only just arrived." And I explained, knowing she would hear the story from Home Sister.

Her name was Wendy Scutt. She was a tallish, sturdily built young woman somewhere in the late twenties or early thirties, which made her one of the younger sisters. I remembered her as a staff nurse in my first year, and later as my ward sister on my first spell of night-duty, in my second year. At Barny's no first-years worked on nights. She used to bounce round Henry Carter in a manner that reminded me of the games mistresses at school, but I had been too much in awe of a sister's uniform in those days to entertain the unlikely thought that the uniform housed a human being, and had had no idea of what she was like as a person. I had since had little opportunity of finding out, as I never worked in her ward again, and since my arrival in the Sisters' Home she and I had discussed little more than the time of day.

She must have known I had once been engaged to Joe. Nothing in her expression or manner showed that. "How very nice for you. May I look at the records?" She ran a finger down the lists. "All these – Chopin? You lucky girl!"

"You like Chopin, Sister? Do you play?"

"Yes." She slid the doors shut. "Not as well as Mr de Winter. What's happened to his piano?"

"I understand he has left it with Mr Swan."

She smiled placidly. "How very nice for Mr Swan! Ready? Then let us make our decorous way across the park. I believe we are in for a lively meeting. As I recollect" – she waited until I closed the lift-gates, then pressed the ground-floor button and kept her finger there – "you have not yet attended one of our meetings?"

"No. This is the first one since I moved up. Does one have to do anything?"

"Unless you have violent feelings on some subject, I would advise you just to sit and look attentive. So much safer as, alas! so many of our respected seniors have the most violent feelings on every subject in the book. At our last meeting I was convinced that but for Matron's presence blood would have been drawn. The subject under discussion was a new form of basic dressing setting for use throughout the hospital. Senior Sister Tutor wants three not four pairs of dissecting forceps, and no Spencer Wells. Sister Private Wing nearly broke a blood vessel in defence of those forceps, and the row split the Sisters' Home down the middle for days after!''

Sister Private Wing, the most senior sister in the hospital, had worn her first lace bow under her chin when Sir Robert was still a student. I had worked three weeks on loan to her department in my first few months of training.

I mentioned this now. "I still only have to see Sister P.W. to feel I'm just out of the P.T.S.''

"My dear, she affects most of us that way, including, it has been whispered, Matron. She'll be retiring soon, and we'll certainly miss her when she goes, even if we do breathe a long sigh of relief. She keeps us all up to the mark. Did you know she actually knew Florence Nightingale when she was a small girl and Miss Nightingale a very old lady?''

"I — yes!" I snapped my fingers. "Of course! Some man in the Wing — I think he was one of our own men — told me that when

I was there, I didn't really believe him. What was his name – Harper? Potter? Something like that. He was in with a back. I forgot what was wrong, if I ever knew it, being so junior then." Then my mind gave one of those mental clicks. "That's who it was!"

She looked at me curiously. "Who what was?"

"I – er – saw some one recently with certain mild symptoms that seemed to be familiar, yet I could not place why. I've just realized where I saw those symptoms before."

She said that kind of thing frequently happened to her. "I have found that when one strikes a chord like that it's generally the right one. One's conscious may make mistakes, but seldom one's subconscious."

I turned this over and over in my mind during the meeting. It was as lively as Sister Henry Carter had anticipated. Sister Private Wing again did battle over the basic setting for a surgical-dressing trolley; admitted herself appalled at the suggestion of disposable masks being used in future. "Disposable this, disposable that! And when do we get disposable nurses?" She then changed from red to purple when Sister Casualty suggested the eight-hour-shift system should be used throughout the hospital and not just in certain departments. "Let me inform you, Sisters," she stormed, "that when I was a junior probationer I began work at 7 a.m. and finished at 9 p.m., with never more than three hours off, and that had to include a meal and a lecture! And we had only one day off a month!''

Matron said pacifically, ''And very excellent nurses you made, Sister. But while the shift system may not be wholly suitable to all departments, I feel it has certain advantages we should not overlook. I believe you would like to enlarge on that, Senior Sister Tutor?''

The Senior Sister Tutor looked ready to throw off her cuffs and up her sleeves. ''Thank you, Matron. We must remember that if our student nurses'' – she stressed the ''student'' – are to attend the many extra lectures now necessary to cover their syllabus and have sufficient time for private studying, they must have longer periods away from their ward work.''

''Nurses without patients! Huh!'' Sister Private Wing snorted. ''And what is a nurse without a patient? A half-baked medical student? Is that the type of nurse we are now sending into the world as a St Barnabas-trained nurse?''

Sister Henry Carter caught my eye as several other senior sisters joined the fight. If I had not been so concerned by my own thoughts I would have been amused, interested, and touched to see how passionately my seniors cared for the future of the profession to which they had given their working lives and were mostly shortly due to leave. But they loved nursing and Barny's and were opposed to change, not, I suspected, because it was change, but because they were afraid it might bring a lowering of standards in the profession which they, and every one else there, including myself, thought the finest profession any woman could choose.

Were we smug, I wondered, looking at the faces. I hoped not. But there was something in every face I looked at that was not always present in the faces of a group of single women of assorted ages. Content. I suspected that was because we knew that what we did was much needed, and women need to be needed.

It was a comforting thought on a night when I badly needed comfort.

After the meeting Sister Private Wing suddenly bore down on me. "Well, Sister General Theatre?" She looked me over, and I turned into a first-year. "Well done, child! I always thought you had an aptitude for surgery. I believe I said as much when you worked in my wing some years ago."

I was surprised the old girl had remembered me. I did not remember her saying anything to me beyond, "Get on, child! Don't dawdle! You are in a hospital, not the Preliminary Training School, now!"

I did not mention that now. I thanked her for her kind words, asked after her department, and was much shaken to discover she obviously proposed to tell me all while I escorted her to the dining-room.

We were in the main hospital corridor when I found the courage to say I remembered one of her patients from my brief stay in her wing. "A Dr Harper, I think, Sister. As I remember, a spinal case."

"Harper? Harper?" She frowned. "I disremember the name, Sister. I seldom disremember names."

"It might have been – Potter, Sister."

"Dr Potter! Yes, indeed. He was a spinal. Poor man! Tch, tch, tch." She clicked her teeth with her tongue. "You must not allow yourself these slips of memory now you are a theatre sister, Sister!"

I apologized meekly, then asked the diagnosis of that former patient. "Sarcoma of the spine, Sister?"

"No, no. Although that was mentioned as a differential diagnosis by Sir Robert when he asked Mr Buckwell of St Martha's to come over and see Dr Potter. He was one of our own men. Mr Buckwell, as you will know, is the acknowledged expert in spinal surgery." And she went on to explain just why such an expert had been necessary in that case. "Unfortunately, on investigation the poor man's condition proved inoperable. Very sad."

"Yes, Sister. Very." I held open the dining-room door. My hand was suddenly very cold.

"Thank you."

Sister Henry Carter had kept a place for me at the junior end of our table. During dinner I asked what she knew about Buckwell of Martha's.

"He comes over occasionally to see various men I've had in with spines. Sir Robert says there's no surgeon to touch him in that line. He's a very nice man." She smiled "Too bad he belongs to Martha's and not us."

"Yes," I said, "it is."

"You keen on spinal surgery?"

"It's one line – or rather one of many – I don't know much about. As you know, any spines here are done by the orthopods. Something Sister P.W. said has made me" – I hesitated – "made me feel I'd like to know more."

She said she could see I was in the right job and began talking about the meeting. After that, for the rest of the meal, the talk was general.

I did not sleep well that night. All next day my thoughts kept going back to what Sister Private Wing had told me, to Mr Buckwell at Martha's, and to Joe. I tried to talk sense into myself, to remember Barny's was a hospital too, and the power of the hospital grapevine. If by any ghastly chance there really was something wrong with Joe's back, some one would have told me. Some one always did.

137

By evening I had had enough. I went into one of the outside telephone booths in the main corridor before going in to dinner and rang the admission desk at Martha's.

"A Mr J. L. de Winter? Come in last evening, you think?" The clerk sounded doubtful, but not as if the name was wholly unfamiliar. "That name's not on yesterday's or to-day's lists, or on to-morrow's bookings. Now, then – de Winter? Would he be from St Barnabas's? Hold on, miss. What's that? Might not be a patient and just stepped in for the evening? Hang on – I'll find out for you." From the sound, the receiver was put down on a desk. Then I heard the clerk's voice very faintly. "Bert. That chap from Barny's as is always coming in here with Dr Durant. Isn't his name de Winter? Thought as I knew it! You did? When?" Bert's answers were inaudible to me.

The receiver clicked loudly as the clerk came back on my line. "Still there, miss? Well, I reckon as you are mistaken about the gentleman being a patient, but he is over here now. Seems he's calling on one of our doctors. If you'll just hang on another jiffy I'll have this call put through to our Medical Officers' Wing for you. I expect you'll be able to get him there."

I had to pretend we had been cut off. I jiggled the receiver rest, ignored the clerk's "I can still hear you, miss. Can't you hear me?" muttered something about having to get some more change before trying again, and rang off.

In the little mirror on the box wall my face was as white as my cap. I was in no mood to sympathize with my face. "You've asked for this, Maggie, my dear." I said aloud, "and, my God, you've got it. Joe's cut his losses with a vengeance, and that's what you've got to do. The snag is – how?"

I never found the answer. I just tried to give the impression I had, particularly on duty. I also tried ringing Martha's again next morning when I judged another clerk should be on duty, then again the next afternoon. Both assured me no Mr J. L. de Winter had been admitted as an in-patient to St Martha's in the last forty-eight hours, or was down on their lists of bookings for the rest of that week. The trouble they took to try to trace the name for me made me feel very guilty about bothering them over what was, on the face of it, the wildest of disturbing hunches. Yet, even after those calls, I remained disturbed. I now remembered, or thought I remembered, that Dr Potter clearly. I recalled his reddish-grey hair, heavy jaw, the fine red hairs on the backs of his invalid-white hands that had slightly nauseated me, the way he used his hands to haul himself out of the armchair when he sat out to have his bed made. His movements had been a caricature of Joe's that day in the sitting-room, and later in my office in the theatre, but the general picture was the same. Of that, I was convinced. Or rather, I was convinced when I was tired, or when I woke in the night. In the mornings, or during the course of normal busy days, I saw the many weaknesses in my hunch, and again reminded myself I lived and worked in a London teaching hospital. All personal feelings aside, that condition was rare enough for any teaching hospital to be glad of the opportunity to study and teach on it, as well as treat it. And Barny's, being a good hospital, was very good about caring for its own. No man or woman on our staff need go elsewhere. If, as with that man in the Private Wing, it was thought that better advice could be found in some other hospital, Barny's was prepared to swallow its pride and ask for it.

All that reassured me − to a certain extent. To be more sure, I asked first discreet and then blunt questions of all Joe's friends in my Unit. That got me nowhere. "Joe? Didn't he say something about the States? Every one seems to be off there these days. Where? Oh, California − or was it Texas − or Maryland? Sorry, Maggie. Try the Dean's Office. They'll have a forwarding address."

They had. A London bank.

Ellen, though reluctant to give credit to men, allowed the boys were just being tactful. "And anyway, men always stick together."

"It wouldn't hurt them to tell me where he's gone."

"Perhaps he asked them not to. He might be afraid you are going to chase after him. Men are so hideously conceited! I don't see why you have to keep on raking up the ashes. And you aren't left high and dry. You've still got Mark Delaney."

I tried again, again without success, to talk her out of her fixation that Mark was in love with me. She had her little ways, but she was a nice girl and longing for me to fall into Mark's supposedly eager arms. She had been shocked by Joe's behaviour to me, but having accepted it herself, she was now very clearly growing impatient with me for not doing the same. Before she left that evening she launched into one of those 'I-think-I-ought-to-tell-you' lectures in which 'pride' figured constantly. "You're just refusing to face facts, Maggie."

"No. Though I'll admit it may look like it. I'm just puzzled because the facts I've been given to face don't match the facts I have long known about Joe's character. A man may change his fiancée, even wife, but not his attitude to living, job, hobbies."

She looked at his radiogram severely. "He shouldn't have given you that. You oughtn't to keep it."

"I know."

She turned on me. "How can you bear to have anything of his after the way he's treated you?"

"Ellen, he fell out of love with me and had the guts to say so. One can't stay in love to order."

"You aren't furious with him?"

"No." She was looking shocked. "Sorry!" She said, "I don't understand you, Maggie. If any man jilted me I'd never forgive him."

I said nothing. There was a short, uncomfortable silence, then we both started talking theatre shop. She left fairly soon after. We had been friends for a long time. We would probably go on being friends on the surface, but after that there would never again be any real basis to our relationship. I was sorry. I liked Ellen, and knew she had been disappointed in me. I wondered if I ought to be disappointed in myself for being sad instead of angry. Perhaps that would come later, when I stopped loving him. If I stopped loving him.

Time went by. I stopped asking questions. No one ever mentioned his name to me. Unless I brought it up, from the day Joe walked out of Barny's, as far as the Unit was concerned, the only S.S.O. anyone remembered was Bill Swan. Anyone, that was, except myself. Weeks turned into months; list followed list; I grew accustomed to seeing Bill's name signing the many notices on my office board; yet when he said "S.S.O. here" on the telephone, or took the S.S.O.'s sink in the theatre, I turned hollow with longing for Joe.

142

Mark dated me on the occasional evening when we were both free; always asked me to the parties the registrars gave in their sitting-room most Saturday nights.

There was one party some two months after Joe left that was extra hilarious even for a hospital party. Mark was on top of his form; the quiet Bill Swan looked in unexpectedly and insisted on doing the Bossa Nova with me; and George Ellis, who was off and had decided not to go away, announced he was going to rule out all possibility of being made to work as he was around by getting very, very drunk.

Later, I remarked to Mark on the high spirits of the Unit boys. ''I've never known George hit the bottle before.''

''And why wouldn't he? When he's free until to-morrow night after a hard week? Arise, my love'' – he pulled me from my chair – ''and if you will not fly with me, at least dance with me. And while we dance, tell me what you mean by doing this line with our Bill!''

''Don't ask me! I was going to ask you. He's not usually a dancing man.'' I had a good look round. ''You all had some good news, or something?''

''Indeed we have! It's Saturday night, the customers are all curing themselves nicely, those poor devils Steve Porter and Tom Ross are holding the G.S. fort, and we are free to dance and make love. What say you, Sister Theatre?''

"We will twist, Dr Delaney. Then you can go and find me some apples."

"Apples? . . ."

" 'Stay me with flagons, comfort me with apples; for I am sick of love.' "

"Solomon? Song of? There now, apples is it to be?" He grimaced. "You're a hard woman, Maggie Lindsay. But I love you the way you are."

One morning the following week Wendy Scutt walked over to breakfast with me and offered me two free tickets for a concert that evening. "The solo pianist is a G.-ex-P. [grateful ex-patient] of mine. He always sends me six tickets whenever he has a concert in London. Those two are in one row. I've four more two rows ahead that I want to use. These any use?"

"Thank you very much. I'm off this evening and not on call."

I met Mark on my way to the theatre after breakfast and asked if he would like to come with me to that concert. "It is your free evening, isn't it?"

"Er – yes. I'm off the call hook, too. Thanks, Maggie. This is sweet of you." He went a dull red. "What time may I call for you?"

He looked and sounded so embarrassed and unlike himself that for the first time I wondered if Ellen might not be right about him. I found the thought more disturbing than pleasing. I was not yet ready to love again.

"Sister Theatre –" Bill Swan's voice made me turn round. "Sister, a word in your ear! Crisis on."

The crisis was in the Obstetric Theatre. A main steam-pipe had burst in the night and the theatre would be out of action all day for repairs. "Any objections to the obstetric department borrowing your theatre and self for a caesar at one-thirty, Sister? Sir Robert'll start an hour later than usual. Thanks. I'll fix it with the accoucheurs."

Sister Obstetric Theatre rang me shortly after I reached the theatre. "Sorry about this, Sister. Will it be convenient if I send down a complete floor staff?"

My theatre nurses were enchanted about the caesar, and as Sandra was off that afternoon, there was no one to take umbrage over the invasion from the Obstetric Theatre staff. I went to early lunch. When I returned my theatre was full of strange forms and strange eyes. The gallery was equally strange, being packed with pupil-midwives and midder-clerks in addition to my own girls and the usual drift of students.

The woman to have the caesar was thirty-nine. She had been married twelve years, and had a poor obstetrical record. "Four miscarriages, Sister," said the staff midwife who was 'dirtying' for me. "The last went to twenty-eight weeks and was abnormal. No arms."

"Oh, God!" I winced. "Does this baby sound right?"

"Aye. The foetal heart's good. But the mother's measurements are far too wee. And she's awful scared."

"The poor dear. I don't blame her. What about her husband?"

"Och, in a terrible state. Mr Bellings (the Senior Obstetrical Registrar) has given him a tranquillizer. Ah — this'll be the trolley now, Sister."

It was not long before the child was born, but apprehension made it seem long. The S.O.S.R. lifted the limp little figure gently. "All there — and a girl. Thank God!" He handed the baby to the sterile-gowned and gloved staff midwife from the Maternity Unit nursery who was waiting to receive her, then returned his attention to the mother. "Something odd going on in here, Charles," he remarked to his assistant as the placenta was removed. "What have we . . . Thought so! Feel this fibroid! God knows how she went to term with this one."

"Going to take out the works?" asked the J.O.H.P.

"Let's have a bit more of a look round."

A few minutes later he said he would have to do a hysterectomy. "She was expecting this."

It was my job to ask, "Has her husband signed his consent?"

"Yes. It's in writing from both."

I had set a second instrument trolley in case a hysterectomy (removal of the womb) might be necessary. The 'dirty' moved it forward for me, propelling it carefully by the lower legs.

Mr Bellings glanced round. "All set? Thanks, Sister."

It was the first time I had ever met Mr Bellings. The obstetric department lived in a world apart from the general side. Joe had been S.O.H.P. during my first year, and neither of us had remembered seeing each other around the hospital until he moved back as Senior Surgical Registrar to the G.S. Unit in my second year.

Mr Bellings was a competent, good-humoured, and very talkative surgeon. He chatted on about the mother's previous obstetric history and fears. "Poor woman had us all on edge with her hunch. So much for feminine intuition!" His hand came my way for a second arterial clamp. "How's that nipper breathing now, Nurse Dunne?"

The staff midwife from the nursery said the baby was breathing quite nicely. "Colour's not at all bad." She adjusted the flow of oxygen into the tented, incubator-type cot sent down from the Mat. Unit. "You got her into this world before much of that anaesthetic got to her. She should do you proud for your half-century."

I asked, "Your fiftieth caesar, Mr Bellings? Congratulations."

He took up the scalpel again, holding it like a table knife, with his forefinger along the handle. As he took it, his fore-finger tapped the handle a couple of times absently. Joe had sometimes done that, and Bill Swan. It was one of Sir Robert's mannerisms that had brushed off on his young men. It should have reminded me of Sir Robert. Instead, I remembered Joe.

His assistant asked who held the caesar record.

"Robbie Stanger with a hundred and forty-four. I expect I'll reach the century before my time's up. May even go over. Old Robbie did extra time in my job, but Joe de Winter told me yesterday that he made a hundred and twenty-nine before he was finished."

I was holding a curved needle at the end of one pair of forceps, a length of thread with another, and threading the needle to it. For a moment my hands stayed poised. "Joe de Winter in London, Mr Bellings? I thought he was in the States?"

"I heard he'd gone over. Apparently not yet. I ran into him over at Martha's. I had gone over to look at some new prem. incubators they're using. He was visiting a friend. Said he'd been on holiday. I forgot to ask where," he added casually, "but it was obviously some place in the sun. He was good and brown, lucky chap."

When Mark called for me that evening I handed this on. "Did you know Joe was back?"

He nodded reluctantly.

"Why didn't you tell me?"

"His news to give." He hailed a passing taxi. "This is luck, getting one so soon. And how did the caesar go?"

I refused to be side-tracked. "Why did Joe leave in such a hurry when there was no hurry?"

"There was some last-minute hitch after he'd left. The man whose job he was going to take suddenly asked to stay on a while longer for some personal reason, so Joe thought he'd take a holiday. I honestly don't know just where."

"Do you know where he's going in the States?"

"I've a notion it's California. I could be wrong."

"The Mayo? Isn't that in California?"

"You tell me, sweetie."

I said flatly, "I can't tell you anything because I don't know anything. I only know there's a perpetual fog of silence round Joe's name. And don't pretend there isn't. I'm not that dumb."

"Then you should be able to understand why no one knowing you both has wanted to rub salt into an old wound." He took my hand lightly in both his. "Mind you, none of us know much. All I know I had from Hugo O'Brien on one of those week-ends I spent with him and Sylvia. Joe's name came up because, as you will no doubt recall, Hugo has an assistant who goes by the name of Frances Durant."

"I hadn't forgotten. She still at Martha's?"

"She is." He gave me back my hand.

"Because Joe's job was postponed?" His expression answered me. "She been on holiday, too?"

"She has. And can we now get rid of the ghosts? As I've told you before, when I'm out with you, I do not care for crowds. So you tell me about the caesar. A fine baby, I hear."

Once at the concert hall he remembered a telephone call he should have made. "There'll be a phone here. I'll see you to our seats, then make a noise like a Big Doctor."

He was away some time. I had exchanged smiles with Wendy Scutt and the other three sisters, two rows ahead, read through my programme, including the advertisements, before he joined me. The orchestra was tuning up as he sat by me.

"All well, Mark?"

"Yes and no. I was too late to talk to the man I wanted. I had to leave a message. Now, what's first?" He glanced casually over my head as he was about to look at the programme in my hands. Then his face froze.

"What's up?" I asked, and was turning my head to look in the same direction before the slowly dimming lights went right down, when he tilted my chin towards him and kissed my mouth. "What did you do that for?"

He grinned. "Now there's a foolish question

150

for a pretty girl to ask a man!'' he murmured. ''Hush, now. We're off.''

The concert opened with Beethoven's second symphony. I had a look round in the interval after the first movement. The hall was packed but it was too dim to see who, if anyone, had been responsible for Mark's looking just now as if he had not known what had hit him. In the lighted interval before the 'Emperor' I had another look. And so, I observed, did Mark. The only people I recognized around were the quartet of sisters ahead. There were two empty seats at the end of the row behind us. I noticed them only because every other seat was taken.

Next day, for no special reason, we became unusually busy. The rush continued for some time, and by the week-end every surgical bed in the wards was occupied. Bill Swan told me Henry Carter had had to overflow into the Private Wing and Sister P.W. was out for his blood. ''But where am I supposed to put the patients? Henry Carter and every other surgical ward has got emergency beds up and down the middles. While there are empty rooms in the Wing, I'm using 'em!'' He smiled wearily. ''And if Sister P.W. has her way I'll end up in one of them myself!''

It was over a week before Wendy and I so much as met at the same meal and I was able to thank her again for that concert.

"It seems months ago now, but it was good. Glad you liked it. Incidentally, there's something I've been meaning to ask you about that night. Was that Joe de Winter sitting in the row behind yours? With some fair woman? I thought it was, but the others said I must be seeing things. I only spotted the particular couple just before the lights went down, and when they went up none of us could see them. I don't know why not."

I had a fair idea. I did not give it. I said I was afraid I could not answer her question, as I had not seen any man looking like Joe in that concert hall.

One of the good things about my job, I reflected as I had to hurry back after lunch to get ready for the afternoon's list, was that it left one no time for brooding on what-might-have-beens. It was another of Sir Robert's teaching afternoons. His long and complicated list was unlikely to finish before six. The instrument settings were as complicated as the cases and needed all my attention.

We were two-thirds through when Sandra came in with a note. She held it up for me to read. It was a message for Sir Robert, and one that had to be handed on, even though I knew the disturbance to his concentration was going to infuriate him.

I said tentatively, "Your sister, Mrs Hall, is

on the telephone for you, Sir Robert."

"Then tell her to get off it, Sister! Ye know I can't talk to her now!" he snapped without looking up.

George Ellis, now Robbie's senior registrar, flashed me a 'watch-out-he's-about-to-blow-all-the-fuses' glance. I had to ignore it.

"Staff Nurse has explained that, Sir Robert. Your sister apologizes for disturbing you, but is very anxious you should contact her directly you are free about the health of her grandson Robin Easton."

His head jerked up. "Young Robin, eh! And what are those bloody young fools his parents – oh, well! Tell m' sister I'll ring her later. Later! Robin, eh! Dear me."

Sandra vanished. The list went on. After it finished Sir Robert borrowed my duty-room for his telephone call. I went along there quite a while later, expecting to find him gone. He was at the desk, frowning at the wall ahead.

I backed out. "So sorry, Sir Robert."

"I've done, thank ye, Sister. Come back. I was just having a think." He got to his feet slowly. "Don't mind telling ye, Sister, I'm not happy. Not happy at all."

There were still occasions in the theatre when he could make me feel as nervous as a first-year, but now I was seeing so much more of him I had begun to understand why Joe and my pre-decessor liked him so much. His fierceness in the theatre proper was partly a defence for his concentration, partly an affectation. He enjoyed being a character. But he was a really great surgeon, he spared himself as little as he did others, and as he was no longer young was often, as now, utterly exhausted when his day's work ended. And yet, if another emergency suddenly came in, he would be able to carry on as well as before, as I had often seen him do. I had always respected him; now I admired him as well.

"You look tired, Sir Robert. Can I get you some tea?"

"I'll go along and have some directly, m'dear. Can you spare me a few moments of your good time?"

In answer, I sat down. "Worrying news?"

"Just so, Sister." He sat opposite me across the desk. "I've talked to m'sister. Sensible woman – though how she could bring up her daughter – but, there it is! Young Geraldine – m'sister's only gel and the youngster's mother – is a pretty little thing though she does her best to hide it – and one of these modern gels with a head stuffed with cock-eyed theories about raising children! She does it by the book, Sister! I ask you! Books! Not that they do much harm if ye know when to stop reading 'em and get down to the job itself! And healthy youngsters can tolerate most things, including cock-eyed parents! But this young

Robin" – he shook his head – "never been a robust child. Too many late nights and too much wrong feeding if you ask me! But, there it is! And he's a good little soul. Bright. Don't like to think of him being so poorly. Fond of him." He glared at me defiantly. "M'sister's been staying with his parents. She had to come back to-day as her husband's not well. Angina. She wanted to bring the lad back with her. Parents refused. Mother says all he needs is a few days in bed to cure his septic foot. Now, m'sister's no nurse – she didn't have a thermometer – but she thought the child was running a fever. Mother told her not to fuss! Refused to get hold of a local doctor. And m'sister tells me the lad had some red lines running up his leg. Red lines! What can one do with lunacy of that nature? I never like making a diagnosis without examination, but it sounds as if the child has obviously a roaring cellulitis blowing up."

"It does." I made the obvious suggestion.

"If I could have the lad brought in here, Sister, there'd be no problem. Or even if I could get to him. But they live in Spain. Right off the map, roughly ninety miles from Gibraltar. The husband paints. Doesn't make much money, but that doesn't seem to bother either of them. M'sister flew home. Only a few hours by air." He paused. Then, "If this hospital wasn't so busy I'd take a day or so off and go out and see for myself. I'll cable them, of course. They probably won't even read it, much less take any advice it may contain. Yet – they're fond of the child. Just cock-eyed.''

"I see. You haven't any colleague from outside you could ask to go out?''

"Sister, how can I ask one of my busy colleagues to drop their own patients and fly off to deal with a silly young woman who hasn't the sense of a two-year-old? Mind ye, if I could get hold of some man on holiday.'' He looked at me thoughtfully. "When ye came in I was thinking about young de Winter. They tell me he's back in town. I've already rung the Dean's Office. They've got some bank as a forwarding address. That'll take too much time, I want to pack some one off at once. Would ye have any ideas how I could reach him more quickly?''

I suggested he contacted a Dr Frances Durant in the pathological department of St Martha's Hospital.

"Path. lab., eh? Hmm. Never thought of that. Much obliged to ye, Sister.''

"Can I get through for you, Sir Robert?''

"I needn't trouble ye any more, Sister, if I may trespass in your office a little longer.'' He stood up. "Thank ye, Sister. I'll let ye know what transpires.''

It was ten days later when he did that while scrubbing up between operations. "A word with you, Sister."

It could not be a private word. We were surrounded by assistant surgeons, theatre nurses, dressers, porters, and the inercom was on, for his students in the gallery.

I moved closer to him, holding my gloved hands clasped high in front of my face. "Yes, Sir Robert?"

"You will recollect my little problem, Sister? About that youngster? Well, you were correct. That pathologist was most helpful. Medical aid was dispatched that same evening with sufficient antibiotics to deal with every bug in the book. Our mutual friend" – he glanced up at the gallery as if well aware that he was broadcasting – "was able to get some sense into those thick parental heads. He even made them contact the local man. Understand he's perfectly competent. That leg's now doing very nicely. I had a letter this morning. No surgical interference should now be needed, but untreated, that child might have lost his leg." He re-lathered his hands and arms, had another look up. "If you young gentlemen ever want to know how to tell a good surgeon from the other sort, I'll tell ye how ye can do it! A good surgeon is never in a hurry to pick up his knife." He caught my eye, grinned like a schoolboy with a shared secret. "Am I not right, Sister?"

I could willingly have hugged his distinguished figure for this compliment to Joe. I saw

Mark and George Ellis exchange 'What-the-hell-is-all-this-about?' glances. I said evenly, "You are perfectly right, Sir Robert. May I say – as always?"

He chuckled. "I don't see why not, Sister. Nothing I enjoy more than being flattered by a charming gel, eh, George?"

George was now looking startled. "Oh – quite, sir."

"Just so," said Sir Robert. "Just so. Well, Sister? What are we waiting for? Let's get on with the job."

CHAPTER SEVEN

Sisters Grow A-Human

Christmas was very near. Our rush went on and, if possible, grew worse.

"Why can't the customers stay healthy?" demanded Mark late one evening after what had officially been our afternoon list. "Why do they have to keep twisting their guts in knots, wearing dirty great holes in their stomachs, getting their gall-bladders and kidneys bunged up with rocks? And if they must indulge in these tedious affairs, why can't they take their innards to another hospital? What's Barny's done to them?"

Sandra paused behind the trolley laden with empty dressing-drums she was taking to the tin-room for refilling. "Perhaps we should stick a large notice outside the main entrance to Cas. saying 'First left over the bridge for Martha's'? Or is it second, Dr Delaney?"

"Now is it any use asking me, dear Staff Nurse?" He switched to his broadest brogue.

"And wouldn't you be knowing I've no head for such facts at all." He held open the door for her, then let it swing shut and came over to my trolley. "She's been much less haemadementic lately. I've been hoping the crisis would at least last long enough to turn her into a permanent angel of sweetness and light. Why that crack?"

"Barny's belongs to her, so Barny's Is Best. She regards your having friends across the river as rank disloyalty to the old firm."

"Is that so? And how in hell does she know so much about my private life?" He was really annoyed.

I looked round and up to make sure no tidying junior had wandered back. "Mark dear, be your age. You know Dolly Bachelor's a chatty soul. You do spend a lot of time with the O'Briens. Sylvia O'Brien's her cousin."

"But a quiet woman. Not the type to make with the talk."

I said, "I've noticed few people talk as much as the quiet ones once they start talking. It's the great talkers like yourself who talk plenty and say so little."

He took a pair of abdominal retractors off my trolley and absently tried to fit them on himself over his gown. "Feeling a touch of the haemadementia, too, Sister Theatre? That sounded awful like another dirty crack. But I'll forgive you as there's something I've got to ask you. Do we have a date for the New Year's Eve Ball?''

The New Year's Eve Ball was the social highlight of the hospital year. Joe had taken me to the last two. Luckily I had a cast-iron alibi for avoiding it this year.

"Thanks, but I'll have to be on call that night now I'm boss. It's the nurses' big night. Remember?''

He slapped his forehead. "Fool that I am! I had forgotten you'll have to pay the price of glory. We'll skip the Ball. There'll be other nights.''

"You mustn't skip it if you're free.''

"If I can't take you Barny's Ball hath no charms for me. As I should be free, maybe I'll slip over the river. The O'Briens are giving a party. I was going to suggest we went over later.'' His smile was uncharacteristically grim. "Should I tell dear Dolly now, to be sure she sets the cat amongst the pigeons?''

I smiled. "I don't think you need bother. Sandra starts her holiday on the 28th. Bachelor's been asked to our Ball by her Welsh young man. Your private life can stay private.''

"That'll be a break.'' He put down the clamps. "I could use some of that tea that'll still be stewing in the surgeons' room. You'll not mind if I love you and leave you?''

"Not at all.''

He had turned to go. He turned back. "For

the record, Maggie, wouldn't that be just how you feel about me? Just your old pal, M. Delaney?''

I hesitated, not wanting to hurt him, yet recognizing we were both too tired for anything but the truth. ''Yes. Do you mind?''

''I'd mind getting the score wrong far more.'' He was gone before I could ask how he really felt about me. He would have told me, and it would have been the truth. Neither of us had had any off-duty that day. We had been working almost constantly since we were called up for a strangulated hernia at a quarter to five that morning. At the end of that kind of day no one has energy left for pretence. And then, as still happened, my mind went back to Joe and the many similar heavy days we had shared in the past, how he used to drift back into the theatre, sit on a high stool, and talk. I had believed him too tired for pretence, believed all he said, yet in his case believed wrong.

I looked at the empty stool under the anaesthetist's end of the operating table. He had generally chosen to pull that one forward and sit on it leaning back against the table. My memory of him was so clear he might have been sitting there now, one arm draped along the table, his shoulders sagging with weariness as Mark's had just now. Whatever else had been false, his tiredness had been honest, and when tired, unlike Mark, Bill, or George, who made

162

for strong tea in the surgeons' room, Joe had always come back directly he got out of his T-shirt and apron, and looked for me.

"Something wrong with the table, Sister?" Nurse Jones, the 'dirty' that evening, had come back into the theatre. "I did carbolize it."

"I expect it's just a shadow Nurse." I brushed a hand in front of my face quite involuntarily as if breaking a cobweb. "Yes. It's quite in order."

Matron sent for me next day to discuss holidays. "You are long overdue for a rest, Sister. You look tired. I want you to take two weeks when Staff Nurse Brown returns."

The last thing I wanted was a holiday on my own around the time Joe and I had once fixed for our honeymoon. But Matron's word was law. "Yes, Matron. Thank you."

I had begun to see a great deal of Wendy Scutt off duty. I was grateful for her friendship. As I had suspected, my friendship with Ellen was now very strained, and we were both glad my job made it difficult for us to meet often. It also prevented my making great friends of my theatre girls, even though I liked Bachelor immensely. The former Sister Theatre was right. I was on one side of the fence, and there I had to stay. Luckily, so was Wendy. We drank tea or cocoa together after work most nights, got along very well, discussing everything but men as men.

I felt she considered the subject interested neither of us. She was an amusing person as well as that far from uncommon figure in the trained ranks of the nursing profession, a young woman utterly dedicated to, and fascinated by, her work, and very content to channel into it all her energy and emotions. She loved her ward as women love their homes; her patients were her children; she humoured, coaxed, and when necessary bullied her residents, in place of a husband. She quite genuinely had no interest in men herself unless they wore patients' pyjamas and nightshirts, or white coats. Consequently, when I told her about my interview with Matron, her reaction surprised me.

"Matron has to stop you working yourself into a breakdown, but knocking off isn't the answer for you at present. It would be far better to let you stay on working. Work's the one thing that keeps your mind off Joe de Winter." She refolded the corners of her apron primly. "Of course, you are still in love with him."

"How on earth did you guess that?"

"One does not have to suffer from a condition to recognize the symptoms, my dear. I've seen a lot of you lately. I know you enjoy the theatre, but it doesn't satisfy you the way Henry Carter does me. I also know you are reputed to be getting attached to Mark Delaney. I think you just like him. Why not? He has great charm." She was briefly silent. "What went wrong? Or would you rather not discuss Joe?"

"I'd love to. But no one ever will."

I then told her all that had happened since the day the previous Sister General Theatre left. She listened as placidly as she would have done to an uneventful ward report.

"What does this Frances Durant look like?"

"I expect you saw her at that concert the other evening." I described Frances. "Right?"

She nodded. "And I've seen her around somewhere else." She frowned to herself. "I disremember exactly where. Not with Joe. Is he back from Spain?"

"I don't know. I haven't had another chance for a private talk with old Robbie. Mark didn't even know Joe had been sent out to see that boy until I told him. Or so he said. Mark doesn't tell me all he knows."

"That I can believe." She pressed her pale lips together, then said briskly. "This tea's cold. I'll put the kettle on again."

We always hoped to be able to close the theatres unofficially on Christmas Day. No member of the nursing or resident staff expected, or would have taken, any off-duty that day, but whenever possible the theatre staffs looked forward to moving in a body into the wards to help serve the patients' Christmas dinners and then with the huge tea-parties given in all our wards on Christmas afternoon. The only nurses from the

G.S.U. Theatre who got into the wards that day were Alcott and Jones, the two most junior. The rest of us managed to get to church in relays and to deal with eleven emergency operations. Two of these lasted nearly three hours each. On Boxing Day we did fifteen operations, all emergencies.

On the day after that a very weary Bill Swan called in at the theatre on his way to breakfast to tell me about an addition to our morning list.

"I've just seen my first morning paper for days. It warned me the holiday is now over and I really must roll up my sleeves and get down to the job. Going to be a real effort, Maggie — in more ways than one."

"Poor Bill! You do look tired. You get any sleep last night?"

"About three hours. Not too bad." He yawned. "Breakfast will revive me — I hope. I'll tell you this — I knew an S.S.O. had what might be described as a full life. I never realized just how full. I can't now conceive how Joe managed to carry on at all his last month."

"Because he was so tired? Or some other reason?"

He looked suddenly very annoyed with himself. "An S.S.O. needs no other reason," he retorted quickly. "Be a bloody miracle if I last half as long as he did. Well — I need that breakfast." He removed himself at the double.

Bachelor appeared in the duty-room door

while I was turning that "how Joe managed to carry on at all his last month" over in my mind. "You look very serious, Sister. Has this morning's list been stretched?"

"Oh – no. No. The *status quo* remains unaltered. Want the dispensary book?"

"Stock-room keys, please."

The rush slackened next day. By New Year's Eve we were really quiet. That night every sister in the theatre block was on call. No one was called up.

I went on early on New Year's Day. Garret and Bachelor arrived a few minutes later yawning their heads off.

"From the look of you girls, you had a good Ball!"

"Sister, it was a riot! But, oh my poor little feet!" groaned Garret. "Why are all young doctors so heavy? I'm convinced all my metatarsals are fractured! I don't know how Nurse Bachelor survived her double act."

"Double?" I queried.

Dolly Bachelor had had man trouble. "I made a mess over their invitations. Evan swore I had accepted his for our Ball – then Dick arrived to take me over to his at Martha's. I had them both glowering at each other in the front hall of our Home, so I said I'd spend the first half over the river with Dick, and the second here with Evan. Could any girl be more helpful?"

I smiled. "Obviously not, Nurse Bachelor.

Did it work out?"

"Sister, it did not! Now they're both mad at me! But that doesn't bother me, as while I was over the other side with Dick – who sulked hideously – I met an absolute dreamboat of a Martha's houseman. He gatecrashed our Ball later. Evan," she added with simple pride, "threw a splendid tantrum. So I left him to it and went back to Martha's with Simon – my houseman. I wouldn't admit this there, but actually it was more fun than our own because it was masked."

Garret said, "That must have made it a real thrill for a theatre girl."

Bachelor giggled. "That's what I told my houseman. Of course, lots of the fun was lost on me as I didn't know many people there to recognize. I spotted Dr Delaney and Mr de Winter at once. No one could miss Delaney's hair and size, or, for that matter, Mr de Winter after seeing him so often behind a yashmak. He was sitting out with Sylvia – she wasn't dancing either, as junior's due in seven weeks. I meant to go and say hallo, but Simon wasn't keen and I had had enough masculine temperament for one night. It was too bad you had to miss it all, Sister."

I said life was a rugged business. "Time to get down to work now, girls. Sir Robert starts at nine-fifteen."

"Why bring up old Joe, Dolly?" Garret

hissed as they ambled off to the changing-room.

"She's not interested in him now. M.D.'s her man. And as he spent most of the time I was there dancing with Frances I thought the old girl ought to know there was another spare man in Sylvia's party . . ." The changing-room door swung behind them.

I returned to my desk and tried to concentrate on work-lists. It was no use. I could not close my mind to Joe's being back in London, obviously for Christmas, and yet not bothering to send me so much as a Christmas card.

"Here's a sweet sight! The one pair of clear eyes in the hospital this grisly morning." An unsmiling Mark filled the doorway. "A happy New Year, dear Sister Theatre. They tell me you had a quiet night last night. The good are lucky."

I returned his greeting. "What brings you in so early, Doctor? They tell me you were living it up behind a mask over the water until the small hours."

"Indeed I was." He sat on the edge of the desk. "I just looked in to say that although last night had its points, it was no great shakes for one man, because you were back here keeping your lamp burning." He smiled drily. "So dear Dolly was there? I didn't see her. What happened to her wild man from Wales?"

"A long, complicated story." With difficulty I kept my tone easy. "Did you know Joe was

169

back?'' He nodded. ''He take Frances?''

''It was a party. If anyone did the taking it was the O'Briens.''

''I see.'' I was so black with misery I clutched at trivialities. ''I hear Joe didn't dance. Why not? He loved dancing.''

Mark said, ''Are you telling me the darlin' Dolly did not observe the strapping on Joe's right ankle? I'll admit it was hidden by his trouser-leg and sock, and she probably wasn't around when he pulled a tendon coming off a plane at London Airport last week, but that should not have bothered herself of the all-seeing eye and all-talking tongue. No doubt,'' he added, ''she did keep account of the number of times I danced with Frances, and was able to give you the exact price of the fine ring on the third finger of the ravishing doctor's left hand!''

''No. Not the ring. You know it was there? That why you didn't tell me Joe was back?''

''You could put it that way.'' He got off the desk. ''And I could use some of that pure, pure oxygen along the corridor, and then one large cup of black coffee.'' He met my eyes. ''Forgive me, Maggie?''

''Sure.'' We were not talking about his hang-over. ''Thanks for looking in.''

Alone, I stared at the wall ahead without seeing it. Joe had done the right thing. A clean break. Hell, but the only intelligent way to make a break. Ellen had been right, too. All my looking back, searching for motives, hunches about his health, had been nothing more than a defensive reaction to save myself having to face the plain fact that a man had stopped loving me.

The telephone on the desk rang and jolted me back to my job. I lifted the receiver mechanically. "Sister General Theatre."

There was a small silence. Then the last voice I expected said, "Morning, Maggie. Happy New Year. Joe here. Joe de Winter. May I speak to Sir Robert, please? He is expecting this call."

He spoke as if we had only parted five minutes back and nothing could be more normal than his voice on the line or request. I felt anything but normal. I had to blink to see the duty-room wall-clock clearly.

"It's not yet eight, Joe. Sir Robert won't be here before nine. You say he asked you to call? Are you in Barny's?"

"No. In my hotel. Robbie's secretary rang while I was out last night and asked me to ring him at the Unit theatre at five to eight this morning. She doesn't usually make mistakes. Perhaps the night hall-porter got it wrong."

"Possibly. Can I give Robbie a message when he arrives? Or will you ring again?"

"I can't really leave any message as it's he who wants to talk to me. I'm not dead clear why. I won't be able to ring him at your theatre later, as by nine I should be sitting in a plane at

London Airport. We've got to leave in a few minutes. I'll try his home first; I expect he'll still be there. In case he's gone out early, would you just say I've rung and my compliments and so on? I'd have liked to come over to Barny's, but there just hasn't been time. You know how it is."

That "we" had jarred like the sudden touching of an exposed nerve of a tooth. I said I knew just how it was. "Off to the States at last? I heard about your job being postponed. From Mark."

"So I gather. Yes. I've been having a holiday lotus-eating in the Mediterranean sun, apart from one very short job for Robbie. But you know about that?"

"Yes." Yet again we were behaving like civilized adults, and I found the strain worse than ever. "Enjoyed the sun?"

"Very much, thanks. I'm fast developing an addiction for lotuses. Or should it be loti?"

"Afraid I don't know. They don't grow in the G.S.U. Theatre."

"How is the old place?" His voice was suddenly his old voice. "Mark said the pressure had been on."

"It has. It's off now."

"Quiet last night?"

"Not one call for the whole block." I glanced at the clock, remembering that other call he had to make, and what he had just said about

172

leaving in a few minutes. It was such agony talking to him as if he had never been more than a casual old friend that I wished he would ring off and go — and yet dreaded the moment when he would.

"Not one call? When did that last happen on New Year's Eve? Not in my time."

"Nor mine, until now." That reminded me to wish him the usual wishes. I did so, then asked if he had had a good evening. "Mark's just looked in. He said it was fun."

"It was. Pity you had to stay in. It would have been nice to see you again, Maggie."

Nice. I winced. "My girls tell me our Ball was quite something. They're all limping round this morning."

"And not only them! I'm a wreck!" He retorted heartily. I had never heard him sound hearty before. "The band was really good! If not the best, one of the three best I've ever danced to! You'd have loved it!"

"Good as that?" I was suddenly very curious. "And how was the floor?"

"Splendid." He might have been a TV commercial.

"So a good time was had by all" — why not add corn to corn? — "as you danced all night?"

"Excellent! After all that twisting my sacro-iliacs will be out of true for life! But I mustn't keep you talking when I know how busy you are at this time even on a quiet morning. Sorry to have disturbed you – my regards to Robbie if I miss him. Don't work too hard. Good-bye.'' He rang off before I could get in another word, say anything about his engagement, or even, as I only remembered when I replaced the receiver, thank him for his radiogram and the records. And as he was now off to the States, it was unlikely I would get another opportunity again.

Then I realized I did not actually know where he was off to. He had not properly answered my question about the States; instead he had waffled on about the sun, made corny jokes about lotuses, been quite nauseatingly hearty about that Martha's party. And why all that nonsense about twisting his sacro-iliacs out of true? And boosting the band and floor? Why ram that down my throat, particularly when I knew from Bachelor and Mark he had not danced all evening. Mark's explanation had been perfectly reasonable.

I reminded myself I had a great deal of paper work to get through and could not afford to waste more time on what was a very trivial matter. I glanced at the calendar. It was over three months since he had left Barny's. He had waited a decent interval before giving a ring to another girl. He did not belong in my life now. Why should I care whether he had or had not danced last night?

I picked up my pen, then put it down again. Whether I cared or not, Joe had gone out of his way to have me believe he had danced. He obviously had not known about Dolly Bachelor, even though he was a guest of her cousins last night. Mark had. And Mark had promptly produced a satisfactory explanation for Joe's sitting out. But Mark had a talent for explaining things away.

My mind shot back to the thoughts his telephone call had interrupted. I brooded on them for a few moments, then dialled the number of the Orthopaedic Theatre and asked to speak to Sister Orthopaedic.

She was doing her paper work and announced herself delighted to be interrupted. "How I detest all these horrid forms! What do you want to know, Lindsay?"

I explained that as we had turned quiet I hoped to give my nurses a class that afternoon. "We do no spinal work in here, as you know, so I thought it would make a change to talk about it. I'm not all that up in it myself, so I wondered if you would be kind enough to help me with my homework."

"Love to. Where do we start?"

I suggested the causes of spinal compression. "I've made a list" – I scribbled as I spoke – "of the extrathecal lesions. Diseases of the bones first; Pott's disease; tumours – "

"Split that, my dear. Primary and secondary."

"Thanks. Next, I've got spondylitis, oseitis, trauma . . . what else?"

"Let me think . . . Yes, our old friend, prolapse and herniation of the nucleus pulposus."

"Hold on. . . ." I wrote fast. "Thanks. I'd forgotten that. Have we covered the bone-diseases?"

She thought it over, decided we had, reminded me she was only a nurse. "But these I have seen. Now, the other types – aneurysms of the aorta, parasitic cysts, tumours of the perithecal tissues – "

"Again, benign and malignant?"

"Right. Our even older friends, sarcomas and lipomas."

"Thanks a lot." I ringed 'aneurysms' asked several questions on the first group, made notes from her answers, before inquiring if the removal of the aortic aneurysm from the base of the spine was not the speciality of Buckwell of Martha's.

"I've never seen any surgeon touch him on that. He came over with his team and removed one in my theatre about two years ago. He has an exceptionally delicate touch. Most interesting man – and case."

"What was the history?"

"As I remember, the man had been unwell for a few months with vague aches and pains he and his family took for rheumatism. Luckily he had a very good GP – an old Barny's man. He was convinced the trouble was more serious, and persuaded him to come in here for investigation. Mr Buckwell came over, agreed on an exploratory op, then found and excised the aneurysm, stitched in a nice little bit of nylon which should, he said, last a lifetime. We had great fun – the automatic heart and everything. It all went most satisfactorily. The man was out of hospital in nineteen days. By now he should have been long back to his normal life and job."

"Very satisfactory." I crossed out 'aneurysms.' "How about sarcomas? As they are usually secondaries, I suppose you don't see many of them?"

"No. But we get a great many tumours of the perithecal tissues." She went on to tell me at length of the surgical and nursing treatment of the various growths that came under that heading. One specific condition had me more than interested. "Only a few years ago, no one would have dared touch it, and the prognosis, depending on age obviously, was from two to five years. It remains that in inoperable cases. It isn't common – thank God. We had a man . . . oh, in the Private Wing long before your time –"

"A Dr Potter?"

She was surprised. "You knew him?"

I explained how. "Please go on, Sister?"

"Basil Buckwell made the breakthrough – I believe about five years ago. It was then he found a way of doing it – in two stages."

I looked at the calendar. "How long between?"

"Months. He won't touch any back until a

patient has been flat in bed at least one month, sometimes more. After the first stage, he gets them up very quickly, and if possible right out and away somewhere. He likes plenty of sunshine and warmth." I nodded to myself. "Then he has the second go." She gave me the surgical details. "Takes hours."

"With what result?"

"Say fifty-fifty chance of a total cure. But as there's no real alternative, most patients are only too willing to chance it." She waited for me to write this down, then suggested my asking Senior Sister Tutor to arrange for the loan of various textbooks from the Medical School Library. "You must like teaching to go into this so thoroughly, Lindsay. Wish I did. I'd always rather do than teach how it should be done."

That left me feeling a fraud. A very worried fraud. I could do nothing about the worry, but eased my conscience by cutting short my off-duty that day to give my girls the class I had originally invented as an excuse. Next day, the nurses who had been off duty asked me to repeat it, then for more similar classes. Senior Sister Tutor provided me with a small library of textbooks and an approving smile. In a very short time I was surprised to discover that my daily classes had become a feature of the G.S.U. Theatre life and I had become a mine of information on diseases of, and injuries to, the spinal column, and its association with the central nervous system.

That information gave me no comfort, but at least in seeking for it and then handing it on to the girls, I kept my mind occupied off duty. The more I read, the more convinced I was that my old hunch had been right. There was a great deal I still did not understand about the behaviour of Joe, and his friends, before and since his leaving, but I had finally learned that leading questions would not get me any answers. The men had closed round Joe. Why they had thought it necessary to do that might remain beyond me, but the fact that they had was something I had at last accepted. I knew enough about doctors to know that when the medical profession decides to close its ranks no direct approach would ever break through successfully.

That's why I had to go about things indirectly. After New Year's morning, I was determined to find out the truth, though what good it was going to do me if and when I did was something I had not yet got round to working out. I was like a person reading in bed at night when the reading-light bulb fails. I had to grope around in the dark for more light, even if I was only going to put it out again.

Sandra had taken three weeks of her annual holiday to go winter-sporting. With a week-end tagged on at either end, that made her away nearly four weeks. The theatre was so much more pleasant without her that I often found myself mentally weighing her efficiency against her disrupting temperament, and wondering whether or not to ask Matron to transfer her. There was no doubt that would earn the whole-hearted approval of my theatre girls and the Unit men. She annoyed Bill, George, and the housemen quite as much as she did Mark. Yet, in bad moments for the patients – and they were the moments that counted – she was an excellent theatre nurse. A formal request – and it had to be that – to have her moved would inevitably affect her future career. I did not want to do that, yet had to think of the good of the theatre. The fact that I found her so tiresome did nothing to help me come to a decision, as I knew my judgement was prejudiced. In desperation I talked things over with Wendy. She advised me to get rid of her. "It's no use trying to be fair to every one, Maggie. One just can't be. Anyway, life isn't fair. And you must think of the theatre. What's best for you will be best for your department. No, I mean that. It may sound selfish, but it's sound common sense. The sister makes or breaks a department. You know that as well as I do."

I did. Yet lack of moral courage kept me dithering. Then Matron sent for me one evening in the last week of Sandra's holiday. "Sister, I am extremely sorry, but I am going to have to ask you to delay your holiday another week.

Poor Staff Nurse Brown has broken an ankle ski-ing. I am going to transfer Nurse Watt to you from Orthopaedic Theatre. She has had some general experience, is well up in the administrative side, as she has so often taken over for Sister Orthopaedic Theatre. I feel sure that if she works with you for a couple of weeks she will be well able to carry on while you are away, particularly as I want your theatre to be spring-cleaned in the second week of your holiday."

I met Sir Robert on my way back to the theatre. He had been delivering a late lecture. We discussed this, then my holiday. He was full of ideas for me. "Does one good to get right away, m'dear. Do ye have a passport? Current, eh? Capital. What about Malta? Majorca? Las Palmas? All very close by air, and if ye fly by night not too expensive. Not booked yet? Dilatory, Sister, dilatory! Never mind. Any good travel agent'll fix ye up – but if ye have any difficulty, have a word with me. M'secretary is an excellent young woman! No equal at getting hold of plane reservations and hotel bookings."

Mark was talking to Rose Garret in the empty theatre when I got back. She asked if she should go to supper. "No calls or news while you were away, Sister."

"I've got some rather sad news about Nurse Brown."

Rose Garret was a nice girl "Oh, poor Nurse Brown; what rotten luck! Still, she'll be insured and not really surprised, as she said she knew she'd break something on the slopes sooner or later, as every one always does. When does Nurse Watt join us, Sister? To-morrow?"

Mark waited until we were alone. "Now here's a turn up for the book, Maggie. That girl" – he gave a long relieved sigh – "did she get in my hair! But what's all this about your going off? Why haven't I been told?"

I reminded him the men's off-duty rota had been altered since New Year's Day and his free time now hardly ever coincided with mine. "Can you imagine old Robbie's reaction if I announced it in the middle of a case? Besides, it's not important. I don't even want it."

"I believe you." He followed me into the duty-room, sat on the desk. "I don't like the thought of you going off on your own. What are you going to do?"

I shrugged. "There are some old friends of my father's I've been promising to visit for years. They live on Exmoor. I may spend some of it with them."

"And the rest?"

"Not sure." I told him Robbie's ideas. "He's sweet, but I don't feel like foreign parts. I like the West Country. I think I'll amble off to some hotel, where I can do nothing, get waited on, and not have a telephone near my room at night!"

"I'm with you there! But — " His manner changed and was suddenly urgent. "Maggie, the time has come for you and I to talk. What time do you finish to-night?"

The telephone rang before I could answer. It was Casualty, to warn the Unit a query acute appendicitis had just been admitted.

"Why," grumbled Mark, "do I have to open my big mouth so wide? Oh, my God!" It was the telephone again. "Not a second acute abdomen!"

I shook my head listening to Bill Swan's voice. "Yes, Mr Swan. Yes. Half an hour. Yes. He's here." I handed Mark the receiver and went into the theatre proper to turn up the heat. Mark joined me a few minutes later.

"You and I must dine together before you make for the West, my love. I've been looking at your off-duty rota. I don't match up yet, but I'll fix it somehow. No backing out, now. This is important."

I could tell that from his manner. I found that very disturbing, and nothing more. "We'll have that dinner, Mark." I looked beyond him as Bachelor and Cotton returned from their supper. "Good."

"Case coming up, Nurses. Appendix. You can take it, Nurse Cotton. Nurse Bachelor, will you 'dirty' please? It's all right, Nurse Cotton," I added as the poor girl stood staring aghast, "you are now quite capable of taking

183

an appendix, and Mr Swan is very easy to work for. I know it's your first, but we all have to have a first."

"Sister – you will be around? Please!"

I had felt like a theatre sister before. It was then I knew I really was one. "I'll be in here all the time, Nurse Cotton. Go and change quickly, then we'll do your instruments together."

Mark lingered after the girls had vanished. "You've come a long way, Sister Theatre."

"In some ways. In others I've just gone round in circles."

He looked about to challenge that, then apparently changed his mind. "I'd best have me a look at this man's chest before I gas him."

Ellen Watt fitted smoothly into the General Surgical Unit. She was not, and probably never would be, as quick as Sandra, but she was very competent, and as an instrument nurse she was calm, good-humoured, and faintly maternal. We belonged to the same set, but it was the first time we had worked together in a theatre, and I was rather amused by her manner of handling the men as if they were so many small boys, warning them to change their T-shirts and not sit around drinking tea while still damp, or that they really must not miss this meal or that coffee-break.

She mothered my girls in much the same way. "Come along, now, chicks, time you were off! Off!"

"Why," I heard Dolly Bachelor ask Rose Garret, "do nurses get odd when they get senior? First we had old bitchy Brown! And here we have Old Mother Watt! We'd better watch it, Rose, or God knows what we'll turn into."

"I don't see we have to," retorted Rose. They were in the tin-room next door to my office. "Look at Sister. She's a norm."

"I always thought she was" allowed Dolly, "but lately she seems to be getting slightly sort of a-human. She just lives, eats, sleeps, breathes, this theatre. I don't wonder poor old M.D. spends so much time over at Martha's."

"Does he?"

"God, yes! Whenever he's free, so Sylvia says. He's always hanging round their path. lab. You know what I told you about Frances, well – " and the tin-room door closed.

I grimaced to myself. A-human? Maybe. That was rather how I felt these days.

I had two more days to work before my holiday. Mark had managed to wangle himself a free evening on my last evening and had booked a table and theatre tickets. When I asked if he had come into money he told me sternly it was to be a special occasion and would I kindly belt up.

I thought about it on my way down to supper on the penultimate night before my holiday, and wished there was some way of getting out

185

of that date without hurting his feelings. It was obvious we were working up for some sort of crisis in our relationship. We had been marking time too long. He had been incredibly patient. As patient as a man could be if he was very much in love – or just plain disinterested.

"Ah! There ye are, Sister! The very person I hoped to see!" Sir Robert came swiftly towards me along the ground-floor corridor. "Can you spare me a few minutes to discuss a matter of the utmost urgency? We can borrow the Dean's Office." He opened a door. "My good friend Dr St John will make no objection."

"Yes, of course, Sir Robert. May I just let the switchboard know where to find me?"

His reply astonished me. "Matron's Office will attend to that. Matron kindly telephoned your theatre for me before I left her. Staff Nurse said you were on your way to dinner. I told Matron we would trespass on the Dean for our talk."

"I see," I said without doing anything of the kind. "Is there something I can do for you, Sir Robert?"

"Won't ye sit down, Sister?" He held a chair for me, then drew one up beside mine. "It all depends. It all depends. Tell me first about this holiday of yours. Matron tells me it starts the day after to-morrow. Did ye take my advice? Going abroad? All cut and dried, eh?"

"Not really, Sir Robert." I told him about

186

my father's friends and vague private plans. "I haven't bothered to book. There'll be no rush on English hotels at this early stage in the year."

"So ye're in no hurry, eh? And free from to-morrow evening? Hm. Just so. Well, Sister, would you have any objection to my suggesting ye alter y' plans somewhat? Start your holiday from to-night shall we say? With Matron's approval, naturally."

I shook my head. "I wouldn't object, Sir Robert." I was very curious. "May I ask why you suggest it?"

He smiled rather charmingly. "Frankly, Sister, I want to borrow you. If ye've no objection?"

CHAPTER EIGHT

Sir Robert Requests A Loan

"Borrow, Sir Robert? Professionally? Outside this hospital? But surely that's not allowed?"

He said I was so right and in no circumstances could I accept employment in my professional capacity elsewhere while under contract to St Barnabas' Hospital. "It would be highly unethical for ye to assist me with one of my private patients, and subsequently pay ye the recognized fee. But, as I have just been at pains to explain to Matron," he went on deliberately; "may I add, to her satisfaction – no one could take exception to my asking if you would give me your help in your own free time on a purely personal matter. I appreciate I am asking a great deal of you." He was now too grave to remember his affected "ye's" and "m's" "The patient isn't even a patient of mine. She's a relative. I believe she needs me – and I need you. If you'll be kind enough to give me your help we shall be breaking no rules. What do you say?"

"If it's all right with Matron I'll be delighted to help you." That was true. I liked the old man, enjoyed work, and was in anything but a holiday mood. "What's the case?"

"A young woman of twenty-seven expecting a second child in three weeks' time. Her right kidney is behaving very badly. It may have to come out without delay. So I face a probable nephrectomy and possible caesarean section. In a private house. So you'll understand why I need a highly skilled theatre nurse with me."

"Yes." Yet I wondered why he had picked me and not one of the private nurses he must employ on his outside cases. Some of them must have had theatre experience. "You want us to go to her?"

"Just so, Sister. Much as I dislike operating in private houses, the circumstances being what they are, there's no question of the gel being moved. We'll have to do a little travelling. Naturally, your expenses will be met as I am asking you to accompany me as my guest. Yes, yes. I have Matron's approval on that score, so no objections, if you please!" He looked at his watch. "As we are pressed for time, I shall give you the full details later. I want to be off to-night. My secretary has already provisionally booked me two seats on a plane due to leave London Airport in five hours' time."

"Five hours?" I echoed weakly.

"We would be ill advised to delay, Sister. The

189

report I had a short while ago was most disturbing, most disturbing. The gel's blood-pressure is rising most alarmingly. If we delay she may go into coma. My poor sister is very distressed. Young Geraldine's a silly little creature, but one's fond of the gel. And it'd be a shocking thing for that young-ster Robin to lose his mother at nine years of age.''

"Geraldine?'' I stood up. "Your niece? The mother of the boy with cellulitis?''

"Just so. The boy's home with his grand-mother. As well. All this would be most upset-ting for a child.''

"But – but – doesn't your niece live in Spain?''

"She does, Sister. But, as I informed you previously, it's only a few hours off by air. Remember my sending young de Winter out?'' I nodded dumbly. "On this occasion I must go myself, so I'm going to take a few day's holiday. I'm due. Overdue! We'll do as he did. Fly to Gibraltar, and on by car. You told me, did you not, that you had a current pass-port? Capital. Capital.'' He patted my arm. "No objection to taking this little trip with me, have you? Good girl. I'm much obliged. Let us make our way to Matron and have another little talk with her. My secretary is along there. She's been in touch with the Spanish Embassy – just let her have your passport *stat*, if you would be so good. I'll return it to you later."

Wendy came along to my room the moment she was off duty. "Is what I hear true? Oh, you lucky, lucky girl!"

"I suppose I am. I feel somewhat shattered."

She flung off her cuffs, rolled up her sleeves. "What's to do? How long'll you be away?"

"He says not more than four days, possibly much less. He's got to be back for a kidney-graft on Tuesday." I rolled two sweaters, put them in my suitcase. "I'm not to take any uniform. He says we must observe the rules, m'dear! He's providing gowns from his own private equipment."

She laughed. "Trust that crafty old man to know every trick in the book. Have you flown before?"

"Yes. And it makes me sick. You wouldn't have any travel pills?"

She said she had none, but was sure Robbie would be loaded with the necessary. "He's always one step ahead – but you should know that from the theatre, Maggie."

"That's true. I just didn't realize he was the same in his private life." I sat on my bed. "I've a grim feeling I'm not going to be high-powered enough for him."

"If you weren't, my dear," she said briskly, "he wouldn't be taking you. Now, then – have a cigarette and leave things to me."

She organized me so well I even had time for a bath, to write to my father, and then rest on my bed. I tried ringing Mark. He was out. Wendy promised to deal with him in the morning. "Not that he'll need telling. Barny's is already buzzing over Robbie's flying you off into the night. I hope Lady Stanger isn't spoiling the story by going along as chaperon?"

A quality of total unreality settled round me like a cloak. I said good-bye to Matron and Home Sister, talked to Lady Stanger, who drove with her husband and myself to the airport, felt my habitual wave of nausea as the engines throbbed life into the grounded plane, swallowed the tablet Robbie produced when he saw my colour. I seemed to be sitting on my own shoulder watching some one who looked like me doing all those things, but could not possibly be myself.

The tablet dried my mouth, stopped the nausea, and made me more detached than ever. I asked what it was, since no other travel pill had had such an immediate effect on me.

"That was a Stanger's Stomach Special, m'dear. I worked them out and first had them made up when I was in the Navy. Shocking sailor. No stomach for the sea. Never travel without 'em now. Remind me to write you a script some time. Now, down to business." He settled himself into a more comfortable position in the seat next to mine and began to discuss in great detail the medical and surgical problems we might have to face. "Won't be the first time I've operated on a kitchen table, and I doubt it'll be the last. Not an experience I enjoy." There was a light in his eyes that belied his words, and reminded me of the stories of Robbie in the last war operating on a ward table in Barny's basement with the hospital literally dropping round his head, before he went into the Navy and won himself a D.S.O. for operating for fifteen hours in a makeshift tent on some beach after his ship had been sunk, and finishing up by giving the last patient a pint of his own blood, because they happened to have matching groups.

He had brought with us sufficient instruments, drugs, and emergency anaesthetics to cover most eventualities. I asked about an anaesthetist. "That local doctor you mentioned before?"

"If he's been contacted. He's the only man in a wide area. That is to say" – he frowned for no reason I could follow – "the only local general practitioner. We'll have to sort that out when we get there. May be tricky. We must expect shocks. To be honest with you, m'dear" – he considered me thoughtfully – "that is precisely why I asked you to accompany me. You'll not object to my saying you're a very young woman, Sister. You've been well trained. And I have observed that you have the calm temperament necessary for dealing efficiently with the unexpected. I've a great respect for your excellent profession, but I've had too much experience of the type of trained nurse who would regard a request to use a scrubbing-brush on a kitchen table as a downright insult – not to mention the mere suggestion that she might have to cook a meal for others as well as herself – that has the species in a real tiz, believe you me! I can tolerate that nonsense in a hospital, not on an unorthodox expedition such as this. For this, I want some one with the essential skill and equally essential adapt-ability of the young. I'll tell you frankly I've no idea what domestic arrangements we may expect to find. You may have to assist me surgically, turn midwife, nurse, comforter of a frantic husband – because God alone knows how that young fool David will react, if he reacts at all. These artist fellows! I dunno!'' He smiled wryly. ''It was my good fortune that you should happen to be due for a holiday at this juncture. I hope ye'll have no cause to regret all your generous action may involve.''

''I'm sure I won't, Sir Robert. I've never done anything like this, or worked anywhere outside Barny's. I think I'll find it all quite fascinating. Thank you for bringing me.''

He looked about to comment on that, then

194

fell silent. When he spoke again it was about air travel. "I'm always crossing the world at odd week-ends to see patients. I never have time to see the countries I visit. Just the airports, and they are all identical. As indeed are the clouds."

"My father said that once."

"Indeed? He live in London, Sister?"

As we talked about my father and then my childhood it suddenly struck me how little we knew of each other's backgrounds, even though we had worked together constantly for so long. But at least we belonged to different generations, and until very recently had moved on different planes in the hospital world. I thought of my fellow-sisters and my theatre girls. The only people I knew very much about off duty were Wendy now, and before that Ellen and Sandra – the last two really only because we had been closer in our original set. Apart from these three, there was that gay little extrovert Dolly Bachelor. My predecessor had said I would find her job lonely. Not till then did I really discover how right she was.

Sir Robert discussed his now grown-up children. "M'daughters manage me. And I enjoy it! Sons are more difficult. They take so much longer to grow up. The youngest lad is for ever sitting in Trafalgar Square. Worries his mother. Convinced he'll ruin his kidneys on those damp pavements. But there it is. And it shows the boy uses his mind, which is more than can be said for his brother! He's either chasing a ball or a gel! Reminds me of meself! Ah, well!" He stifled a yawn. "I think, if ye'll forgive me, I'll have a little nap. We may find ourselves very busy once we are down."

I watched him drop off, thought how impossible it was to think of sleep myself, and then the next thing I knew was our attractive young air-hostess shaking me gently, as it was time to refasten our safety-belts.

Sir Robert rubbed his eyes. "Does going down worry you?"

"Yes."

He patted my hand. "And me. Know what our trouble is?" I shook my head. "Just a pair of cowards, m'dear." We smiled at each other, and I felt much better. Then, because the old habit was still there, I caught myself thinking, I must tell Joe how sweet the old man's being . . .

I cut the thought short, and looked out of the window by my seat. The sky was very pale. Below, the mountains of North Africa framed the southern sea-line like great black Bedouin tents. Then a grey-green dot ballooned hugely. I glimpsed a white sand beach, a row of fishing-boats with yellow sails on the oily dawn sea, and then we were down.

The car Sir Robert expected had not arrived. After we had been seen by the various officials, he left me drinking coffee in a small, empty reception lounge while he made inquiries about the absent car.

"Miss Armstrong cabled that young fool David last evening. He sent a car here for de Winter. We'll give him a little longer, then hire one this end and drive out." He went out, leaving the door ajar, and I heard him talking about hired cars with some one outside.

We had left London freezing in a mid-winter night and flown into a golden early spring morning. There was a great vase of yellow mimosa on the table by my chair, and the – to me – mild morning air held a mixture of the sea, petrol, and the scent of wild geraniums. I looked round, remembered telling Robbie I expected to find all this quite fascinating. Fascinating. The irony of my being here alone at this very time hurt like an operation without an anaesthetic.

I wondered what Joe had thought about that honeymoon we never had when he flew out to see Robin Easton, or if he had even thought about it at all. Now we were away from Barny's and Sir Robert was being so human, I should be able to get some real news about Joe out of him. All these last few months in London, apart from that Robin Easton business, he had avoided mentioning Joe quite as constantly as his juniors. In his case, there was nothing odd about that, since he was not given to gossiping with the nursing staff – and that included theatre sisters. His conversation on the way out showed he had left a good many of the barriers that traditionally hedged a hospital pundit back in London. It should not be too difficult to get him to talk, but what good that talk would do me was another problem.

I realized the subject had become an obsession with me, particularly since New Year's morning, and as ever I tried to rationalize myself out of it, without success. I was like a patient I once nursed – an old lady admitted with an apparently mild gastric disorder that on investigation proved to be advanced carcinoma. "I know as I got nothing to fret me, duck," she said. "Me stomach's settled real lovely after them powders, and I feel much better in meself. But me bones got the wind up something cruel, duck, so I reckoned as I best bring meself up for the doctor to have a look-see for hisself. Reckon me bones'll heed the doctor. I can't be doing nothing with them."

Sir Robert's voice outside brought me back to the present. "Capital! Capital! Best news I've had in years! Now, be a good fellow and go along to that room there and wait for me. You'll find my young assistant there. I shall be with you directly."

I gathered together my gloves and handbag as slow, rather heavy footsteps came towards the lounge door. The steps surprised me. From Sir

Robert's remarks I had assumed they belonged to David Easton. They did not sound the steps of a young man.

They belonged to a young man. He pushed open the door with a stick, then stopped dead, leaning one hand on the door-knob, the other on the stick.

My bag and gloves slid to the floor. I was too transfixed with astonishment to remember them or get up. "Joe! Robbie never told me you were out here!" I looked from his face to his stick, then back to his face again. He went on staring at me as if he refused to believe his eyes. He was much thinner and very tanned. Beneath the tan his colour had drained away. I stood up slowly, went closer. "What was that about good news? Aren't we going to have to do a nephrectomy plus a caesar on a kitchen table after all?"

My voice had spoken for me. It was a voice I now recognized as my 'Sister Theatre' voice. It would have sounded strange to him. I had only begun using it after he left Barny's.

He looked surprised, but less shocked. He still breathed as if he had been running. "The caesar's off the list. She had her baby before I left."

"She did?" My profession was now my armour. "I thought it wasn't due for three weeks? A live baby?"

"Fine. Not even visibly prem. She must have

had her dates wrong." His voice was almost normal. Then, "Maggie, what the devil are you doing here?"

"Robbie asked me to come."

"And what does he think he's doing dragging a Barny's theatre sister out here on a private case?"

"We haven't broken any rules." I went back to my chair, as my legs were feeling most peculiar. "I'm on holiday. He's not employing me. I'm his guest. How about you?" And as there was something that had to be said I said it at once. "I see you've been ill. I'm sorry. I didn't know."

"Robbie didn't tell you?" he demanded.

"No one's told me anything." I folded my cold, cold hands in my lap. "But you can tell me something, Joe?" I saw a muscle twitch in his taut cheek. "What make is this baby? And how has it's arrival affected the mother's blood-pressure? Robbie had the idea she was heading for a uraemic coma, or eclampsia, or both."

He did not answer immediately. He looked at me in silence for several seconds, then moved over to a hard chair against the wall and lowered himself on to it stiffly. "The old man wasn't far wrong. I spent most of yesterday having dark thoughts along those lines. She hadn't been at all well these last few days. Early yesterday morning her pressure rocketed." He sketched the upward curve of a graph in the air with a flattened hand. "Just like that. It had me checking the size of their kitchen table, made me stop acting like a guest and chuck my weight about like a Big Doctor. I had been trying to warn David what might happen. He's a good man, but it just didn't sink in.''

"Robbie's given me a general picture of that ménage.'' I managed to smile. "He doesn't dig these artist fellows.''

"I wouldn't have said they were his cup of tea, though I like them a lot. Snag over this business has been their leave-Nature-to-Mother-Nature routine. Childbirth is a natural process, and so on. A couple of weeks in any Mat. Unit knocks that one out. Still, as Geraldine had no trouble with her first baby and no medical attention beyond the nearest handywoman, they were convinced they had a point and I was just making the usual medical song-and-dance. I did tell David the damage to her right kidney obviously started then, but as she was only eighteen at the time and that's an ideal age for having a baby, she got away with it.''

"He didn't believe you?''

"Doubt he even heard. He's devoted to his wife, but he started a new picture this week, and when he's working he just switches off from all other contacts. So yesterday morning I took things into my own hands. I got David out of his studio more or less bodily and told him his wife would probably die if he didn't drop this back-to-nature lark. Enough got through to make him borrow Pilar's bike – she helps in the house – and cycle the seven miles to the nearest village for the local doc. Man called Alvaro. He qualified in Madrid. Good. But he wasn't home. His wife said he was delivering breech twins twenty miles off. The nearest hospital to the Eastons' house is over fifty, and anyway I didn't think it would be safe to move her. So David cabled Robbie from me. When he got back I asked Pilar to scrub the kitchen, and got busy boiling up everything I had in the way of instruments in a fish-kettle on an oil stove. Real Sunday-paper stuff.''

''You had instruments?''

''Enough for an emergency caesar. Robbie fitted me out with a little black bag when he sent me out the first time. The anaesthetic was the big problem. I only had a little chloroform and largish bottle of ether. I didn't fancy the prospect of a caesar under open ether, quite apart from having no one but David around to give it.''

''How about standing? Can you do that without a stick?''

He hesitated visibly, then, as I was hoping as I had never hoped before, the force of the old habit that had let him talk the way he had was too strong. Doctors and nurses together talk shop as instinctively as they breathe. Because we were only talking shop, we were both breathing more easily.

He said, "I can't stand without a stick for more than a couple of minutes. I should have had to prop myself up. A bit tricky."

"Very." The atmosphere between us was still tense, but somewhere the bells were ringing. I did not yet know exactly what was wrong with him, but there was now no doubt about my getting all that out of Sir Robert at the first possible opportunity. That the condition was serious was obvious; whether it was also dangerous was still an open question. The bells were ringing because that remark he had just made showed he had realized his ill-health was not a dirty word to be avoided. I was not going to force him to talk about it, but if it came up in the conversation it came up. I asked about the baby. "Normal delivery?"

"Couldn't have been more classic." His face was transformed by his old smile. "God, Maggie! Talk about a lucky break! I disremember being so relieved to see an infant. He only gave about twenty minutes' warning. Directly he was born her pressure began to sail down, the way it does. I was just wondering if there would be any hope of getting a hold-everything cable off to Robbie, when Miguel — he runs the only local taxi — came out with the cable telling us Robbie had decided to come out. As I'd sent the false alarm, I thought I had better come and break the news. Miguel brought me in. We'd have got here sooner if we hadn't had a puncture." He folded one arm on the other, and, as on that night in his room, the knuckles of his exposed hand were white. "She must get rid of that kidney. If you two take her back with you I'd be a lot happier."

"When'll she be fit to move?"

"A day or so. There's nothing like a successful childbirth for giving a woman a new lease of life. According to the books, she should now be dead, and junior, if alive, a sickly prem. I left her drinking tea, making plans for the next one, and junior bawling his head off."

"Who's looking after things? David?"

"In theory. In fact, Pilar's mother and posse of sisters. She's got six. I think they were all there this evening with a few aunts and female cousins thrown in. Pilar's a good, sensible kid. She's only sixteen, but no teenager. They haven't been invented in her village yet. Too far off the map." He looked round. "Oh, there you are, sir." He got on his feet by pushing on the back of that hard chair and his stick simultaneously. "I've put Miss Lindsay in the picture. Quite a surprise," he added drily, "finding you had brought her along."

"Good God, boy!" retorted Sir Robert sternly. "What's surprising about my bringing an experienced theatre nurse when y'cable warned me I might have to perform a pair of major operations! How many pairs of hands am I supposed to have, eh?" He looked Joe over openly and clinically. "Y'stance has improved considerably since I last saw ye! Turn round, boy. Let's have y'stick." He removed this as he spoke, handed it to me as if we had been in a ward, flattened his hands against Joe's shoulders. "Get 'em as far back as ye can. Good. Not bad at all. Buckwell should be pleased with ye. Get much pain now?"

As Joe's back was to us I could not see his expression. There was none in his voice. "Not much more than an ache."

Sir Robert held out a hand for the stick. "Here y'are, boy." He waited while Joe turned round. "When does Buckwell want you back in Martha's for the second stage?"

Joe glanced at me. I met his glance as I would have done had we really been in a ward and he one of the patients. "He hasn't told me." He smiled rather grimly. "You know what surgeons are like when it comes to telling patients about themselves."

Sir Robert was in fighting form. Knowing him, and Joe, I was convinced that was intentional. "Ye don't have to grumble about that. What can he tell ye that ye don't know for yeself? Eh?" He turned to me for sympathy. "If there's one thing I can't abide, m'dear, it's operating on a fellow-surgeon! Impossible patients! Everything always goes wrong!" He glared at Joe. "Not that much seems to have gone wrong with the job Basil Buckwell's doing on you, m'boy! Sound man, Basil. That's why I sent ye over to him. No man, in my opinion, to touch him when it comes to spinal tumours. Mind ye, his technique is unorthodox – but pays off. If ye'd been born a few years earlier, Joe, you'd have been on y'way out now. As it is, you've a very good chance of getting away with it. But there it is. There it is. Well?'' he demanded, having let in not just some fresh air but a veritable hurricane. "What are we waiting for? This gel's had a long night! She needs some breakfast!" He held the door for me. "Then we'll decide what to do next."

We had breakfast in a hotel dining-room that overlooked a steeply-terraced garden. There were scarlet, pink, and white geraniums scrambling like weeds over the narrow terraces, banks of rose-coloured azaleas, and a languid fig-tree sprawled against a lower wall, its leaves already powdered with a fine white dust.

I looked at the garden while Robbie rambled on about what he had said to the Dean and the Dean to him ". . . if we don't turn out more qualified men per year, then we may as well face it, this Health Service of ours is going to grind to a halt. What we're trying to do is run a twenty-four-hour service with what amounts to a twelve-hour medical staff! Any self-respecting trade-union official would shout for a general strike if the members of his union were asked to work half the hours we expect of our young men. A forty-hour week indeed! Tell that to the average house-surgeon, who calls a fifteen-hour day a normal day's work!''

Eventually the conversation returned to Geraldine Easton. Sir Robert agreed with Joe about her returning with us. ''Let's settle everything this end while we're here and in easy reach of London by telephone.'' He pushed back his chair. ''Be back for ye later, m'dear. Come on, boy!'' He stomped off without waiting for Joe or even looking back, which allowed Joe to follow at his own speed.

He took his time. He stubbed out a cigarette, got on his feet using the same methods as before. ''So you really didn't know, Maggie?''

''No. Did you ask the boys at Barny's not to talk? Believe you me, they did not.''

''That was decent of them. Not many knew.''

I asked, ''Joe, why? You didn't want pity?''

''I don't know about not wanting that.'' His smile was self-derisive. ''I do know one doesn't honestly need it. One gives oneself so much. I think – I had better get after Robbie before he starts bellowing for me.''

''Yes.'' We both knew he had not answered my question. I did not intend to repeat it. ''He detests being kept waiting.''

I made myself watch his walk clinically. It was good. According to all the books I had read on what I now knew was the right subject, most patients at this stage would still be using two sticks. ". . . but the more the patient can be encouraged to rely on his own muscles, the better the ultimate prognosis."

There was good as well as bad in his knowing so much. He had read all those books, and seen for himself on hundreds of occasions the quite astonishing physical difference the right mental approach to an illness can make. He had the right temperament, build, and previous physical condition to make a good operation subject. All those were tremendous assets now, and when he had to have the second-stage operation. The books I had managed to get hold of had said approximately 20 per cent of all such cases could be cured surgically. But most of them had been written five or more years ago, before Buckwell's breakthrough with his then very new technique of grafting. Sister Orthopaedic Theatre had put the figure up to fifty. And old Robbie had been genuinely pleased just now. He was far too shrewd to have attemped any form of an encouraging act. But a cure still meant being left with a permanently weakened back. Joe was a surgeon. Surgeons have to have strong backs. If Robbie was right – and he was seldom wrong – Joe should get away with it, and with his qualifications he could always earn some sort of a living. Yet unless something not far short of a miracle happened, I could not see how his particular talent was going to be much use to him, or anyone else, again.

I was nearly falling over backward mentally in my efforts to view things with the detachment I had learned from my job. Suddenly, I could no longer keep it up. I was too distressed, too bitter, even to remember that before I was out of my first ward I had learned never to ask why. And I understood why he had not said a word about this at Barny's, and had asked the boys to keep it quiet. I understood, because I had seen pain, real pain, the type that takes over the individual so often, in the wards. That type, whether of the body or the spirit, is a very private affair. It turns a human being into a statue who scarcely dares to risk movement even by breathing, and while it lasts the sufferer is drawn into a secret, silent world of one inhabitant. It is not a question of not wanting to share it: it cannot be shared.

In his place, I would have done as he had. I would have wanted to get away even from him. Then, for the first time since our meeting, I remembered Frances, and that this must be as much hell for her as it was for me. They must have met and fallen in love when he went over to Martha's path. lab. for the various tests he must have had before Buckwell was willing to touch him. Those were the 'injections' Dolly Bachelor had let out. 'Injections' was a useful euphemism frequently used by hospitals, since it covered a lot and explained nothing.

But all this did explain why she had not yet given up her Martha's job. I thought she was right to do that, to stay right away from him — if she had — while he was still warded, but if I were her now during these waiting weeks, I would be out here, fine job or no fine job. Possibly that was because I was a nurse and not a doctor. Doctors saw patients at regular intervals, but for comparatively short periods. Nurses were with them all day, or all night. It was not nearly so easy to remain academic about a patient once he or she turned from a patient into a person, as happened after only a couple of days in a ward. And people during convalescence need the comfort of understanding companions very much more than when at the height of their illness. Then they need skilled care.

Joe would probably deny this strongly. That must have persuaded her. The way I felt this morning, it would not have persuaded me. Matron would have had to find herself a new theatre sister fast, I thought fiercely. And then I thought no, she wouldn't. If Joe and I had been still engaged when he went into Martha's I would not have been Sister Theatre. I would have known he was ill, and when Matron offered me the job would have turned it down as I did before, thinking I was getting married. Matron would have understood. So the question would not have arisen.

Nor did it now, I reminded myself bleakly; nor did it now.

CHAPTER NINE

A Spring Morning In Spain

The sun shone as we drove slowly down the already crowded main street. The lights were off in the all-night cafés, the doors wide open. The scent of fresh coffee roasting, of baking, and scrubbing soap mingled with the scent of musk from the Indian shops.

Joe sat between Sir Robert and myself in the back of Miguel's large and much worn American car. Sir Robert had arranged the seating. "Sister and I are the tourists. Be sure and tell us what to look at, boy!" He smiled across at me. "As it would look as if this may turn into a fine old wild-goose chase, m'dear, the least we can do is get in some sightseeing." He peered suddenly through his window. "Take a look at that, Joe! Over there by that window with all the brasses! What's a youngster like that doing with an arthrodesed hip? But that's what some fool of a surgeon's done to him, eh?"

"Looks like it, sir. Could be a pin, of course,

or a plate in after a road accident.''

"Possibly.'' Sir Robert continued to look put out until he spotted an untreated bursa on a youngish woman's elbow, then an early case of disseminated sclerosis. As we slowed at the Gibraltar frontier, Joe murmured to me, ''Any passengers left undiagnosed on your plane out?''

A stream of Spanish workers was pouring in over the border, each holding the permit that allowed its owner to pass in for a day's work. A solid, delightfully incongruous figure in the blue uniform of a London policeman watched the Spaniards with a typically impassive face.

The Spanish guards at the second frontier delayed us only briefly. The customs check seemed more a social occasion than anything else. Neither Sir Robert nor myself spoke any Spanish, but Joe had acquired sufficient at one time and another to translate for us and answer their questions. Before finally waving us on, the guards asked several questions that, from their bows in my direction, seemed to concern me. As we drove on into the small frontier town of La Linea, Sir Robert asked why those amiable fellows had been so amused.

"It wasn't amusement, sir. Admiration.'' Joe glanced my way, smiling slightly. ''They decided your Sister Theatre has the complexion of a lily, the eyes of an angel, and the ankles of a racehorse — amongst other attractions.''

"Is that so? Most observant fellows, if I may

212

say so, m'dear! Most observant! And what was all that business about a novice? Didn't I catch that word?"

"Not novice. *Novio.* That's a – oh – serious suitor. My Spanish isn't up to much. I had tried to explain why you were visiting your niece. They got hold of the impression that had to be Miss Lindsay. This is still an old-fashioned country, and as they saw from my passport that I'm single, they assumed that as I was travelling with an uncle and niece, I must qualify."

"They did, did they? Hm. It must save a great many complications havings things so cut and dried. I have often observed – " But we never heard Sir Robert's observation in that context, because just then our driver swerved violently to avoid a little group of women walking towards the border with baskets of clean linen on their heads. He was flung against his window. I would have landed in Joe's lap, but for his quick steadying arm round my shoulders.

He had reacted instinctively, but as he gripped me his arm muscles suddenly turned tense, as if he had had an electric shock. And that was how I felt. He removed his arm almost immediately. It was just as well. His nearness was disturbing enough. His touch had reminded me far too vividly of the times he had held me in his arms. I edged as far away from him as possible and stared out of my window until my face grew less hot and my ears stopped drumming. If this kind of thing was likely to happen again the sooner I got right away from him the better.

Sir Robert stifled a yawn and talked of the arrangements he had just made by telephone with Bill Swan to admit Geraldine Easton and her baby to Catherine Ward on the day after tomorrow. "Glad we've got the ambulance and plane reservations all settled." He yawned again. "This is very pleasant." His eyelids drooped and his head began to nod. In the clear light of that Mediterranean morning he looked much older than he did in London and, despite his sleep on the flight out, very tired.

Joe looked from him to me. "Sleepy, Maggie?"

I shook my head. "How long from here?"

"Two to three hours."

I said quietly, "Let's let him sleep in peace."

"Yes. He needs it."

He was, I sensed, as grateful as myself for an excuse for silence. Sir Robert's brisk presence awake, even when absent, as when we had waited in that reception lounge, had served as a constant reminder of our professional selves, and consequently allowed us both to retreat behind our professional armour. Asleep, the old man looked oddly gentle and as defence-less as people do in sleep. He looked nothing like the great surgeon with the world-wide reputation for being one of the biggest names in modern surgery. And because his defences were down, ours seemed to have gone too. I no longer felt anything like a theatre sister. I very much doubted Joe now felt anything like a surgeon. I was only the girl he had stopped loving, and he was the man who did not want my love. Our physical proximity must have made the past embarrassing for him as it was dangerous for me. We had known each other too well to be able to make successful small talk. But unless we talked shop there was now no other kind of talk open to us. Our past hedged our present with forbidden territory and 'No Conversational Entry' signs.

The road grew narrower and rougher and for a while hugged the coast. The sea was very blue and flecked with minute specks of white, as it was still early in the year. Offshore dozens of little fishing-boats bobbed like corks, and behind us the rock pointing like a giant finger into the sea began to merge with the horizon. The mountains we had to cross lay ahead, purple shadows on the skyline. Then we turned inland and the shadows turned to massive black rock.

I tried to think of Mark, to use him as a refuge from Joe and the effect of his silent presence. I avoided looking at his profile, yet was conscious of every slight movement he made, every breath. I told myself I was being a fool and, as Mark would say, rubbing salt into the wound. I reminded myself of everything Ellen and my theatre girls — including Sandra

– had ever said about Mark's feelings for me. I worked hard to get myself in a state of indignation for Mark over my own behaviour towards him. Dolly Bachelor thought me a-human. Was it any wonder my relationship with the poor man had been so bogged down? He was a good man, a kind man, and he had been quite incredibly and uncharacteristically thoughtful to me ever since Joe left. He might have been a big brother, only he was not my brother. I had no brothers, but from observing those of my friends, I had noticed the only men who behaved to girls like brothers were their brothers. Yet Mark, for all his talk, had never once persuaded me he felt more for me than a great kindness. Perhaps that was his way of loving. And then I had to look briefly at Joe. It might be Mark's way, and a good way. It was not my way – yet.

The car bumped and jolted. Sir Robert slept on. We passed small villages with white-walled and flat-roofed cottages; larger villages with roofs of the houses all shining brown tiles; skirted the high wall of a monastery or convent on a hill; caught the occasional glimpse of an elegant golden-stone house with iron-grilled windows standing aloof at the end of an avenue of eucalyptus-trees.

The mountains were very near. The last valley was carved into pocket-handkerchief fields, each neatly edged with a low rough-stone wall. The women working in the fields looked round and then waved as we went by. Miguel drove more slowly and waved back vigorously.

Joe said quietly, "His mother comes from here." He jerked a thumb. "Her sisters, cousins, and aunts."

In one field a young man was ploughing rhythmically, his plough drawn by a solitary ox. He looked as if he had all eternity in which to finish that field and had been there since eternity began. I watched him and thought. I've got until the day after to-morrow.

The mountain road was cut out of the rock face, and the drop on the off-side was sheer. I never had a head for heights, and for most of that winding, tilting climb and then descent sat with my eyes closed.

Joe's voice said, "You can open them now, Maggie. We're nearly down."

Beyond the mountains the country was flat and yellow, and then it grew more undulating. We drove up a hill to yet another white village, which at first sight looked more African than Spanish. Joe told me it was the last village. "Seven miles more, that's all."

The Eastons' house stood on a terrace half-way up a hill. At the foot was an olive-grove; above was a carpet of thyme and heather. The house was much bigger than I had expected. It was built of yellow stone with a long, low flat roof, and stood round three sides of a patio tiled with red and white diamonds. The patio had a trellis of vine as a roof, and the vine was in flower. The afternoon sun filtered through the trellis and set the diamonds dancing.

A girl lay reading in a bed pulled outside one open doorway. By an open window a few yards from her, an attractive dark-haired younger girl sat sewing. Behind her was a basket-work cradle on a truckle stand. Through the wide door of a room across the patio we could see the back of a fair man in a blue shirt and jeans working on a canvas fixed to an easel.

Joe at my elbow read my mind. "I've never been able to blame them for taking risks to live here either."

Geraldine Easton was twenty-seven and the mother of two sons. She had been married ten years. She looked a young seventeen. Her long-ish, light-brown hair was tied into a school-girl ponytail. She put down an erudite-looking book on political economy to welcome us warmly.

"Now you are back, Joe, I'm getting up," she announced later when we were all supplied with long glasses of fresh limejuice. "I only stayed in bed because I promised you I would until your return."

Her uncle put his glass down on the tiles. "None of that nonsense, young woman! You're staying where you are!"

She smiled as if he was a sweet but tiresome

child. "Darling Uncle Robert, don't fuss! I'm not ill now. I've only had a baby."

Sir Robert turned to me. "Didn't I tell ye how it would be! How can one begin to teach those who will not learn! Well! Where's that husband of yours, gel? Let me talk to him!"

"Darling, we can't disturb David yet! He's working." Geraldine was adamant. "He's having trouble with the new picture."

"And that permits him to ignore our arrival?"

"He's not ignoring you, Uncle Robert. He's just not aware you are here."

Joe agreed. "Once David's working, the house could fall in without him being aware of it – provided it didn't knock down his easel with the rest."

Sir Robert said no doubt that was all very fine if you were one of those artist fellows, but such an attitude was beyond the comprehension of a simple surgeon. Joe and I looked at each other, then away, quickly, as Sir Robert produced all his favourite 'simple surgeon' clichés, ending as we expected with ". . . and a stitch in time saves nine on the operating table as elsewhere, young woman!"

Geraldine patted her uncle's arm. "Darling, you musn't be cross or think I don't appreciate all you've done for me. You've been simply wonderful, thinking of everything, rushing out here with Miss Lindsay, and I really am grateful, and so will David be when he realizes everything. But the baby and I can't possibly leave him and fly home with you. There's no need now I've had the baby, and I do so hate hospitals. I'm not letting you or anyone else cut me up — but that doesn't mean I don't adore you!''

Sir Robert cleared his throat to explode. Joe said quickly, ''I thought we agreed the other day that there's no point in postponing the inevitable, Geraldine?''

She considered him thoughtfully. ''Have I truly got to have that kidney out?''

''I'm afraid so. Sorry.''

''Soon as this?''

''Sooner the better.''

''You mean that.'' She was not asking a question. ''Oh, hell!'' She sighed. ''All right. I'll do what you want, Uncle Robert. Now don't let's talk about it any more.''

David Easton came out of his studio when the light began to fade. He was a short, sturdy man, a few years older than his wife, with an attractive voice and pleasant, if very absent-minded, manners. He thanked Sir Robert and myself warmly for the trouble we had taken and proposed to take for his family, then obviously forgot who we were and what we were doing in his household.

His habit of drifting away in the middle of a conversation or meal infuriated Sir Robert, but amused Joe and myself. I enjoyed being a guest in that house. No guest there could ever feel in the way, since most of the time it was apparent that neither host nor hostess recollected their guests' existence. Now I had met the Eastons, I well understood why Joe had chosen to stay with them. The architecture of their house was ideal for anyone in his present physical condition; their attitude to him was even more ideal. They accepted him as part of the furniture and, when they remembered his presence, treated him as a combination of the Delphic Oracle and an elder brother, and ignored his health as completely as they did their own. That was far more restful for him than Sir Robert's blunt acceptance of a regrettable situation, or my trained nurse's 'lets-call-a-fact-a-fact-and-forget-it' technique. Joe knew there was no real question of my being able to forget his health, but the Eastons did. With them he need never feel self-conscious about his slow walk, inability to manage without a stick, necessity to sit whenever possible, or to prop himself against the nearest wall when standing for more than a very short period.

The baby was enchanting. Pilar and her female relatives had weighed him on the kitchen scales. He weighed six and a half pounds. His very marked resemblance to his great-uncle was the one thing that cheered Sir Robert since our arrival at the house. The old man was petulant with the fatigue he refused to admit and, though genuinely fond of Geraldine, thoroughly annoyed that his worst fears had not been proved right.

For a little while that evening Joe and I were alone in the stone-flagged hall the Eastons had converted into a dining-room. Pilar had cleared the table and was washing up in the kitchen with two of her sisters. Geraldine's bed had been pushed back to her bedroom. Sir Robert was with her. David had vanished.

Joe talked about the difference twenty-four hours had made. ''It'll be a long time before Robbie forgives us for not saving the drama for him. He would have so enjoyed getting down to it with a penknife and a few hairpins on the kitchen table.''

''I had that impression on the way out. Of course, we would have spoiled the fun for ourselves. We've a crate of instruments and dope.''

''Nonsense, Maggie. The lot could have fallen out of the car on the way here.''

''On that mountain road?'' I shuddered. ''It was steep enough.''

''Poor Maggie! You missed the view. It was worth seeing.''

''And poor Robbie missed his drama,'' I said firmly. I did not want to be reminded of that car ride. ''Do you think he's going to take out her kidney, or leave it to Bill Swan? She's a pretty close relative.''

''I should say he'll do it. It's not as if she's his wife. And that kidney may be a tough job.

Robbie was always very good at doing his own dirty work." He pushed his cigarettes towards me absently, then looked surprised when I took one. "I thought you had given it up?"

"I'm still fighting it. Not enough will-power."

"That doesn't tie up with Robbie's views on you as a theatre sister." He lit his own. " 'An excellent gel, m'dear! Capital, capital!' "

"Thanks." I was surprised at the pleasure that gave me. "He's been very good to me."

"And to me." He studied his cigarette. "As you now know. He knew which strings to pull, and pulled the lot." He looked round. "Including this place. Before I came out to look at Robin's leg I'd been staying with Margery and her husband in Casablanca."

I had wondered about that period of time. "Is she the sister married to the French architect?"

"That's right. He's putting up some new flats there. They were very decent to me, said come on out at once when I wrote inviting myself, as Buckwell was very keen to have me get somewhere warm and dry. But I couldn't stay on with them indefinitely. I wrote to Robbie before I left them saying I was coming home for a follow-up and not sure where I'd go next. I had Cornwall in mind as just about the warmest, if not the driest, place for an English winter. You know the rest."

"Yes." Then, as one subject had been nearly choking me since that morning, I had to mention it. "Joe, Mark told me a few weeks back that you are now engaged to Frances. I've been meaning to congratulate you. Kept forgetting. Of course – I do."

He looked at me quickly, and then as quickly back at his cigarette. "So Mark told you?"

"Yes. And about her staying on in her job. Very sensible."

"It would be more than foolish to let a girl chuck up a promising career for a man in my present set-up, Maggie. It would be bloody selfish and bloody silly."

I nodded vaguely. There was no point in reminding him there were two sides to that question, since Frances was clearly seeing it from his side. She might even be right. I did not think she was, but she might be.

He asked about Mark. "Think he'll get into Homer's firm?"

"Sure of it." I explained why at some length, since Mark was one of the few safe subjects we could discuss.

He said drily, "Mark's got a good P.R.O. in you, Maggie."

"Why not? I'm very fond of him, and he's been very good to me – and, incidentally, to you. You did ask him not to talk about your back?" He nodded, watching me very closely. "Well, he not only kept his mouth shut on the main issue, but when necessary – as I only now realize – he produced instant – and reasonable

224

- explanations to cover up for you." I told him about the evening he left Barny's, New Year's Day, that Beethoven concert. "You were there with Frances?"

"Yes." He stubbed out his cigarette and promptly lit another. "Maggie, I hope you won't misunderstand why I didn't want you to know."

"I don't think so. Isn't it obvious? The less people in on any secret the better its chances of being kept. I don't blame you for not wanting to talk, Joe. In your place I would have done the same." I suddenly remembered I had never thanked him for that radiogram and the records. I did so now, added, "It was your leaving them behind that first gave me my hunch that there was something odd going on."

"You had a hunch?" He asked curtly.

"Yes. I just couldn't prove it."

"Until Robbie did it for you. Unintentionally."

I said, "Of course." I thought I was being honest at the time. Later, in bed that night, I wondered if that was true, or whether Sir Robert was once again two steps ahead. I suspected he was, but was too sleepy to work out why.

No one called me in the morning, and I slept on until after eleven. When I was dressed and went to look for the others David was in his studio, Pilar singing in the kitchen, Geraldine, Sir Robert, and Joe were on the patio. Geraldine's bed had again been lifted out, and she was reading her political economy. The men were playing chess.

I apologized for oversleeping. "I feel most ashamed. It must be nearly lunch-time."

"Lunch indeed! Let me tell you m'dear, we have only just finished breakfast! It was served at 10.45."

"Darling Uncle Robert," protested Geraldine, "that's early for us. We usually have it at eleven."

"Eleven!" Sir Robert echoed impatiently. "By that hour I reckon to have half a day's work done!"

"Which is very clever of you, Uncle." Geraldine closed her book. "Maggie, come and sit by me. No, of course you mustn't do anything. For one thing there's nothing to do, and for another, it would offend Pilar. She'd be badly shocked if I let a guest lift a finger." She smiled. "And she is quite disturbingly hard-working and capable. Here she comes with your coffee."

The men went on with their chess. Geraldine and I discussed the advantages of being an expatriate. She still refused to admit to that way of living having any serious disadvantages. "The rent we pay here wouldn't cover the smallest flat in London. Then there's Pilar – I loathe housework. An English char three mornings a week would cost more than she does full time. But even those aren't the main attractions." She looked over to the studio. "David can work here. The sun is something one can depend on. We like the people even though we don't see much of them. We like being in this house too much to want to leave it for more than the odd evening. Uncle Robert thinks we are nut cases, and so do most of our friends at home. Do you?"

I said truthfully, "I did, until I got here. I could still say you are taking a lot of risks with your own and your children's health. But you'd do that every time you let them cross a road at home, or crossed one yourselves."

"You're not going to give me a lecture on cutting my family off from all the advantages of modern living in a modern city?"

"Did you expect me to?" Joe had his back to me, so I could watch him with impunity. "When you must know how very much you are giving your family in exchange?"

She said, "We know. But with the exception of Joe, and now yourself, every other visitor we have ever had has spent most of his or her visit taking me into quiet corners and warning me we are heading for disaster if we persist in our foolish ways." She grimaced. "That's one reason why I'm really dreading flying home with you. The thought of leaving David and having an operation is bad enough, but it's going to be hellish while I'm in hospital, as all our relations will descend on me with more lectures, and I won't be able to get away."

I suggested she confided some of this to Sister Catherine. "If she suspects your visitors are going to upset you she'll have them out of her ward before they've barely had time to deposit the flowers and grapes."

"Is she allowed to do that?"

"In Barny's, as in most good hospitals, a ward sister pretty well makes her own rules. If anyone should question that she'll have the backing of the entire medical staff to support her. Technically we may all now be civil servants, but what the doctor says still carries all before it. Sister Catherine'll be well able to keep your relatives out of your hair."

"And she won't mind my asking? But hospital sisters are such fierce women! Oh – dear oh me! What have I said!" She smiled apologetically. "Yet it's really your fault for being nothing like my idea of a hospital sister, or even a nurse. All the nurses I've ever met bustle around, say 'we,' and act as if their patients are backward toddlers. You are so quiet, Maggie, and you sit so still. I noticed that yesterday as well as now. Is that anything to do with your working in the operating theatre?"

"Possibly." I looked again at the back of Joe's head, and remembered my thoughts on mental and physical pain. "A theatre in action is a very quiet place."

A car drove up the dirt road – it was actually only a cart-track – running up the hill from the olive-grove. Geraldine recognized it as belonging to the local doctor and called Pilar. "David's going to be furious, but he must come and talk to Dr Alvaro," she explained to me before giving Pilar instructions in Spanish.

I was a little surprised, remembered what Geraldine had said on that subject yesterday when we arrived. Later, when the four men retired to drink sherry in the hall, she said, "Lots of things don't matter here, but good manners matter very much. Alvaro hasn't come to see me. He wanted to meet Uncle Robert. That reminds me –" She summoned Pilar again and arranged for a message to be taken to Miguel to ask him to drive Sir Robert into the village that evening to return the call. "Alvaro's pride would be hurt if he didn't. If you hurt a Spaniard's pride you're in for trouble. But then" – she watched the men through the open hall-door – "one could say the same of most Englishmen."

"One could."

She looked at me keenly, then back at the men. "Joe looks a far more typical Andalusian than Alvaro, until he starts talking. Not because of his accent, but because he doesn't use his hands. Now, when he's just sitting listening he could be the Spaniard in that quartet."

I agreed. I realized we were now having one

of those conversations in which the important words were those left unsaid. I was not sure why. I waited for her to give me the lead.

She talked about the portly, middle-aged Spaniard with thinning light-brown hair, then his wife and five daughers. "I find the Senora rather frightening. She's so chic and serene. She makes me feel I must do something about my hair. But David likes it done this way."

"Then I shouldn't let any other opinion bother you."

"That's what Joe said." She hesitated. "There's no getting away from it – you and he are awfully alike. Of course, you've known each other a long time."

"Yes." I was still waiting.

She said. "He told me he was once engaged to you and that it broke off and about – well – "

"Frances Durant?"

"Yes." She gave me another keen look. "Do you mind his telling me?"

"I can't say I enjoy the thought of being discussed, but it's not going to make me take great umbrage, if that's what you mean?" She nodded. "Taking umbrage isn't one of my hobbies. Possibly because I'm neither Spanish nor English."

"As Joe would say – darling, you and me, both. Oh, hell! Here they come!"

I too wished the men had stayed a little longer on their sherry. I wanted to ask her to explain

230

that conversation, since most of her remarks had been so obvious and she did not strike me as a girl given to stating the obvious without good reason. I had no opportunity to do that then, or later, since that was the only private conversation we had during my stay in her house.

When Miguel arrived for Sir Robert that evening David Easton suddenly decided I must see something of what he called "the real Spain" before I left. "Why don't Joe, you, and I go down to Luis' with Uncle Robert, Miguel, and bring him back to join us in the *taberna* later? They make the best *tortillas* and serve the finest shrimps in Andalusia there. You'll like it, Maggie. Joe and Luis are great pals."

"It's a good place," agreed Joe unenthusiastically, "but we can't all leave Geraldine."

"Why not?" demanded David. "Pilar'll be here – and probably Carmencita and Maria as well. The brat's fine. He'll just snooze. The girls'll look after Geraldine."

Geraldine backed him up. "You may not have another chance, Maggie. This is your last evening."

"Last?" echoed her husband. "It's tomorrow you are taking Geraldine back? Then I'm not going out. Joe can take Maggie. You two won't mind leaving me behind, will you?"

Sir Robert joined us at that point. He had been tidying himself for his formal call and looked very spruce in a professional dark suit he had brought with him, he now explained, for much this reason. "Didn't I tell ye we might have to deal with the unexpected, m'dear?" he asked me. "So I brought along all the tools of m'trade." He fingered his neat hospital tie. "Just in case I had to show the flag! And what's all this about some outing for you youngsters? Staying behind are ye, boy? Quite right. Quite right. Y'wife needs ye to-night. These two young people will have a good time on their own, eh, Joe?"

"Yes, indeed, sir," said Joe politely. "If you are ready, Maggie, let's go." He did not add, and get it over. He might as well have done. His reluctance was so apparent to myself, if no one else, that I thought momentarily of producing one of my nasty headaches. Then I realized that if I did Sir Robert would certainly insist on providing me with the antidote, and anyway it was not fair to intrude on the Eastons' very natural desire to have that evening alone together. So I only asked if they would give me three minutes to get my bag and a coat and I would join them in the taxi.

CHAPTER TEN

Dr Delaney Calls

In the darkness the village looked more African than ever. The streets were narrow; most of the houses faced inward. Some were lit with oil-lamps, others with electricity. There was a flashing neon sign outside the wine-shop, and the first thing I noticed inside was a huge television-set. It was not in use.

Joe said, "We'll go downstairs."

That bothered me for him until I saw the stairs. They were stone, set wide, curving, and shallow. He managed them fairly easily.

The large converted cellar below was lit with oil and candles for effect, not necessity. There was an electric switch on the wall near our table, and a row of unused, unshaded electric bulbs hanging from the shadowy ceiling. The tables were covered with scarlet linen cloths, and there were coloured posters of bullfighters pinned round the walls.

I said, "Joe, this can't be real. It's too right."

"I know. One's seen it all in a dozen movies. But those were the copies. This really is the original. It's no tourist trap. They still get very few in here. It's too inaccessible, and there's no main road to anywhere inside of thirty miles whichever way you chose to go." He smiled at some one over my head. "You must meet the boss, Luis."

Luis was a small, thin man with the face of a weary poet. I thought him around fifty. Later Joe told me he was thirty-four. He welcomed Joe with dignified warmth, bowed to me, then turned back to Joe with a quite charming smile and long comment in Spanish that had Joe smiling rather mechanically.

When we were alone again he asked if I wanted a translation. "Or did you gather you met with Luis' complete approval?"

"Roughly. Spain seems a country to boost a girl's morale. I've always heard Spanish men were much given to making gallant remarks, but, like this set-up, I never really believed it was true. Have you caught the habit yet?"

He shook his head. "Wouldn't be wise if I did. They don't much care for foreigners making verbal passes at their own girls. Until you arrived Geraldine was the only English girl I'd heard of around here."

"Frances hasn't been out then?"

Luis was back with a jug of wine and a plate of shrimps to keep us going until the *tortillas* arrived, so he just shook his head.

Luis asked a question in which the one word I understood was *novio*. Joe's reply resulted in his hand being shaken again.

"Get the gist of that, Maggie?" he asked when the proprietor left us.

"Again, roughly. Wouldn't he take no for an answer?"

"It wasn't quite that." He coloured very faintly. "I gave him the wrong impression – intentionally. He'd have been a bit upset if I hadn't."

"This is an old-fashioned country and so on?"

"That's right. And a particularly old-fashioned part of the country. Nice girls here don't go out with any other type of male friend. In point of fact, here most girls wouldn't even be allowed out alone with a fiancé. But as we are English and officially expected to be mad, that he'll overlook. It hasn't upset you?"

For one wild moment I considered answering that truthfully. My training, if nothing else, prevented me. The habit of dealing gently with the sick and convalescent was too firmly in-grained to let me hit back even when hurt. "Not at all. I'm all for seeming to abide by local customs. Do you come here a lot? That how you know him so well?"

"Miguel brings me in about once a week. Sometimes more. It depends on our post. He brings it out – generally in the evening, unless it contains a cable. Time isn't all-important here, which is a constant joy to me. Geraldine and David have got used to it. But though time isn't a god, things get done."

I glanced at our fellow-customers. Most of the tables were taken. There were only three other women there amongst the many men. Every one was talking rapidly, quietly, intently. "Things also get discussed, it appears."

He looked round with patent affection. "Luis once told me only death silences an Andalusian."

He had turned the 's' into a 'th,' as Geraldine did. I remarked on it, then asked how he had learned so much Spanish so soon. "I never remember your knowing any."

"I did some at school. Not much, but enough to start me off here. And as hardly anyone here speaks English I had to pick it up or stay dumb. I brought some books out with me after Christmas and have been doing some homework for something to do. Luis has been a big help, and as he's only a couple of years older than myself, we see most things the same way."

"He's only that much older? I thought him at least fifty."

"If he was he probably wouldn't be alive. The forties-to-sixties men are largely missing. The Civil War."

"I'd forgotten that. I suppose they haven't?"

236

He shook his head. 'Not that they talk about it – to strangers, that is. Luis did tell me he remembered his father and two uncles being killed. He didn't say how. I didn't ask. They are all great talkers, but they don't like personal questions, or talking politics with foreigners. They make very good company, but, in my experience, don't give much away."

That applied to our conversation. We talked constantly, yet might have been strangers. I found myself waiting, as one did with a strange man taking one out for the first time, for him to give me the conversational leads. Yet there was one big difference to eating out with a stranger. There we would both have sought for mutual ground. Now we were searching for the safety of the ground we had trodden together in the past.

A man sitting against a wall began to play a guitar. The rhythm fascinated me. It was simple and complicated. "Joe, is this a type of flamenco?"

"No type. Again the real article." His face had lit up the way it always did when he heard good music. He produced an old envelope, noted the tune on the back. "This is one I haven't heard. I'd like to try it on a piano some time."

"Is there one around?"

"The only one I've seen belongs to the Alvaros. I dine with them occasionally, but it's always very formal." He smiled. "They'd both be appalled if I suggested bashing out a jolly tune on the old joanna. They'd let me, of course. A guest can do no wrong. But they wouldn't ask me in again, which I wouldn't like. They are a nice pair, and their kids are quite enchanting."

"Geraldine told me they had five girls." I had another look round. "Pity they don't have a piano here."

"Luis is talking of getting one – *mañana*. I hope he does."

"Yes." I remembered how he had always used the nearest piano as a safety-valve. "How about learning the guitar?"

"I've been thinking of that, but have put it off as I don't know how long I'll be here and don't want to accumulate too many possessions. There isn't much space in hospital, even in a private room, as you know."

"Buckwell did you in their Private Wing?" I asked, thinking back to those telephone inquiries I had made and wondering how they had been so unsuccessful. "When did you go in? When you left Barny's?" He nodded. "I suppose they suddenly had a bed for you, hence your sudden removal?" I spoke as if all this had just occurred to me. I dared not tell him the truth about it or those calls. That would have given far too much away.

"That's right." He lit another cigarette, changed the subject by drawing my attention

238

to a portrait of Luis behind the bar. "You can see it now those chaps have moved off. David did it."

"Can I go over for a better look? Will anyone object?"

"No. As you officially belong to me, the wolves won't howl."

I said, "They look remarkably harmless wolves."

"My dear Maggie," he replied smoothly, "they may be. But you are not."

I stood up. "And you, my dear Joe, seem to be picking up the local customs fast." I walked over to the picture, exchanged bows and mime explanations with Luis, looked at the picture for a few seconds without seeing it at all, then, realizing I was going to have to discuss it, made myself take it in.

"It's odd," I said, sitting down again, "but rather impressive. Did he do it all with a knife?"

"Yes. He's laying off that technique now. That was done two years back. He's still feeling around, but I think one of these fine days he's going to be really good. There's one dealer in London who's now very interested in him. I took four canvases back with me on my last visit home. They've all sold."

"I hope you told Robbie?"

"I did." He grinned. "He still thinks they are pathological cases. I did once. They are devoted to Robin, but were acting up like a pair of morons over his leg — like David with Geraldine all this week. Yet on balance I think they've got so many of the right answers." He refilled our glasses. "They've asked me to come out again after my next op."

"And will you?"

"*Mañana*, Maggie. Now tell me about the rest of your holiday. What was that you said in Gib about going down to Exmoor?"

We talked Exmoor, then Devon, then the whole West Country, in such detail we might have been preparing a guide-book. Then the guitar-player started again.

I was grateful for the excuse for silence, just as I had been on the drive from Gibraltar. But then I had needed silence as a refuge from his touch; now, because he had become so untouchable. I listened to the gentle, haunting, and to me quite unbearably sad tune, and thought, This can't be me, and that can't be Joe. This has to be some sort of dream, bordering on nightmare.

The candlelight accentuated my sensation of unreality, softening the lines of Joe's highcheekboned face and the faces of the other men around that were so uncannily similar to his.

"Joe, have you any Latin blood?"

He blinked as if waking from a private dream too. "Not that I know of. Both sides of my family come from Kent, and as far as I've been able to trace them always have, as you know."

"Of course." The atmosphere between us was suddenly much more strained. My thoughtless remark had knocked down a 'No Entry' sign. "You were born on the Romney Marsh. Weren't any survivors washed up there from the Armada?"

"If they were I never heard it. We had the Danes, and the Vikings, and the Normans. Frances," he added – I thought deliberately – "has the notion that one of my solid Saxon ancestors must have fraternized with the occupying troops, hence my name and colouring. She could be right, but I never heard it from anyone in my family. Ah! Here's the old man!" There was no hiding the relief in his voice. "And looking exactly as if about to do a ward round in his pundit's suiting." He heaved himself to his feet. "Over here, sir! Try some of this wine – it's good."

We flew back from spring and back to winter early the following afternoon. From the air England was hidden beneath a thick carpet of cotton-wool. Our hostess told us it was snowing in London, but the airport was still open. "We are lucky. Yesterday every airport in the south of England was closed, but this morning was fine, so they were able to get the runways clear. This snow only started about an hour ago."

Sir Robert was relieved. "Not that I much care for the idea of going down in this, m'dear, but I have to be back for that kidney-graft tomorrow. Wouldn't have suited me at all to be stuck out in that cock-eyed household another twenty-four hours, not to mention delaying your holiday again. I'm deeply obliged for all ye've done, Sister."

We were over in England, so I was 'Sister' again. I sounded it as I said, "Not at all, Sir Robert. I haven't really done anything, but thank you for saying that."

An ambulance and Lady Stanger were waiting for us when we arrived. She followed in her car, while Sir Robert and I travelled with Geraldine and her baby to Barny's, then waited while we were up in Catherine Ward, after previously insisting that I spend that night in her house.

Plump little Sister Catherine took the baby from me. "So this is my lodger? What a nice little fellow! My nurses are delighted to have a baby lodger!" She paused until Sir Robert vanished behind the curtains for another word with Geraldine. "Well, Sister? You seem to have had a most exciting time!"

"Oh, yes, Sister. It wasn't dull." I touched the baby's face with one finger. "He's been a model baby." I then gave her a brief account of the trip, which did not include Joe's name. She would almost certainly get the whole story from Geraldine, and if she then thought my reticence odd that was just too bad. Once she heard his name, and about his condition, she would want all the medical details, and they were now something I could not bear to discuss even with Sir Robert. Now I was back in the hospital atmosphere I understood better than ever why Joe and his friends amongst the residents had clamped down on that story. His medical case-history would fascinate even those few members of the staff who were above listening to grapevine gossip. Every one of his symptoms would be discussed in minute detail, every possible prognosis considered. It was an interesting case, made the more interesting by his being so well known in Barny's and the inevitable effect it must have on his professional future. Once the news got round it would be a very long time before the general interest began to fade. No sensitive person enjoyed being the object of so much talk, or the thought of what having to listen to that talk would mean to his friends. Far, far better try and prevent it all getting started.

Sir Robert returned. "Shall we now go and pay our respects to Matron, Sister Theatre."

Matron announced herself most happy to see us back. "Spring-cleaning has started in your theatre to-day, Sister," she added, after hearing Sir Robert's version of our travels. "All general surgical work is now being done in the Ortho-paedic Theatre. Staff Nurse Garret and Nurse Cotton are working there on loan."

I noticed Sir Robert had also omitted Joe's name in his explanation. Out in the main corridor I asked bluntly, "Sir Robert, did you avoid mentioning Joe de Winter intentionally?"

"Just so, m'dear. Just so. Can you see the reverse serving any useful purpose? As I've just informed young Geraldine. I didn't have to tell a good nurse like yourself. Good nurses know how to keep their mouths shut. The boy doesn't want a parcel of silly old women of both sexes prattling over his prognosis. Well? I want to see Bill Swan. I shall be about fifteen minutes. Will you join m'wife in the car?"

"There are a few things I would like to collect from my duty-room. May I nip up there first?"

The theatre corridor was empty, the whole department very quiet with that strange lifelessness of all hospital departments when temporarily closed to patients. The theatre seemed to have died a little, the way a ship does in port, or an aircraft when grounded.

The duty-room door was open, and Dolly Bachelor was writing at the desk. "Sister!" She bounced up. "I thought you were in Spain!"

"I was. We've just got back," I explained why I was there.

"I'm not surprised you left things behind going off in that hurry." She made for the door. "I must go and check the anaesthetic-room."

"Don't let me turn you out, Nurse Bachelor . . ." but she was gone without asking one question about my journey. As she was normally such a chatty, friendly girl, her vanishing would have puzzled me if I had not had so much else on my mind. Consequently, I was only grateful to be spared telling the tale again and to be left alone.

But the desk telephone reminded me I must let Wendy and Mark know I was back. I rang Henry Carter first. Wendy was off duty. Her staff nurse thought she had gone to see some show with Sister Matilda. ''I'll tell Sister you rang, Sister Theatre. And that you'll be back in ten days.''

Charlie on the switchboard said I was dead out of luck, I was. ''Dr Delaney's off until eleven. Went out for the evening not a half-hour ago. Any message, Sister? You'll be in touch? Right. I'll see as he gets it.''

Lady Stanger had the heater on in her car and was knitting placidly. ''I get most of my sweaters made waiting for Bob. I hope he doesn't keep us too long. You look fagged out, my dear. Was it all very tiring?''

She had been a ward sister at Barny's before she married. She asked a few questions about her young in-laws, but was far more eager to talk nursing shop and compare my experiences with those of her own days.

We spent most of that evening on the subject, before at her insistence, retiring for an early night. When she drove me to the station next morning she asked me to spend the last week-end of my holiday with them. "I really did enjoy talking to a fellow-nurse again. Neither of my girls are interested in nursing, and though Bob and I talk Barny's most of the time, naturally he doesn't see things with a nurse's eye. Do say yes, m'dear."

I did as she asked, intending to write with some polite excuse while I was away. My one desire at that moment was to get right away from anyone with any connection with Barny's or Joe. Our final good-bye in Spain had been even worse than I had anticipated. He had been so polite, so damned polite, and so utterly untouchable. He had asked me to give his regards to dear old Mark. "One of these fine days perhaps the four of us can meet up in London. You, Mark, Frances, and myself. Tell him that from me, will you, Maggie?"

I spent that night in a hotel. By morning I had had enough of my own company and rang my father's friends.

Exmoor was powdered with snow. My friends warned me to expect a lot more. "Last winter we were snowed up for weeks. It will be nice to have you stranded with us."

They were very pleasant people. They knew nothing about hospitals, had never heard Joe's name, remembered me only as a schoolgirl. "And you are now an important sister in the

246

theatre! You must tell us all about it!"

I did not attempt anything of the sort, as they were not really interested in anything but their farm, milk-yield, and the effect the next general election was going to have on farm subsidies. I found their attitude restful for a couple of days, then the reaction set in and I wanted to be back in my own world. I wrote to Lady Stanger thanking her again for her invitation and telling her the time I expected to arrive at her house, then sent postcards to Mark and Wendy.

It snowed fitfully most of my days on the moor. On the last morning the snow was much more constant. My host fitted chains to his car. "Change your mind and have this week-end with us, Maggie, and I think I can promise you a much longer holiday."

I said untruthfully there was nothing I would enjoy more, but must leave or offend the Stangers.

"Isn't this Sir Robert a big noise? You can't do that!"

Lady Stanger welcomed me like an extra daughter. "The same room as last week, my dear. Dinner will be an hour later than usual as Bob has a meeting. Never marry a surgeon." She flicked shut the window-curtains. "Either he's in the theatre, lecturing, or at a meeting! Luckily I knew what to expect, but it can be very lonely, particularly now the children have grown up."

"I expect so." When she left me to unpack I found myself thinking how much I would love to be lonely for Joe, in those circumstances. I wandered over to the dressing-table, studied my reflection dispassionately, as if it belonged to another person. "Not bad-looking," I said aloud, "and quite intelligent. Isn't it time you woke up, for good? He doesn't want you or need you. He's engaged to another girl, and he must love her the hell of a lot to have asked her to marry him before having this second op. And she must love him the hell of a lot to have said yes. They both know there's a chance he may end up in a wheel-chair. The fact that he doesn't mind having her to push it shows just how much she must mean to him – and how he's changed. Your Joe," I added much more slowly, "would have waited until he was in the clear. He hasn't. Do you need any more proof that he's no longer yours to love?"

I stayed some little time staring into the mirror and thinking over that last thought. I could guess why it had only just occurred to me and not hit me at once that first morning in Gibraltar when I discovered my hunch was right. My subconscious had sat on it, because it did expose a weak streak in Joe that I had never suspected and was still only too anxious to avoid admitting. I could not put that off any longer. A lay person might just possibly have thought he had every right to get engaged at

248

this juncture. No one with any real experience of illness would agree. Frances might have insisted on their being engaged, but he should have refused to tie her down until after his second operation. If a husband or wife was crippled after marriage that was one thing; marrying a man who might well be crippled was another. The only people who could possibly imagine there was any romance in such an arrangement were those who knew nothing about the physically disabled. There was no doubt Frances must love him, but it was not fair to her, or any girl or man, to be put in the position that he had now put her. I still loved him, was desperately sorry for him, and had seen for myself the courage with which he was facing his illness. But I knew too much to be able to excuse what he had done to Frances Durant. How could she have said no? How could any girl? And how he had changed! I was surprised and saddened. I should not have been either. I knew illness too closely not to be aware it brought out the worst as well as the best in human nature.

Lady Stanger knocked on the door. "A visitor for you, my dear. Dr Delaney – oh, bother! The telephone! Go on down to the sitting-room – remember the way? I'll take this call in our bedroom."

My postcard had told Mark I was coming up

for the week-end. I had given him no other address as I had not wanted him to contact me until I had that breathing space. It was kind and ingenious of him to call here and so promptly, but I wished he had waited.

At the sitting-room door I braced myself for the inevitable agonizing reappraisal, then went in quickly. "Mark, this is very nice of you –" and my voice stopped abruptly.

Frances Durant was standing by the open fire. She turned apologetically. "You expected Mark? Didn't Lady Stanger –?" and she broke off, then answered herself. "Of course! She's met me in Martha's as well as at Dr Homer's party last Tuesday. She called me Dr instead of Mrs?"

I gripped the back of the nearest chair. "She should have said Mrs Delaney?"

"Shall we sit down?" And when we were sitting, "Yes. I didn't mean to tell you quite so abruptly, but perhaps it's the best way. I'm Mark's wife."

I was first too astounded for speech, and then too angry. Joe might have been weak, but Mark – and she – had been down-right wicked. An acute emotional shock is just about the worst thing anyone can have before a serious operation. Why, and how, they had found themselves in the position to administer that shock to him did not at that moment concern me. I could only think of Joe's angle.

She said, "I can see this has upset you. I'm sorry. May I explain?"

My voice returned. "You can try."

"You're very angry. I hoped . . ." She paused nervously. "Or rather, I thought . . ." Again she broke off. I let her flounder. I was in no mood for helping hands. She said at last, "You must feel, with good reason, that Mark has treated you – well – badly."

"Me?" I demanded. "You think I care that Mark's married you? For myself? I wouldn't give a damn if he married a whole harem. But I give several for what his marrying you is going to do to Joe. Or had you forgotten him?"

"Joe? Joe de Winter? He's why you are so furious?" She began to laugh. "For dear old Joe?"

I had never hit anyone in my life. I came very close to it just then. "Yes. For dear old Joe. He's due for an op shortly. Or had you forgotten that little detail too?"

She controlled herself. "I'm so sorry. No. I haven't forgotten Joe or his op. Those are two of the reasons why I'm here. I've been wanting to talk to you for some time, but the position was somewhat tricky."

"That I believe."

Her huge green eyes were very intelligent as well as very attractive. The way she was studying me reminded me of her specific branch of medicine. I could have been something rather dangerous under a microscope. "It was the ethical set-up that mainly tied my hands. I did some tests on Joe before Basil Buckwell decided to operate. That made him my patient. He talked about you – in confidence. But even without the professional angle, I would have had to keep quiet as he asked, since he had been so very good at keeping quiet about Mark and myself."

"He knew – ? For God's sake, how long?"

"Nine months, one week."

"Nine?" I echoed incredulously.

"That's right. Joe, my boss, and the Inland Revenue boys were the only people we told. My boss is a pet. He didn't even tell his wife, as she's got a cousin at Barny's."

I was too staggered to do more than clutch at inessentials. "That's why Mark was always crossing the river!"

She flushed. "You must think him an awful heel. If it's any consolation, he feels one."

I waved that aside. "Where did you meet?"

"At the Smithe-Grey's. We married four weeks later. We were quite crazy, because as you'll know Mark can't afford a wife financially or professionally. But as I already earn more than he does, we decided to take a chance and keep it quiet."

"I see." I did. It was the kind of impulsive thing Mark would do, despite Dr Homer's views on married residents. And then he, Mark, would have not been unamused by the need for secrecy. It must have appealed to the infantile streak in his nature to have taken Homer for a ride all this while. And yet at the same time, when Mark's responsible side was uppermost, it must often have made him acutely anxious. I could see his wife's angle easily. He was a very fascinating man. It was only then I fully appreciated why she was so on edge about me.

I said, "I won't pretend he didn't seem to be making a play for me whenever we had an audience. He never continued the act when we were alone. You've never had to worry about him and me."

"My dear girl, he's my husband. Of course I worried," she retorted bluntly.

"Then why," I asked equally bluntly, "did you allow him to date me?"

"He said he had to back up Joe's story. And you were in a tough spot, his very old friend, and needed a shoulder. Don't blame me for that little lark. I didn't like it at all." She smiled wryly. "Show me the wife who would. I just had to go along with it partly because I like Joe, partly because he and Mark are such old pals and I didn't want to be the kind of wife who goes about trying to bust up her husband's friendship with his old pals. If you have to blame anyone blame those two men. This was all their idea. And you actually gave it to Joe in the first place."

"Me? How?"

"Don't ask me how you knew of my existence! But didn't you once ask Joe if he was going to marry me?"

I remembered that evening in his room, and nodded weakly.

"That made him realize the one thing that would stop you asking awkward questions would be to have you believe there was another woman involved. I gather he was right?"

"Yes." I went on to tell her about Sandra's various references to her name.

"Sandra Brown. I should have guessed. Mark detests her, and even back at school she had the makings of a queen-bitch. Mark was always scared of her guessing about us. She'd have got the news to old Homer like a bat out of hell."

"Faster." A slow wave of wonder, happiness, and sadness, began to flood over me. "Joe used you as a red herring. To get away from me before I discovered about his back?" I smiled for the first time since I walked into the sitting-room. "No wonder he looked so odd when I told him Mark had told me you two were officially engaged."

She knew all about that. "Mark had a letter last week giving him hell for adding that touch. Joe said it was enough to make you suspect the whole thing, it was so phoney. He wrote, and I quote, 'only a self-centred moron would start handing out engagement rings in his present set-up.' I was furious with Mark. We had a flaming row. We'll have another after to-night, as he doesn't know I'm here. But I can see no sense in letting the nonsense continue. Thanks to Robert Stanger there can't be much left for you to know about Joe's condition – which knocks out one of his reasons for wanting you kept in the dark. The other two" – she ticked them off on her fingers – "have worked out the way he planned it. You are now no longer tied to him in any way. You haven't messed up your Barny's career by turning down promotion to be free to sit by his bedside and hold his hand."

I took a long breath. "So that was why?"

"Yes."

There were some drinks and glasses on a cabinet against a wall. I was too dazed with a sheer, blinding joy to worry about the future, much less if Lady Stanger would object to my helping ourselves. I poured two sherries.

"Thanks." She raised her glass to me. "We can both use this."

A minute or so later she said, "I rang Basil Buckwell to-day. Those ethics kept niggling. So I asked if I could hand Joe over to my boss. I knew it would be all right with Hugo. I used some idiotic excuse to Basil about finding it hard to treat a friend. As one of the big advantages of being a woman is that all men are perfectly prepared to accept one is an emotional idiot, Basil took it without a question. Handing over doesn't actually put me in the clear, but I'm not worrying about that. I want you to get this straight, and then I want me to be Mrs Delaney officially. That's why I gave that name to Lady Stanger. I'll tell Mark it was a slip, and as I've seen you it's time he faced old Homer with the truth. I made him take me to Homer's party the other evening – minus wedding-ring – so that the old man could look me over. We had a splendid tête-à-tête about bugs. I don't know if he liked me or not, but I saw he did Mark."

"He does. Mark's work has been very good recently."

"That's fine. It'll strengthen our hand. All this cloak-and-dagger stuff was amusing for a while, but now it's getting a hideous strain." She smiled. "This may amuse you – I've been calling on Mark in Barny's while you've been away. The grapevine has got busy, and your theatre nurses do not approve. Mark says the temperature drops to sub-zero whenever he sees any of them now."

"They're nice girls." That explained why Dolly Bachelor had been so anxious to avoid me the evening I returned from Spain. "But they are apt to judge people by their face values. They weren't all that wrong about Joe. They were all convinced he resigned" – my voice shook – "because he was behaving like a little gentleman for my sake."

She said gently, "There was nothing else he could do. Not being the man he is. I'll admit

256

I did think you had a right to know exactly why he wanted to break off your engagement, but now I am coming round to thinking he did the right thing. Having that diagnosis confirmed was bad enough without having you officially involved and unable to uninvolve yourself.''

''Not unable. Unwilling.''

She said, ''I do believe you, but try switching the situation as it then was between you two. No matter how much Joe loved you, would you have wanted to risk there coming a day when he would try not to think of you as a helpless burden, and yet find himself thinking it? And you're a woman. Think of the blow that would be to any normal man's self-respect. When he asked you to marry him he was able to offer you what he thought was most likely a glowing future. Suddenly it looked as if it was all gone. Whether it is or not is still very much an open question. But the fact that you have already had to get on without him has shown you that you can. It may have been hell, but from what I've heard from Mark and the men around Barny's you are making a great success of that hell. That means your job must fascinate you, and that whatever happens to your private life your professional life should be assured. If Joe's actions hadn't forced your hand you might never have discovered you could be such a high-powered theatre sister.''

''I wouldn't have discovered it. I expect I

would have gone on nursing, but not in a theatre. It would have reminded me of too much I wanted to forget. As I had to stay . . ." I paused. "Yes. If I still can't have Joe I know now where I belong and what I want to do with my life. You're right. He's shown me that."

"And at the time you had no suspicions?"

I told her the truth, then asked about those telephone inquiries.

"Those admitting clerks probably saw him coming in with me for those early tests. Once he was admitted to our Private Floor, he used his mother's name, Marden. He told Basil he wanted privacy. He's not the first patient to ask that. The hospital had no grounds for objecting. He's single, no parents living, no family in this country. He gave Robert Stanger as next-of-kin." She smiled again. "A crafty man, Robert Stanger. I wonder what he would have thought up if you hadn't happened to be due for a holiday when he wanted to take you to Spain. Of course, he'll swear blind he only took you along because you were efficient. He wasn't hamstrung by ethics, but, like the very few people who knew the truth, knew Joe's anxiety to have it kept dark. A very, very crafty and clever man, that."

"And kind. He's always had a soft spot for Joe."

"And not only Joe, I gather. Has he told you yet that Joe's due back in Martha's next Wednesday? He knows, because Basil told me this morning he had told him. Joe should have had the letter and cable recalling him by now. He'll probably fly back that day. I suppose," she added slowly, "you couldn't pay him another flying visit? If you are short of cash I'll gladly lend you the fare. The least I can do — as one 'other woman' to another. He'll probably be very annoyed with you and furious with me, but what the hell! Being annoyed'll take his mind off the future. And I doubt he'll stay annoyed."

"You think I should go back to Spain?" I demanded. "Now?"

"If you can't get away to-night, to-morrow. I'm sure the Stangers won't object. Why not? Don't you want to see him?"

"Of course, I do. But . . ." I hesitated without knowing why, since there was nothing I wanted more than to be with him. "Joe likes to make his own moves."

"But the whole point is, he can't. Now can he?"

"No," I said. "No. It has to be me." I stood up none too steadily. "I must ask Lady Stanger if I can borrow her husband's secretary. I've no idea how much it's going to cost, so I may want to borrow some money. As one 'other woman' to another, Mrs Delaney" — I smiled at her — "thank you very much for everything. Do help yourself to another sherry. You deserve it."

CHAPTER ELEVEN

La Señorita Inglesa

Sir Robert said any understanding of the female mind was beyond the powers of a simple surgeon, but he was gratified his secretary had been able to render me all the necessary assistance.

Miss Armstrong had produced a seat for me on a London – Gibraltar flight next morning. I did not sleep much that night. The snow had stopped; I kept watching for it to start again. I was convinced every airport in the country would be closed before I got away.

When Lady Stanger came to call me I was up and dressed. She now knew nearly as much about my affairs as I did myself. She asked me to spend my next free week-end with them. "There's nothing like a Barny's training for teaching a woman perseverance. No, my dear! Don't thank me! I don't know whether it's a sign of getting old, or just plain immaturity, but I love a romance!"

Frances rang before I left. She had not yet

had her flaming row with Mark, as she had decided not to tell him she had called on me until that night. "He would be bound to feel himself forced to send off warning cables under the O.P.A. It'll be far better if you catch Joe off his guard. How do you feel?"

"Queasy. Robbie's loaded me with travel pills."

She laughed. "There's one thing bothering me. Where are you going to stay? With the two men?"

"No. Robbie said that wouldn't do at all. You know I told you he met that Spanish doctor? Well, his wife was at school in England. Robbie did one of his human dynamo acts late last night, got a call through to them, and asked if the Señora would be kind enough to entertain a young female friend of his wife's as a week-end guest. She's never even met me, but she said yes."

She said she was glad to hear I was going to be properly chaperoned. "Will she let you talk to Joe alone?"

"God knows. I don't know anything."

"You'll be all right. Oh, hell! I've just thought of another snag: will this female or her husband tip Joe off?"

"Don't know that either. They live some way from the Eastons."

"Just another chance you'll have to take. You'll be all right," she repeated, "and what if you do come back with a pair of black eyes? I'll lend you the raw steak I shall certainly need after my ever-loving hears what his wife has done!''

The car Miss Armstrong had ordered by cable was waiting when I reached Gibraltar at one o'clock local time. It was newer and better-sprung than Miguel's taxi. The driver was a Mr MacDonald. He was a stocky, middle-aged Gibraltarian with a strong North American accent superimposed on an Andalusian lisp. He told me he was bilingual and frequently forgot whether he was using English or Spanish. As a young man he had worked some years as a cab-driver in New York. He was very interested to hear my father was there, and while we waited at the first frontier asked me to visit him. ''New York City is the greatest Señorita.''

''Yet you came back?''

He shrugged. ''I'm a Rock Scorpion, Señorita. Born on the Rock. I've got all my folks here. New York City was a great spot, but I got real lonesome for my folks. I guess a guy needs to be where he belongs.''

Two of the guards at the Spanish frontier recognized me from my last visit, obviously took my return as a personal compliment to themselves, and greeted me with wide smiles, bows, and cries of, ''Ah, ha! La señorita inglesa!'' plus a great deal more which I did not understand, but which had my driver looking somewhat self-satisfied. Then one of their questions made him turn to me. "They want to know if the sick lady and her baby are better?"

"Much better, thanks. Mrs Easton – the lady – has had an operation and hopes to be back here very soon."

The guards beamed when this was handed on, then launched into a long discussion that clearly concerned me, but was conducted at such a rate that I was not even able to catch the odd word I might have understood.

When we drove on, Mr MacDonald asked about my uncle, the famous English doctor. "He couldn't make the trip this time?"

"No. He's working. He's not really my uncle. He's – " I hesitated, trying to find the right word.

"Kind of guardian?"

"Yes," I said truthfully, "you could call him that."

He nodded as if he approved of this. "Seems there are a lot of doctors in your family, Señorita. Or going to be. Those guys were saying the young English doctor you are going to marry lives out here. Is he staying near the house of this Señora Alvaro you are going to visit with?"

"Fairly near," was the only comment I felt I could make.

He nodded again. I asked if he knew the Alvaros' village well? He said it was some years since he had taken a fare that way, but he remembered enough and knew Miguel. "He comes into my garage to stock up with spare parts when he brings a fare into Gibraltar."

He ran three cars, had two of his sons working for him. He was a pleasant and very chatty man. By the time we were a few miles from La Linea I had heard about his Gibraltarian wife, four children, Spanish mother, Scottish father, and maternal grandfather from Ronda who had, he said, been the best wine- and tobacco-smuggler in the business. "It was too bad the old man wasn't around in New York City in the old boot-legging days. I'm telling you, Senorita, he certainly knew all the angles."

It was a bright, dry afternoon, far removed from the freezing slush I had left behind. The traffic was as sparse as previously. We met the occasional car, a few scooters, an ox-cart, several much-laden donkeys. It was siesta time, and the little white villages had a timeless air. There were old men snoozing against walls; barefooted children playing a type of hop-scotch in the still light dust; and every now and then an old woman all in black came slowly out of a house with an earthenware jug on her head, looking as if she had stepped out of some biblical print.

In the valley before the mountains the same women were working in the same fields. The young man with the ox-plough was missing. My mind went back to the thought I had had while I watched him, and then the tension and bitter, black despair of that other drive. So much still remained unchanged, yet because I felt as if I had come alive again, anxiety had become a challenge.

The sickening twists of the mountain road were exciting instead of terrifying. I kept my eyes open and saw the yellow plain below rolling wide and open as the sea when we reached the crest. I glanced back. Far away to the southwest the sun was shining on the roofs of a large town on a hill. The tiles glistened and sparkled. It could have been Bunyan's Celestial City. Then the road curved, and it was gone. I was glad I had not missed it this time.

I concentrated on the view, intentionally, in the rare intervals when Mr MacDonald was silent. I dared not let myself wonder whether I was doing the right thing or not. Joe had gone to so much trouble to avoid me. Was it fair to invade his privacy? Was it fair not to? I remembered my instinctive hesitation when Frances made her suggestion. She was convinced I was doing right, and so was Lady Stanger. Sir Robert had given me every assistance, but no opinion. He and I knew Joe far better than the others.

I had thought along those lines all my waking hours last night. I refused to let myself think on them now. My job had taught me to control my thoughts as well as myself. That was necessary in the wards, doubly so in the theatre. And not only in the theatre, I thought, not only in the theatre.

Once down on the plain I realized it was cattle-country. The yellow land was speckled with tiny dust clouds hovering over ambling herds. A little later, we drove by about fifty head of cattle under the leisurely guidance of two young men on small tough-looking horses.

My driver jerked a thumb. "Cowboys, Señorita. They don't look much like John Wayne, eh? But that's what they are."

"Are there many farms round here?"

"I guess not what you'd call farms. That herd'll most likely belong to all the folks in one village. Some'll own a few beasts, some just one, some'll share a beast with the neighbours. The men from the village will take it in turns to do the droving."

Some way on he slowed again as we passed some black bulls grazing on scrappy scrub in a well-wired paddock. "Take a look at those, Señorita. Fighting bulls! And mighty fine ones at that! You been to the bullfight? You ought to get to see one. They are the greatest!"

After that he talked bullfights and matadors for miles. The land grew hilly again, we were nearing my journey's end, and I began to feel so peculiar I wondered whether to take another of Sir Robert's pills. I did not because they made me so muzzy. I was not at all sure what lay ahead, and I needed a clear brain for dealing with it.

On the flight out I had been tempted to drive straight to the Eastons' house to get my first, and inevitably tricky, meeting with Joe over as soon as possible. On reflection, I decided against that. Señora Alvaro had been extraordinarily kind in inviting a total stranger as a week-end guest, and she might be offended if I delayed introducing myself. As she had spent five years in a convent in Sussex, I guessed – or, rather, hoped – she would not be unduly shocked if I later asked to hire Miguel's taxi and drive over to the Eastons during the evening. If she was it would be just too bad. I had come all this way to see Joe, and I was going to see him even if it sparked off an international incident.

At the last village my driver said he must ask the way to the doctor's house. There was a little crowd of men standing outside Luis' wine-shop. One of the men answered my driver's query with a polite explanation that took around ten minutes.

Mr MacDonald turned over his shoulder. "We go on through, take a left turn." He waved at the tavern. "Seems they've been making a fiesta in there all week. The boss has a new piano, and there's some Englishman staying here who plays it real good."

I sat on the edge of the back seat. "That why they are waiting?"

There was another long explanation. My driver translated briefly: "Seems they are just taking the air. This guy – the piano-player – seems he's gone to Madrid."

"Madrid? Oh, no!" Both men stared at me. I took a grip and asked the driver to inquire if the English piano-player was the man staying with the English artist. "Or if he doesn't know that, could you ask if he walks with a stick?"

I was already hideously sure of the answer even before the Spaniard illustrated his reply by leaning on an imaginary stick and limping round in a little circle. He used the name Luis several times.

Mr MacDonald was very upset. "But maybe this guy has it wrong. You wait here. I'll go talk to this Luis."

I was far too disappointed to be embarrassed by the appraising glances and comments of the men who had now grouped themselves round the car. They moved aside to let my driver return with Luis, then closed in on us again.

Luis, looking now more a tragic than a weary poet, spread his hands helplessly directly he saw me. "Aie, aie, aie! La señorita inglesa! Aie, la pobrecita Señorita!"

My driver said, "He says the Englishman didn't know you were coming."

"No, I – I wanted to surprise him."

The expressions on the faces of the men around now reminded me of Sir Robert's last evening. They listened to the exchange of remarks between my driver and Luis, then all began talking at once.

Again the driver translated. "Seems your gentleman had this cable telling him he must get back home early next week. He came in last evening to say as he guessed he'd like to take a look at Madrid as it was his last week-end and he didn't know when he'd get back to Spain. Miguel took him down to Malaga airport first thing this morning."

I had never burst into tears in public in my life. To my horror that happened. I was very ashamed, until I saw my behaviour had clearly met with the full approval of my whole audience.

Luis bellowed something. A few seconds later a youth in a white apron appeared with a glass of wine for me. The wine pulled me together. I asked if anyone knew where Joe was staying in Madrid and if he was coming back or going straight on from there to London.

No one knew his address. Luis told me via MacDonald that he had suggested several places where Joe might care to stay, but he had not made up his mind on any particular one when he said good-bye. He was not expected back.

The crowd offered sympathy and suggestions. Mr MacDonald discussed the matter in detail with Luis. They talked and talked and talked. And I sat and wanted to kick myself for being such a blind, senseless fool, not only now, but all these last months. If I had not let my fixation about his loving Frances cloud and distort my intelligence, I would have long realized he had had to shed his white coat at Barny's, but not his whole character. Certainly illness brought out the worst as well as the best in people, but more than that, it turned people into caricatures of themselves. The brave became braver; the weak weaker.

Joe was a quiet man. Quiet, not weak. In many ways he was very like Robert Stanger. Neither man was given to acting on a crazy impulse like Mark, but both preferred action to the reverse. That was why they were surgeons, not physicians. If only I had had the sense to remember that I would have realized that once he had that recall, and knew what hell the strain of the next few days would have to be, the last thing he would have done would have been to sit out the dragging hours on the Eastons' patio, or in Luis' tavern, accepting the inevitable with a resigned and increasingly gloomy shrug. He had never been able to stand around helplessly in the face of defeat – and a lot of people were alive at that moment who would have been dead but for that. Throughout his S.S.O. time, when a situation turned tougher, his mood always matched it. ''God knows we can't make matters worse,'' I remembered him saying hundreds of times, ''and crying woe, woe, won't help, so we may as well go ahead along a new line. It may even turn out to be the answer.''

Eventually Mr MacDonald finished his conversation. "Life is shorter than death, Señorita. I guess maybe we should go on, eh?''

Ever since that talk with Frances last evening all my energy had been concentrated on getting to Joe. I had not even worked out what to say to him when we met. I just wanted to be with him, and to achieve that I had been prepared to regard walking out on the Stangers, the money I was spending, and my being a self-invited guest in a strange household in a strange country, as minor details. It was only when we reached the doctor's house that I fully appreciated that last point. It would have been difficult with Joe. Without him it was going to be grim.

The house was built along the same lines as the Eastons', but even from the outside had a much more formal air. Señora Alvaro, a plump, youngish lady in elegant black, came out to welcome me. I expected a very civil but very formal reception.

"Miss Lindsay, how nice of you to visit us! Such a long way to come! What a pity you did not let Mr de Winter know of your visit, but, of course, you wished to surprise him! We are all so disappointed for you.''

Later I learned she had heard the news through Luis. He had sent one of his younger brothers up on a scooter while my driver was still thrashing out my problems with the crowd outside his tavern. One of the Señora's three maids was Luis' second cousin; the scooter-riding brother was her *novio*, and only too happy to deliver any messages at any time to her house.

The doctor was out. The household, with the exception of an aged gardener, was exclusively feminine. The Señora in nearly perfect English introduced me to her two elderly aunts who shared her home, five fascinating little daughters, and a middle-aged lady whom I took to be the housekeeper by her bustling air, but later discovered was a distant cousin of the doctor's who had moved in with them when she lost her husband several years back.

"Poor Antonia," said the Señora calmly, "she is very trying because she will never rest. She had no children, which is very sad. But she is one of the family, so, naturally" – her hands fluttered constantly as she talked – "we could not leave her to live alone."

She was a charming hostess, friendly, even gay when we were alone with the other females. The atmosphere was very much more formal during the brief periods when her husband was present, and at meals.

After only a few hours in time I felt as if I had stepped back at least half a century. The step was by no means wholly unpleasant. I found it rather restful, for a limited period, to live like a Victorian woman in England. The Señora was another great talker. She never stopped unless her husband was there. She told me about her early life in Madrid, of her parents' modern ways that had resulted in her having part of her education in England. She had enjoyed her schooldays, apart from the weather. "It rains every day! And if the rain stops for ten minutes all you English people say, 'Isn't it a nice day!' "

In Spain, she said, men and women still inhabited separate worlds. Her world was her home. There, as I observed, she was supreme. It was that, plus her insight into English life that she had gained as a girl, that explained my presence. "I remember my English schoolfriends were constantly travelling by themselves – you have so much freedom! I have always liked the English, and was very happy to be able to entertain you in my own house."

She said she seldom had guests staying in the house unless they were relatives. She never went out unless escorted by her husband, one of the aunts, or "poor Antonia." I gathered Joe was the first unrelated male guest her husband had entertained at home. "But Mr de Winter is English." She shrugged expressively. "My husband is a good man. He knew it would give me pleasure to meet your fiancé. Such a charming man! So sad he has been ill. Was it an accident? My husband did not tell me, and I never like to disturb him with questions. He prefers his work to remain outside his home."

I said Joe had had a spinal complaint without giving any details.

"He will be better soon, and then you will be married. I think" – she considered me – "you will be very happy. Mr de Winter has the face of a good man."

I said, "Yes, he is. Thank you, Señora. I hope we will be very happy."

She could not have been more hospitable, yet every hour seemed endless. That night in bed I remembered my anxiety in London last night and how much better it would have been if the snow had closed all the airports. And then I thought about Joe in Madrid, and how difficult if not impossible, it was going to be to see him before he had that operation. I had to be back in Barny's on Monday night, as I was due on duty Tuesday morning. Sir Robert had told me the spring-cleaning was over and my theatre working again. Tuesday morning would be the gynae list, Tuesday afternoon Sir Robert's teaching list – and he said it was going to be a long one. I would not be free until late that evening, and having been away would probably find myself on call for the night. If I went across to Martha's in my free period on Wednesday, if he had arrived – and I did not know what time he was expected – he would almost certainly have asked for no visitors again, and they would not let me see him. In any good hospital only a husband, wife, parents, or children were allowed to batter down that particular request – and they would have to struggle. Even an official fiancée only had rights if the patient named her as next-of-kin.

Next morning the Señora returned from Mass looking perturbed. Her husband had been called to a case several miles away and Luis' young brother had arrived on his scooter while she was at church with a message from her parents-in-law. They lived near a village twenty miles off. Her father-in-law had had what sounded to me like a minor stroke in the night, and his wife was anxious her son should see him. "We must go to her," she added anxiously, "as she will need the comfort of her family. I have already sent a message to my husband and ordered Miguel's car. It distresses me to have to ask this – but will you excuse us if we leave you alone for a few hours?"

"Of course! I'm so sorry about your father-in-law. Naturally you must go."

It took me a long time to persuade her I did not consider this an affront, but eventually she was reassured. Miguel arrived not in his car, as it would not have been big enough, but in a minibus he had borrowed from an uncle. The Señora, the two aunts, poor Antonia, the five little girls, and one maid to look after them all seated themselves in orderly rows in the mini-bus. Rosaria and Pepita, the two maids left behind, watched with me until the bus drove off in the direction away from the village, then sighed sadly and retired to the house, talking quietly together.

I stayed until the dust died down in the road, and thought of the many old patients I had nursed. I had forgotten nearly all their names, but could remember so many old faces. And so many of them had been so alone. "You can't blame the young folk, dear," they had said. "They've got their own lives to lead. It's not that they don't want the bother – they just haven't got the time."

Was it only that? I thought of the way the Señora accepted the old aunts, poor Antonia, her mother-in-law's need for the comfort of the family, not as so many demanding respon-sibilities, but as natural a part of her life as were her children.

I went back into the house to a solitary lunch, feeling disturbed and rather ashamed. Pepita hovered helpfully. Then I remembered how much domestic help the Señora had, how much room in her house, and consequently how much time at her disposal. Perhaps all those old patients were right. The fundamental problem involved was not irresponsibility or selfishness; it was that price tag on female emancipation, lack of time.

That reminded me of how much I was at present wasting. If only I had known where he was staying in Madrid I could have got a message to him.

Could I? Saying what, I asked myself. And if you had sent a message, supposing he had not answered it? What then? Take off after him? On your salary? When all this has already cost much more than you can afford?

I had told Señora Alvaro I was quite happy to be alone. I was not enjoying my own company at all.

Directly I finished eating I went out on the patio. I would have liked to have gone for a walk, but did not think I should without permission from my hostess. I could not sound out either of the maids on the subject as neither spoke a word of English.

Pepita appeared with a cane armchair, followed by Rosaria with two large cushions and a rug. Their gestures invited me to seat myself, and they then tucked me up as firmly as if I was a delicate invalid, with wide smiles and obvious 'now-you-have-a-good-rest' remarks.

I did not feel tired, but the sun, rug, lunch, and two disturbed nights combined to make me very sleepy very soon. I did not go right to sleep, but drifted in that pleasant plane between sleep and wakefulness. I heard the girls chattering away in the house; then some time later the *putt-putt* of a scooter; then a man's voice speaking rapid Spanish, and squeals from the girls that translated as coy in any language.

I wondered drowsily if the ladies of the household would approve, closed my eyes to show anyone looking that I was too dead asleep to hear a single thing, and that time went properly to sleep.

The noise of an engine woke me with a start. I felt I had slept hours, looked at my watch. It was only twenty minutes, and too early for the family to be back, as they had only been gone two hours. The engine had sounded more like a car than a scooter. It might be the doctor back for some reason, or perhaps another of the girls' young men. I shut my eyes again, in case it was my host. I was very grateful to him, but found his heavy formality and halting English quite as much of a strain as I suspected he did me. The girls' voices were much more subdued, yet much closer. I heard footsteps, pretended to be oblivious to the lot. *La señorita inglesa* was having a siesta from which she was incapable of being disturbed.

I then heard the faint click even a stick with a rubber tip makes on stone. I jerked my eyes open. Joe was standing by me, leaning on his stick. Behind him Pepita and Rosaria were beaming with delight.

He said drily, "This is a long way from Exmoor, Maggie."

278

"Joe!" I sat up. "What are you doing here?"

"Feeling very much that this is where I came in."

My heart was making the most abominable noise. It was a long time since I had stopped believing in fairy-tales, but he was there. "I thought you were in Madrid."

"I was."

The girls produced another chair, then retreated to the house, giggling quietly. He said they had told him the family was out. "Luis drove me up from the village." He sat down, managing rather better than when I last saw him. He did not look better. He looked tired, on edge, and in what the last Sister Theatre used to describe as one of Mr de Winter's silent-volcano moods. "Beware the fury of a patient man, my dear."

I was too pleased to see him to bother with being wary. "He said you weren't coming back."

"I didn't intend to, until I heard from him that you were here." He produced cigarettes, and when I refused lit one for himself. "Well, Maggie? What's the angle this time?" He looked steadily at me. "I'm interested."

"I'll tell you, when you've told me something first. How could Luis contact you?" I demanded, to give myself just that much more time to get things under control. "He said he didn't know your address."

"He didn't. But as he had given me a list of possible hotels, he assumed rightly I might have checked in at one. They were all run by either relations or old pals. He wired one man with a message for me, asked him to spread the word. It got to my hotel while I was out last evening. I got back after midnight. I flew down to Malaga this morning, hired a car to bring me out to the village."

"Joe, I'm sorry you've had all this travelling –"

"That doesn't matter." He cut me short tersely. "Let's get down to it, Maggie. Minus the tactful cotton-wool."

That night in Luis' tavern I had felt my hands tied by my training. I had dealt gently with him, treated him as if he was a patient. That was the right technique with patients, but I suddenly realized how that must have jarred on him. He was too accustomed to nurses' technique not to have seen through my act and not to have known that in using it I was turning him into something less than a man. An object for pity, sympathy, even love; but an object. In Barny's we were trained to view our male patients that way, since otherwise nursing in a men's ward would prove intolerable for nurses and patients. But I was not his nurse. I could not be sure what I was to him, yet his present hostility coming on top of all I had heard from Frances made me suspect I was possibly the last woman in the world he wanted as a nurse, for the same reason that he was the last man I would want as my doctor. So I hit back.

"I've no intention of using any. Not that I would say you have any right to objections on that count, in view of the amount you have used on me."

He stiffened. "I don't follow you."

"You should. From what Frances Delaney told me . . ." I repeated most of what that was. "I hope Mark squares things with Homer," I added, "but I would suspect even Mark'll have a tough time talking the old man round. He won't enjoy being fooled any more than I have." I let that sink in. "I never guessed you were such a good actor, Joe."

His face tightened as if I really had hit him. "Frances had no right to do this to you!"

"I don't agree. It wasn't her idea in the first place. She's sick and tired of pretending. She wants Mark to risk that showdown. He wouldn't do it while I was still in the dark."

"So she unburdened on you and heaved on to your shoulders a set of burdens that were not only hers to shed." He was very angry. "I can't tell you how sorry I am you had to find out that side from her. I'm sorry you had to find out anything. I never wanted that to happen for a long time yet. I don't hold with rushing in with news until one's certain what the news is going to be. What I could do to Robbie and that woman!" He shrugged.

281

"What's done is done. No use crying woe, woe."

I was watching him very closely and growing slowly very happy. "Are you so jealous of your burdens, Joe?"

"Why not? Since they belong to me."

I let that go for the moment. There was something I had to say on that, but I had to have the right words. "Why didn't you tell me the truth? Did you think I couldn't stand it?"

"No. One can stand anything when one has to. I simply didn't see why you should have to."

"Sharing it might have helped."

He lit another cigarette before answering. The afternoon had grown warmer. There was no breeze. He wasted three matches before he could keep one alight long enough to be any use. "Oh, yes. It might have helped to pull out all the emotional stops and let rip. That's a big relief for the ripper," he said drily, "and hell for the person on the receiving end. I had to hurt you, Maggie. I wasn't prepared to give you hell as well. Nor to let you do what you would have insisted on doing." He was silent for some seconds. "You must have it all added up." He sounded weary, defeated. "What are you going to do now?"

I had been asking myself that most of the last forty-odd hours, without finding the answer. Suddenly I knew, and the right words came unsought. "Nothing very much. I haven't a lot of time. I have to go back to-morrow. A splendid man called MacDonald is calling to drive me back to Gib at twelve sharp. And as Señora Alvaro has been quite fantastically kind to me and has had to rush off to a sick father-in-law, I can't leave here until she gets back. You in any hurry?"

He shook his head as if uncertain he was hearing right. "David isn't expecting me. Any time I turn up will suit him. I told Luis I would probably get a lift down with Miguel when he brings back the family."

"Do you think the Señora would object if you took me out to dinner chez Luis? I'd like to hear that new piano."

"I doubt she'll take exception to that. If that's what you want to do? Just that? You've come all this way just to eat shrimps and *tortillas*?"

"No. To see you. To tell you what I have to."

"And then go back?"

"I must. I'm on duty Tuesday morning. It looks like being a tough day. The theatre needs me, is my responsibility. I could have got out of that as a staff nurse. Not a sister." I paused. "Which was why you made me take the job, wasn't it?"

"Yes." The tension had left his face. He even looked much less tired. He breathed as if he had been running. "Maggie. Thank you very much."

"For coming? Or for asking you to stand me a supper?"

"Neither. No – that's not true. For both, and so much more. For what you haven't asked. For what you are not going to do. Understand?"

"Yes."

We smiled at each other: the sword was back in its sheath and we were at peace. I had no need to tell him how much I still loved him, of the anxieties that remained unchanged, the fears lurking in the still shadowed future. He knew all that, just as I knew all about him. I knew him better now than I ever had even during those theatre years when we had been so close.

The last time we were together I had thought he needed comfort. That was because I had then been thinking with my emotions and not my head. To insist on sharing his burden, to stay and offer him comfort, would be to crush him under the greater twin burdens of gratitude and guilt at having another person so involved. It could do even worse damage. It could destroy the two things so vital to anyone in his present position. A white-hot motive for wanting to recover as best he could as soon as possible, and his self-respect. I loved him. So I left him as I had said. He saw me off at Gibraltar. We did not discuss what he was going to do when he left me then, or when he was back in London.

On the drive, Mr MacDonald clearly assumed Joe's return had been delayed for some reason, but was as clearly well satisfied with the general situation and beamed on us like a grizzled Cupid. At the airport he asked Joe to be sure to let him know when the Señorita came back, as he, Joe, knew that with him the Señorita would be looked after real good. "You will be together again soon, eh?"

Joe said, "We hope so." He looked at me, and I felt I was in his arms.

The taxi driver considered us both, then used the same words Señora Alvaro had used last evening about her father-in-law's chances of getting over his mild stroke. "Hope is a candle that cannot burn out because it is lit by the Hand of God. We will see you back soon, Señorita, eh?"

CHAPTER TWELVE

Sister Theatres Do Not Faint

On Tuesday afternoon George Ellis came into the theatre ahead of Sir Robert to warn me the old man was in a filthy temper. "If I don't have an ulcer before the day ends it'll be a something miracle." He began scrubbing up, then glanced over his shoulder. "Of course! You've been away, Sister. Good time?"

"Yes, thanks, Mr Ellis." I smiled rather wryly behind my mask. My holiday had so altered my whole attitude to life that I felt I must have altered physically. I half expected questions on that score, and certainly about my trip with Sir Robert. I had forgotten how long a fortnight is in the life of a hospital, and how wrapped up every one in a hospital is in the affairs of their own department. Even Wendy, though very interested in all I had to tell her, could hardly wait to tell me about the latest crisis in Henry Carter. ". . . my dear, those stitches just gave while I watched. The man's viscera just welled out through the wound. Our new houseman was taking notes across the ward. He had never seen an abdominal wound burst before – my dear! He wanted to push the lot back! As I told Mr Swan, I had to be very stern with the boy to stop him doing more damage. Naturally, all we did was cover everything with sterile towels, give him a shot for shock, and pack him down to the theatre in his bed. But really, Maggie! How some of these young men manage to get themselves qualified is beyond me! That boy hadn't the intelligence one would expect in a pre-clinical student!"

The list was a long one. Mark was anaesthetizing. He gave me a guarded smile when he came in with the first patient. Wendy had not mentioned him last night, so I guessed he had not yet had his showdown with Dr Homer.

Sir Robert growled throughout the afternoon. Our dressers changed each Tuesday. One of the new boys, after hours of standing doing nothing, backed against a wall. Sir Robert glanced up and happened to notice. "Hey! Yes, you boy! Something wrong with your legs?"

The dresser sprang to attention. "No, sir."

"That's good. They can carry you out of this theatre. Get on, boy! Out! Up to the gallery! This is an operating theatre, not a street corner! I'll have no lounging around in here! Out! fast!"

The poor boy scuttled off, his face scarlet above his mask. George Ellis caught my eye as

Sir Robert continued to mutter into his mask on the problems of a surgeon who had to try to teach surgery to a set of lazy layabouts who couldn't even take the trouble to stand on their own feet.

A new junior had taken Nurse Alcott's place during my absence. She was being taught how to 'dirty' by Dolly Bachelor. A little later she dropped a small kidney dish as she removed it from a sterilizer with bowl forceps.

"Good God, Sister!" snapped Sir Robert. "Do we have to have this constant clattering and banging? How am I supposed to concentrate, eh?"

"I'm so sorry, Sir Robert. It was an accident."

"Ye don't think I thought the gel was throwing things on purpose, do ye? I don't know." He looked round at my trolley, scowling. "That silk ye're about to give me, Sister? Why can't I have nylon?"

I did not remind him that on the last occasion when he had done that specific operation at that point he had stated a preference for silk. I had the necessary nylon in reserve. I re-threaded the needle quickly. "I'm sorry, Sir Robert."

Later, I heard the new girl ask Bachelor, "Is he always like he was this afternoon, Nurse?"

"Oh, no," replied Dolly cheerfully. "Sometimes he get really tough."

Later still I was in the duty-room checking through the off-duty rota with Ellen Watt, when Sir Robert appeared in the doorway.

"Can ye spare me a minute, Sister?"

Ellen vanished tactfully. He came in, shutting the door behind him. "Well? Have a good trip?"

"Yes, thank you, Sir Robert."

"Hm." He looked me over. "Am I right in assuming we may shortly expect your resignation?"

"No. At least – I've no plans that would entail that at present."

He leaned against my desk. "That so, eh? Hm. Can't say I'm sorry. Never could stomach unnecessary changes in my theatre. Ruins the concentration." Suddenly he smiled. "Should have guessed ye'd be a sensible girl! Well, I can't hang around gossiping like this. I've got work to do."

Mark came into my duty-room very early next morning to tell me he had asked Dr Homer for an interview, to talk about Joe, and to apologize. "How do I do that, darling?"

"By skipping it – and Joe. I don't want to talk. You know Frances rang me last night? And she's going to keep me in touch." I smiled. "Good luck with Homer."

"And, by God, I'll need it, angel." He blew me a kiss. Dolly Bachelor went down the corridor just then, and gave him such an old-fashioned look that I suggested it might be as well if we gave the grapevine a little to buzz over in advance. "I don't believe Joe would now mind. Wendy Scutt knows the truth. There's

289

no need to go the whole hog, but just tell a couple of people I was with him on my holiday and he's now in Martha's. No one'll be allowed to bother him, and the story should smooth a few rough edges.''

''Maggie, me darling,'' he said, ''if I wasn't a married man, for this I would marry you myself!''

I never asked Mark what he had said, but that evening Wendy told me the entire Sisters' Home had got hold of the story. ''Needless to say, my dear, they all knew! They just knew there was more in Mr de Winter's resigning than met the eye!''

Ellen had gone away that evening for two days off. When she got back the grapevine had already lost interest in Joe and myself and was buzzing with Mark's marriage, inevitable resignation, and obvious ruin. It came as something not far removed from disappointment, despite Mark's genuine popularity, when the hospital discovered that although Dr Homer had not been best pleased, he had admitted that in view of the improved quality of Mark's recent work, Dr Delaney must be the exception to prove his rule. The hospital consoled itself by making corny jokes along the 'even-Homer-sometimes-nods' line.

Mark told me it just proved how much 'Hearts' resembled St Paul. ''No doubt he agrees it is better to marry than to burn, and one M. Delaney is a highly inflammable type. You don't know how I wish I'd had the guts to get this over before, Maggie."

"You couldn't do that. Because of Joe and me."

"Nor I could! I feel much better! A hero, no less!" He turned serious. "Isn't this the day? Any news?"

I shook my head. "I don't expect or want any until Frances rings to-night. Buckwell should have done him by now. He was first on the afternoon list. He shouldn't yet be round. News now would have to be bad."

He looked at the clock. "True. You off this evening? Frances is working. Let's go out for a drink. I'm not on call."

"Nor me. Thanks, Mark. I'm off at six."

At ten to six Bill Swan rang me from Casualty. "We've got a man here with a busted aneurysm. Chest. Branch of the thoracic aorta. He got jammed against the shaft of his steering-wheel. There's no time to get the automatic-heart boys. He needs corking fast. The S.C.O.'s doing a boy-in-the-dyke. His thumb'll have to stay where it is until we get this man under. Coming up now, as he is."

"Right. Have the path. lab. got his blood group?"

"Yes. Five pints'll be along *stat*."

"And what about his personal details, Mr

Swan? Do Casualty know anything?"

"No," he snapped, "and if I don't stop talking and follow him up fast, he'll probably bleed to death before anyone has time to find out." From the sound, he had slammed down the receiver.

It was a major emergency; haemorrhage always was. That was why we always had an emergency setting ready for instant use on such cases. All I had to do was change into a sterile gown and gloves. If the man arrived from Casualty before I was scrubbed up it would be one of the rare occasions when we just pulled on sterile gloves. Occasionally we could not even delay for that. But rush or not, it was still my job to find out as much as possible about any patient operated on in my theatre.

Ellen arrived to take over the theatre at six. The patient, in his outdoor clothes, was already on the table. I asked her to ferret round for his identity.

"Then want me to take over, Sister? You are off," she murmured.

I shook my head. The job had started. Bill was worried, working at the tremendous speed essential for what he had to do, and, for some reason that was most probably just tiredness, in an unusually bad temper. If he had to curse anyone it had better be me.

He was doing a dangerous, difficult, and very messy job well. He gave his surgical assistants and myself hell in the process. When it was over he surveyed the theatre distastefully. "God, what a filthy mess! The whole place is awash with blood!"

I said, "It'll wash off, Mr Swan. Blood's clean stuff."

"Doubt they'll get this chap's car cleaned up so easily, from what the cops said. He had a little kid sitting in the front with him. Boy of about four."

"Did they bring him in?" I asked anxiously.

"Yep. B.I.D." (Brought in dead). "His brains were bashed out by the windscreen. When the cops discover who his mother is" – his voice was harsh – "she'll be up."

And he would have to face her. I was no longer surprised by the shortness of his temper.

Frances rang me later as arranged. "So far, good. He's round. Buckwell did graft. Joe'll be in isol. thirty days."

My theatre was busy during those days. That alone made them bearable. My nights off call were not. I lay and thought of every possible and impossible complication in the books, that I had seen, heard of, and a few I worked up for myself.

The Delaneys entertained me on the rare occasions when the three of us were off together. Frances had a flat in a mews just round the corner from Martha's. We never went into the hospital itself. They were excellent hosts, but I was glad when those evenings ended.

Wendy Scutt was the person whose company

I most enjoyed during those weeks. She listened to all my horror stories, then demolished them one by one.

"Why a coronary at his age?"

"You can have a coronary at any age."

"Certainly. But it's an unlikely post-op complication for a young man – and he's now over the fourteenth day! You, my dear," she said severely, "are thinking like a first-year! Remember how one suffered from all one's patients' complaints? And after all medical lectures always had all the symptoms? I well remember having carcinoma of the stomach, leukaemia, tubercles – oh, yes, and a head tumour because I had the odd headache – in my first six months!"

I had to smile. "I had chicken-pox. There was quite a lot going round at the end of my first year. But because my spots came out in a bunch on my hands and face and not in batches as it said in the book, I was convinced the S.M.O. didn't know his job. Had to be smallpox."

On the subject of Joe's future she was as firm as on his present. "Why all this nonsense about 'only a miracle'? To start with, what's so unusual about a miracle? Haven't you seen a good many in your theatre? I have in Henry Carter. But even if his back is too weak for much standing – Maggie, that man has got a specialist's degrees already. He's had years of general experience. He'll just have to specialize in some fiddly line like hands. Didn't you tell me that when you

294

did that tendon-graft last week you had all your surgeons perched on stools all morning?"

"Yes, but – " The telephone in the corridor outside rang. She went to answer it.

"Just what you need, my dear. A nice strangulated hernia is waiting for you. No, leave me those tea-cups."

I buttoned my cloak. "Wendy, I do realize, despite my gloom, that things are going along quite nicely. But it's too early yet to know if that graft will take. He's still in isolation."

"For the usual thirty-days, didn't you say?" She shrugged. "No one can answer that one yet."

"Supposing it doesn't take? Then what?"

"It'll be up to him to make the next move."

"And I'll have to go on doing nothing?" I demanded urgently. "And let him die, alone?"

She said, "Maggie, you've seen death. When is it not lonely? But whether it is any lonelier than life is something I have often wondered." She came out to the lift with me and opened the gate. "Have a good case."

One Tuesday afternoon some five weeks after that conversation – five weeks that seemed more like fifty years – Sir Robert had another long teaching-list. There were nine operations on that list; all but the last were unusually complicated even for old Robbie when teaching. The last case was a student with a broken ankle.

He should not really have been done in our theatre at all, but as the Orthopaedic Theatre was having its hectic turn and the boy was one of our students, Robbie had decided to do the job himself.

It was a clean break, needing only a simple reduction and plaster. It was the kind of operation I could have taken with my eyes closed and one hand tied behind my back. Sir Robert set the fracture. I moved from my instrument trolley to the one set for plaster that was waiting beside me, when some movement in the gallery above made me glance up more than a little wearily. It had been a heavy day. I guessed the students above had themselves had enough and were beginning to move off, which would certainly infuriate the old man.

The gallery was moderately full and still. I looked all round, wondering if I had imagined the disturbance, and then my heart seemed quite simply to stop. Joe was sitting on the end of the second bench from the front.

"Plaster slat, please, Sister," prompted Sir Robert impatiently. "We don't want to be here all night!"

"Sorry, Sir Robert. Just coming." My voice did not sound like mine. I did not feel like me. I had never fainted in the theatre even as a junior. Theatre sisters did not faint. But the green walls were doing the most extraordinary things; the plaster slat I was trying to prepare lurched on a rocking trolley, and the floor was pitching upward. I felt too odd to waste time signalling my 'dirty,' as she was the new junior working on her own for the first time on the last case as it was so simple. Ellen was busy by the sterilizers and had her back to me. Bachelor, the anaesthetic nurse for the list, had come in with the student and was standing by Mark. I beckoned her. ''Get some ammon. aromat. *stat*.''

''For the junior, Sister?'' she whispered.

I could not answer. I felt her grab me as I went down, and heard Sir Robert's outraged, ''God bless us! Sister's down!'' Then the green walls crashed in on the upcoming floor.

I came round to find Mark lowering me on to the examination couch in the anaesthetic-room. His mask was down, his green cap pushed back on his red hair. He was smiling broadly. Beside him, Dolly Bachelor's round face was rounder than ever with astonishment.

''Sister, Sister'' – Mark reached for my pulse – ''this is a sad business. But you'll live. Do you have some brandy there, Nurse Bachelor?''

''Ammon. aromat., Dr Delaney. Sister asked for it.''

He took the medicine glass from her, sniffed it. ''Foul stuff. It'll do. Here, Sister. Slowly now, or you'll choke.''

''Thanks.'' I sipped obediently. ''I'm most terribly sorry. What about the case?'' I tried to sit up, but his hand on my shoulder held me down. "Nurse Bachelor, has Nurse Watt taken over?"

"Yes, Sister. It's all under control. But what about you?" The poor girl was still very shocked. "I never guessed you wanted that ammon. aromat. for you!"

Mark said Sister was under control, so would she be a dear girl and go back to the theatre and take a look at his student man. "Call me if he turns blue. He should be fine. I switched off the lot." He waited until she disappeared. "Maggie, my precious, you will never ever live this down! Sister Theatre herself passing out cold over a simple reduction! Now what could have caused it, I wonder?" He looked over his shoulder. "Would you have a line on the diagnosis, Joe?"

Joe came in slowly. He was stooping a little, but had no stick. He stood by the couch, his hands in his pockets. He did not hold on to anything, or lean against anything. His tan had faded, and so had the shadows under his eyes and a good many lines. He looked years younger than on his last appearance in my theatre. He did not say anything.

Mark looked from him to me. "I've a notion that student man may be dark blue after all. You'll forgive me if I leave you." He went out, closing the door.

That made me sit up. "Joe, open that. Matron would have a coronary if she were to come in now."

298

"She'd have my sympathy." He did as I asked. "I nearly had one just now. I had hoped to surprise you. Not shock you like this. How do you feel?"

"Not nearly as shocked as my staff." I swung my legs to the ground and sat on the edge of the couch. "I hate to think what Robbie's going to say."

"And that worries you." He took one of my hands, peeled off the glove, then held my hand between his. "Sweetheart, I am sorry. It was another of my bright ideas that didn't come off."

"Oh, yes, it did! Oh, Joe" – I sighed – "any time was the right time. Tell me quick – what's the verdict? I know it must be good or you wouldn't be here, but I want to hear the words."

Sir Robert stamped in before he could answer. "Well, Sister? This is an odd business! Never had a Sister Theatre faint before. But there it is. Better now? Capital! Capital!" He turned on Joe. "So ye've come back, eh? And about time! Buckwell says he's pleased with ye! Turn round, boy." He examined Joe's back through his jacket the way he had that morning in Gibraltar. "That's more like it. How about bending? Good. And standing still tiring?"

Joe turned round. "Not nearly so much, sir."

"Well, don't try to run before ye can walk, boy! And how's the spare part settling in? No reaction, eh? I don't know. What with all the grafting this and grafting that we're doing these

299

days, it'll soon be a wise patient who knows his own body! But we must move with the times. And when are ye going to be able to do some work?"

Joe looked at me. "Buckwell says nothing for a year, and then taking it in easy stages for another. No standing for more than half an hour at a time."

"But ye don't agree, eh? Hm. You youngsters are all the same. Always in a hurry. Ye've got to reach my age to realize the young are the only people who have plenty of time. There it is. Well? What's ye own opinion?"

"A year's far too long. A few months – "

"And then ye'll be fit to stand all day? Nonsense, boy!"

Joe said, "I know that, sir. Buckwell's advised me to scrub any ideas of that, and I have. It means dropping general surgery, which is a nuisance as that's the type I prefer, but so few general jobs can be done sitting down. They let me watch several cranial jobs across the river. Their Mr Anstey did most of the op sitting on a high stool."

Sir Robert allowed that to be sensible, since brain operations lasted so many hours. "Ye've not had much cranial experience, Joe. Ye'll need a post-grad."

"I thought that would be a good way of using up the easy stages period. Do you think it would be an idea if I talked to Mr Sellars?"

Joshua Sellars was our own cranial specialist. Sir Robert said he did not think talking would do any harm, and he supposed he had better have a word with Mr Joshua Sellars himself. "But there's to be no showing y'face in this hospital even as a post-graduate inside of six months, boy! Wait that time, then come and see me. And be sure Buckwell knows what you are planning to do before ye ring m' door-bell. Then we'll talk." He turned back to me. "Fainting, eh? Hm. That's what comes of all this overworking and failing to take ye appointed off-duty. Time we had a proper break with none of that rushing in and out of aeroplanes on what you chose to call your last holiday. Well? I can't waste any more time standing around gossiping like this. I've got work to do." He allowed himself to smile at last. "No more work for you to-night, Sister. Can't have my theatre sisters fainting all over the place like this! The staff nurses are managing nicely. Get off duty and have some fresh air. And you, boy – see she does!" He stomped out again and, like Mark, closed the door behind him.

Joe said very quietly, "We'll have to risk Matron having that coronary. Robbie'll take great umbrage if we open it. You wouldn't want to upset him again after fainting all over the place." His eyes were alight with laughter, and more than laughter. "Would you?"

I shook my head. "Life is hard for a simple surgeon."

"My God, darling" – he barely breathed the words – "You've got something there, but you are using the wrong tense. Was. Not is." Suddenly he seemed to explode. I was in his arms, and he was kissing me as not even he had ever kissed me before.

Dolly Bachelor's horrified gasp: "Oh! Sorry – Sister! –" and quick slamming of the door made him raise his head, but not let me go.

"Joe!" I held his face in my hands. "We can't go on like this! I'm on duty."

"No, you aren't." He caught one of my hands and kissed the palm. "I looked at your off-duty rota on my way up to the gallery. This evening you are down to be off at five-thirty. And you are not on call. It's gone six now."

"But I am still Sister Theatre."

He let me go then, moved a little away, "Maggie, you know what Robbie said about taking a break? How long a break could you take?"

"That would depend on my reason for taking the break."

"Would a honeymoon be the right sort of reason?"

"No." I said firmly. "Matron wouldn't allow that. When she gave me this job she made it quite clear it would only be given to a single woman."

"I should have remembered that." He sat on

the edge of the couch. "Sweetheart, I'm sorry. You've been so good to me, you've given me more than I would have dared to expect from any woman, even – once – you. I've done nothing but take, and I'm now doing that again. But I'm not taking your job from you until I've got something more concrete to offer you than a chat with Robbie in six months' time. When I've worked things out, will you still marry me? And will you mind waiting?"

"I wouldn't mind waiting. But we are not going to. Have you got any money? Enough to support us both somewhere cheap for the next six months? Because my last holiday just about cleaned me out."

He was on his feet. "Yes, but –"

"But nothing! We've done enough waiting. I don't know for sure what it did to you, but I have the impression much what it did to me. My nurses were beginning to think me a-human." I smiled. "I suspect Bachelor'll change their minds on that. And you, my darling, had better change your mind about not marrying me until you've got a job of your own, because you are going to marry me just as soon as Matron can get hold of a new Sister Theatre. She'll find one. She'll have to."

"Maggie." He took my shoulders with his hands. "I am not going to let you do this for me. It's not that I don't want you. I want you so much . . ." He raised his hands, held them out. They were shaking. Then he put them in his pockets. "I'm not letting you throw up the job you've come to love yet."

"It's not a question of your letting me, Joe. I'm telling you what I am going to do. Don't forget we are still in my department. I may faint all over the place, get seen by one of my staff nurses when I'm being kissed by an ex-S.S.O., but I am still Sister Theatre. And what I say here goes!"

He was smiling. "That cuts me down to size." His smile vanished. "This is what you want?"

I kissed him, and he asked no more questions. Later he said, "I'd like us to go back to Spain."

"I'd love that."

"And I," said Joe, "love you. Without you I have felt only half alive. And yet, even without you, just thinking of you, gave me a kind of strength. When I left you here and went into Martha's the first time I was dead scared about a lot of things, but never that you would stop loving me, any more than I would stop loving you. It was odd, that. I felt safe on that one thing. And at the toughest moments on the blackest nights I always felt that if I put out a hand you'd be there. Understand?"

"Yes," I said, "yes." And I thought; no man could ever give his woman more.

THE END